AR QUIZ#. 502393
BL- 4.7
Pts -12

ORDER OF THE MAJESTIC

MATT MYKLUSCH

ALADDIN

NEW YORK LONDON TORONTO SYDNEY NEW DELHI

ALADDIN

An imprint of Simon & Schuster Children's Publishing Division
1230 Avenue of the Americas, New York, NY 10020
First Aladdin hardcover edition May 2019
Text copyright © 2019 by Matt Myklusch
Jacket illustration copyright © 2019 by Owen Richardson

For information about special discounts for bulk purchases, please contact
Simon & Schuster Special Sales at 1-866-506-1949 or business@simonandschuster.com.
The Simon & Schuster Speakers Bureau can bring authors to your live event.
For more information or to book an event contact the Simon & Schuster Speakers Bureau
at 1-866-248-3049 or visit our website at www.simonspeakers.com.
Jacket designed by Karin Paprocki
Interior designed by Mike Rosamilia
The text of this book was set in Goudy Old Style.
Manufactured in the United States of America 0419 FFG
2 4 6 8 10 9 7 5 3 1
Library of Congress Cataloging-in-Publication Data
Names: Myklusch, Matt, author.
Title: Order of the Majestic / by Matt Myklusch.
Description: First Aladdin hardcover edition. | New York : Aladdin, 2019. | Series: Order of the Majestic ; 1 |
Summary: Thirteen-year-old daydreamer Joey Kopecky discovers magic as he is caught in an epic battle between two
powerful, ancient orders in an alternate New York City.
Identifiers: LCCN 2018043315 (print) | LCCN 2018050425 (eBook) |
ISBN 9781534424876 (hardcover) | ISBN 9781534424890 (eBook)
Subjects: | CYAC: Magic—Fiction. | Adventure and adventurers—Fiction. |
BISAC: JUVENILE FICTION / Action & Adventure / General. | JUVENILE FICTION / Fantasy & Magic. |
JUVENILE FICTION / Social Issues / Friendship.
Classification: LCC PZ7.M994 (eBook) | LCC PZ7.M994 Ord 2019 (print) | DDC [Fic]—dc23
LC record available at https://lccn.loc.gov/2018043315

FOR MY BROTHER,
WHO TAUGHT ME MY FIRST
REAL MAGIC TRICK

Contents

1

Gifted and Talented

Joey Kopecky didn't mean to become the smartest kid in the state of New Jersey. It just kind of happened out of the blue. He had gone to bed one night an average, unremarkable student and arrived at school the next morning a genius—on paper at least. Halfway through the seventh grade, Joey was shocked to find out he had aced a barrage of state-mandated aptitude tests, scoring higher than any student ever had before. Perfect hundreds across the board. Joey had always been good with standardized tests, but it turned out he was better than good. Way better. And the price he had to pay for that was terrible.

It was Monday morning, April 22. Earth Day. It wasn't a national holiday or anything (not really), but Joey wasn't going to school. He wasn't ever going back to *his* school. Instead, he and his father were riding a commuter train bound for

Manhattan, on their way to decide what Joey was going to do with the rest of his life.

"You ready for another one?" Joey's father asked him.

"I can't wait," Joey lied, staring out the window.

"All right," Joey's father said, punching numbers into his phone. "What's the square root of 361?"

Joey grimaced. The whole ride, his father had peppered him with random questions, eager to explore his intellect like some newly discovered continent. For Joey, the game got old real fast.

"I don't know, Dad. I told you, it's not like I have a calculator in my head."

"How about some history?" Joey's father scrolled through his phone. "What year did Lincoln give the Gettysburg Address?"

Joey shook his head. "I'm not Wikipedia, either. Sorry."

More scrolling. "What's the capital of Albuquerque?"

Joey was about to say he wasn't Google Maps, but he stopped himself. "Albuquerque doesn't have a capital. It's a city, not a state."

Joey's father beamed. "See that? It was a trick question, but you caught it just like that."

"Gold star for me." Joey gave a sarcastic thumbs-up. "Doesn't exactly take a genius, Dad."

His father put his phone away. "What's eating you?"

Joey looked at his father. "Let's see if you can figure this one out. A train leaves Hoboken at eight a.m., headed to New York at sixty miles an hour. If the city is thirteen miles away, and a kid on the train has to be there at nine a.m., at what time is his life officially ruined?"

"Joey." His father sighed. "We talked about this."

"This one's a trick question too. *I'm* the kid on the train. Did you catch that?"

"Yeah, I got it. How about we dial back the negativity a little?"

Joey grunted. "My life was ruined when you and Mom signed me up for this school."

"This school is one of the best in the country. Maybe the world. We had to jump through a lot of hoops to get them to take you in the middle of the year like this. They don't usually do that."

Joey turned. "What middle of the year? There's no middle of the year at Exemplar Academy. They don't break for summer. They don't break *ever*. It's all one continuous year there."

3

"Just like the real world. You might not appreciate it now, but this is an unbelievable opportunity."

"Emphasis on 'unbelievable.' You heard what my old teachers said—"

"I remember what they said," Joey's father cut in. "That's why they're your *old* teachers."

Joey scrunched up his face. Joey's teachers at Francis A. Sinatra Junior High had been convinced his perfect test scores were some kind of fluke. A glitch in the grading machine, perhaps. At home the reaction was different. Years of slacking had come back to bite Joey in the neck. His lackluster academic track record was now the reason his parents suddenly thought he was some kind of prodigy. *He's not lazy. He just needs to be challenged more!* They were acting like he was the next Tony Stark. It was a disaster.

Joey's mom and dad wasted no time enrolling him in a special school for gifted and talented students. Joey didn't know if Exemplar Academy was the best school in the world or not, but he was pretty sure it was the most demanding. Their motto boasted "Our Students Change the World," which Joey thought was a lot of pressure to put on a thirteen-year-old.

He looked around the train. It was filled with people carrying homemade signs, on their way to various Earth Day marches, demonstrations, and events. A young girl passing through the train car handed Joey and his father pamphlets that read SAVE THE PLANET in big, bold letters.

"Thanks," Joey said, tucking the paper into his pocket. "I'll get right on that."

Joey's father frowned at him. "Don't be mean."

The girl continued down the aisle, unfazed. Joey felt bad afterward about being snarky with her. He wasn't trying to be mean; she had just gotten him in the wrong place at the wrong time with the wrong message. He didn't want to change the world. When did that become his responsibility? Just because he'd scored in the ninety-ninth percentile on every test that mattered, he was expected to do the impossible all of a sudden? Joey didn't care what anybody said—he *wasn't* a genius. He was a normal kid. He had tried explaining that to his mom and dad, but they were too proud of his test scores to listen to reason. For them it was like winning the lottery. They had visions of Ivy League scholarships dancing in their heads.

The truth was, Joey was not a great student. He was a great

test taker. That was why he had always done well enough in school, earning Bs and the occasional C without trying very hard. His days of getting away with that were over.

"This is a total waste of time. I'm going to flunk out of that school in a week." Joey squirmed in his seat, attempting to get comfortable, smushed between his father and the window as a group of eager environmentalists crowded in. He opened his phone, looking for a digital escape. Every part of him wanted off that train.

"You're not going to flunk out of anything," his father told him.

"I don't belong there. The kids at Exemplar are all super-brainiacs."

Joey's father smirked. "Don't take this the wrong way, but you're a super-brainiac too."

"*Dad*," Joey said, in a lecturing tone. "How many times do I have to tell you? Those test scores . . . They don't mean anything. There's a trick to doing well on tests like that."

The way Joey saw it, a real genius would have known the subjects he'd been tested on backward and forward. That wasn't him. He was an expert on Star Wars, Harry Potter, and the Marvel Cinematic Universe. That was about it.

When it came to literature, he had encyclopedic knowledge of comic book continuity. Not exactly the stuff global leaders were made out of. Joey hadn't done well because he understood the material on the tests. He had done well because he understood the questions on the page. There were hints to what the answers were hidden inside of each question. Joey spotted traps that test makers laid to lure students into choosing wrong answers and clues that helped him zero in on the right ones. That had been always been enough for him to get by, but he couldn't get away with those tricks forever. At Exemplar Academy, Joey was finally going to come up against a real challenge, and when that day came, things would get ugly.

"Try to relax," Joey's father told him. "You already got into the school. The hard part's over with. What you have this morning is just a placement test."

Joey scoffed. "The PMAP isn't just another placement test, Dad. It decides your whole life."

"I know it feels like that, but—"

"It does. At Exemplar, the PMAP is like their bible."

For the first time in forever, Joey was actually worried about a test. The Predictive Model to Ascertain Potential was known in kid circles as the "What Will I Be When I Grow Up?" test. It measured a student's potential for success in any given field and identified their ideal career choice. Every student at Exemplar Academy got their own personal curriculum with courses geared toward the job recommendation on their PMAP. Joey's new school was going to plan out his whole education based on one exam.

"What if this test says I should do some job I hate? What happens then? I have to study that until I go to college?"

"Don't get all worked up. The PMAP just helps the school point you in the right direction. It's a competitive environment. You want to hit the ground running."

"Finally, something we agree on. I'm taking off as soon as this train hits the station."

"Ha ha. Very funny."

"I'm serious. There's gonna be a Joey-shaped hole in the wall like something out of a cartoon. You'll see."

"I'd rather see a Joey-shaped *person* appreciating how lucky he is. This school is going to open all kinds of doors for you." His father put a hand on his shoulder. "I know this is hard, but I promise you it's going to be worth it. Try to remember, whether you think you can or think you can't . . . you're right. I happen to think you can do any-thing you put your mind to."

"Thanks, Dad, but if that's true, what do I need this wacky school for?"

"This wacky school is going to get you where you need to go in life."

Joey frowned. "Where's that? You think these people at the testing center have the answer? They don't even know me."

"They're supposed to help you figure it out, that's all. Why don't you tell me what you want to be when you grow up? Any ideas?"

"I've got lots of ideas." Joey counted them off on his fingers: "Tomb raider, paranormal investigator, masked vigilante, Jedi knight . . ."

"C'mon, Joey. For real."

"Is boy wizard an option?"

"You want to know why you're going to this school . . . ? This is why. We have to put that big brain of yours to work on something meaningful."

Joey sighed. "All I know is I don't want to hate getting out of bed every morning. I want to do something I actually like. Something cool."

"Like what?"

Joey was quiet. He had no idea.

"Everybody wants their life to be like something out of a movie. You've got to prepare yourself for reality. You think I dreamed about being an accountant when I was your age? No, but I was good with numbers. That was me. We play the hand we're dealt." Joey's dad punched him in the shoulder. "You're holding aces, kiddo. It doesn't matter what you do. You can't lose."

Joey went back to his phone and tuned out the world as the train rolled on toward the city. *Easy for you to say*, he thought. *It matters to me.*

The testing center was located on the north side of Manhattan's Theatre District. Joey and his father took a cab, but they ended up getting out before they hit Forty-Second Street. An Earth Day rally setting up in Times Square had snarled traffic, and they had to walk the last few blocks. As they made their way through the crowd, Joey read the signs people were holding up:

SCIENTIFIC FACTS, NOT ALTERNATIVE FACTS!

CLIMATE CHANGE IS NOT FAKE NEWS!

Joey gave the demonstrators credit for passion and creativity, especially the person channeling Dr. Seuss. It was good to see this many people take to the streets to show they cared about the environment, even though he was pretty sure at this point it sadly wouldn't make much of a difference.

They arrived at their destination. It was a bland, monolithic skyscraper, every bit as welcoming as a supervillain's fortress. Joey stared up at the building from the sidewalk. The testing center looked like the kind of place fun went to die. Exemplar Academy had arranged for Joey to be evaluated by the organization that had designed the PMAP, the National Association of Tests and Limits. The NATL wrote just about every standardized test in America, including the ones that had gotten Joey into this mess. His father dropped him off outside and gave him a hug. "I'm late for a meeting. You'll have to go up without me. Don't worry. I'll be back before you're done in there."

Joey nodded, looking grim. "Wish me luck."

His father thought for a second. "How about I do you one better?" He reached inside his pocket and took out an old foreign coin. Joey watched as his father went through his usual routine, holding the coin up in his right hand, closing his left hand over it, and then making two fists. When he opened them back up, both palms were empty. Joey's father made a show of searching his pockets for the lost coin, then grinned and fished it out from behind Joey's ear. "There it is." He wiggled his fingers, and the coin danced across his knuckles, back and forth. Joey had seen this sleight-of-hand trick a hundred times before, but he still liked watching it. The smile on his face was a reflex. "I know it's silly, but I've always thought this coin was good luck," his father said, flipping it high into the air and catching it. "I don't think you need any, but here. Just in case." Joey's father took his hand and dropped the coin into it.

Joey blinked. "You're giving me your lucky coin? Really?" Joey couldn't believe it. His father took that coin everywhere he went. He'd had it since he was a kid.

"I'm just lending it to you. Don't lose it, okay?"

"I won't," Joey promised, examining the coin. It was an old, dirty bronze token about the size of a fifty-cent piece. The coin looked like it might have been taken out of a pirate's treasure chest or stolen away from some ancient lost temple— or both. It had a square hole in the center surrounded by words and symbols that Joey couldn't make sense of. Neither he nor his father recognized the language or had any idea where the coin had come from—not that it mattered. Joey didn't need to know. There was just something cool about the coin. He liked it. He always had.

"I mean it, Joey. Take care of that for me."

"I know. I will. Jeez, Dad, you're like Gollum with this thing." Joey clutched the coin to his chest and stroked it like a pet. "*Yesss . . . my preciousss.*"

"You know what? I changed my mind. Give it back."

"*No! Curse you! Filthy hobbitses!!*" he joked, backing away.

His father laughed. "Feeling better?"

"A little," Joey admitted, closing his hand around the coin.

"Good." Joey's father reached out and messed up his hair a little. "You're gonna do fine. Go get 'em, buddy."

"Thanks, Dad."

Joey pushed through gleaming revolving doors, entering the NATL building. Holding tight to his father's lucky coin, he fought the urge to keep going all the way around and back out onto the street. As Joey signed in at the lobby security desk, he felt like he was checking himself into prison, but he pressed on. It was no use fighting. The NATL had been deciding children's futures with their tests for more than fifty years. That wasn't going to change just because he didn't like it.

Joey got on the elevator and rode the car up to the twelfth floor. A bell chimed and the doors *whooshed* open. Joey stepped into the reception area of a bright, antiseptic office. The color scheme was a mind-numbing blend of white and off-white. Artful black-and-white photos of No. 2 pencils and Scantron sheets hung on the walls. The place looked like it had been decorated by a textbook. A set of glass doors led to the main waiting room, where a bunch of other kids sat quietly, dressed in white plastic suits with drawstring hoods, the kind that scientists wore in sterile labs.

"What the . . . ?" he said to the nearest kid, but one of the other shrink-wrapped children shushed him, gesturing to a sign on the wall that read ABSOLUTELY NO TALKING.

Okaaay . . . Behind the reception desk, an old lady with a pinched face regarded Joey skeptically. The nameplate on her desk identified her as MRS. WHITE, which matched her pixie-cut hair but not her wardrobe. She wore all black with

14

thick, red horn-rimmed glasses. Mrs. White gave an impatient sigh as Joey approached. "Can I help you?" she asked in a pointed voice.

Joey nodded. "I'm here to take a test."

Mrs. White slid her glasses down and looked over the top of the frames. "And you are . . . ?"

"Joey Kopecky. I'm supposed to take the PMAP. You guys set it up through my school."

Mrs. White turned to her computer. After a few minutes of furious typing, she said, "Oh yes. Kopecky. Mr. Perfect Score." She gave a haughty "Hmph," and mumbled something under her breath. "Aren't you the clever one?"

Joey smiled awkwardly. It didn't sound like she meant it as a compliment. He pointed back toward the other kids. "Is there some kind of biohazard situation in here I should know about? How come you don't have a suit on?"

Mrs. White admonished Joey with her eyes. "In this building, Mr. Kopecky, we ask the questions."

Joey put his hands up and leaned back from the desk. "Sorry."

Mrs. White tapped her computer screen with the eraser of her pencil. "I'm afraid you're mistaken. I have you scheduled to retake New Jersey state aptitude tests one through six. Nothing here about a PMAP."

Joey blinked. "You want me to take the tests again?"

Mrs. White put on a condescending smile. "That is what 'retake' means."

"The same tests I got perfect scores on?"

Mrs. White ignored the question as her printer sprang to life, spitting out papers with Joey's name on them. She placed the documents inside a manila folder and took a vacuum-sealed package out of her desk. Handing both to Joey, she said, "You can put these on over your clothes. A test monitor will be out to collect you as soon as an exam room opens up."

Joey stared at the plastic suit, complete with latex gloves, booties, and goggles. "What do I need this for?"

"All testing at this location is performed under strict observation in controlled environments. We have to make sure you don't bring any unauthorized materials in with you this time."

Joey's eyes narrowed. "This time? You think I cheated last time?"

"Did I say that?" Mrs. White shook her head. "No. We just

think it's amazing how no one's ever gotten a perfect score on any one of our tests before, let alone multiple tests. Why, you'd have to be a genius!" Mrs. White lifted a teacup to her lips, a challenging look in her eyes. "Are you a genius, Joey?"

Joey opened his mouth to argue, then snapped it shut. This little curveball was the answer to his prayers. A way out of Exemplar Academy. All he had to do was retake the tests, get a bunch of answers wrong, and everything would go back to normal. Still, he didn't like what he was being accused of. Maybe he wasn't a genius, but he *knew* he wasn't a cheat. "You can't make me retake those tests just because you don't like how I did on them."

"It's not that we didn't *like* your test scores," Joey heard someone say. "They simply didn't tell us anything." A tall, slim man wearing a formfitting charcoal suit strode to the reception desk. His black hair was slicked back with styling gel. "But we're not going to learn anything new asking the same questions all over again, are we?" The man shook his head, answering his own question. "Thank you, Dolores," he said to Mrs. White. "I'll take it from here."

Mrs. White nearly choked on her tea. "Mr. Gray? But I thought—his file said . . ."

"Change of plans. We missed something. That is, we almost missed him."

"What's going on?" asked Joey. "What do you mean you almost missed me?"

"I'm sorry. Where are my manners? John Gray, Department of Alternative Testing," the man said, offering his hand. Joey shook it. "Let's see what you have here. I'll take this . . . ," he said, collecting Joey's file. "We won't be needing this . . . ," he added carelessly, dropping the plastic testing suit on Mrs. White's desk, spilling tea everywhere.

"Oh!" Mrs. White yelped.

"Yikes." Mr. Gray winced at his mistake. He sucked air in through his teeth as Mrs. White struggled to save her papers and keyboard from the spill. "I am so sorry, Dolores. I didn't mean . . . Ooh, that's ruined, isn't it?" Mr. Gray looked at Joey and nodded back the way he'd come. "I think we'd better go," he said in a low voice.

"Right." Joey threw Mrs. White a half-hearted wave. She didn't notice, as she was focused solely on her tea-splattered workstation. Joey followed Mr. Gray and booked a hasty retreat, power walking down the hall away from the desk.

Mr. Gray led Joey through a maze of cubicles filled with

white-suited students taking tests. Test monitors hovered over the children, jotting down notes on tablet screens. The office was as quiet as an empty library. NO TALKING signs were posted everywhere. "This way," Mr. Gray whispered, guiding Joey up a staircase. The thirteenth floor was even weirder than the twelfth. It was lined with glass-walled exam rooms occupied by students wearing large bulbous helmets that covered their eyes and ears. The helmets looked heavy and uncomfortable, far too big for the children wearing them. They rested on support braces each test taker wore around their neck and shoulders. "Sorry about the confusion back in the lobby," Mr. Gray said, as if none of this were in any way unusual. "Must have been some kind of mix-up in our files. It happens." He was speaking normally again, no longer feeling the need to whisper.

"What is all this?" Joey asked, gawking at the odd, cumbersome headgear. "I don't have to wear one of those things, do I?"

"What's that?" Mr. Gray said, distracted. He was leafing through Joey's file as he walked. Once he realized what Joey was talking about, he laughed. "Oh no. Those are noise-canceling helmets. Don't worry. You won't need one. You're

19

going to be in here." He directed Joey toward an office with opaque, frosted glass on the door. As far as Joey could tell, it was the only room you couldn't see into from the outside.

Behind the door lay a spartan workspace. It had white walls with no decorations of any kind, not even a clock. There was an empty desk in the center of the floor (more of a table, really) with two identical chairs, one on either side. The room's only distinguishing features were a surveillance camera near the ceiling and a series of shelves filled with puzzles, board games, sports equipment, and toys, all arranged neatly in plastic bins.

"What's with all the toys?" Joey asked.

Mr. Gray took the seat opposite him. "Those aren't toys. They're office supplies. I need them to deal with people like you."

"People like me?"

"Students who are going to 'change the world.'" Mr. Gray tapped Joey's file. "It says here you're going to Exemplar Academy. Very nice."

Joey groaned. "Don't remind me."

"What? That's a good thing. The world needs smart people."

"It definitely does, but come on . . . changing the world?" Joey shook his head. "You've got the wrong guy."

"Is that so?" Mr. Gray took stock of Joey, trying to get a read on him. "You wouldn't be out there holding a sign this morning if you didn't have to be in here with us?"

"Not likely," Joey said. "Those people . . ." Joey paused, thinking about the eco-warriors filling up Times Square. "Don't get me wrong. Their hearts are in the right place. I'm just not sure they make any real difference in the end."

"What would make a difference, then? You're the genius. What would your sign say if you had one?"

"I'm not a genius. And I don't know what would make a difference. My sign would probably just say something funny like, 'Earth is the new Krypton.'"

Mr. Gray furrowed his brow. "What's that mean?"

"You know . . . Krypton. The planet Superman came from? It blew up."

"I'm aware of Superman's origin."

"Then you know. Think about it. Krypton . . . that's us right now. When I was little, I couldn't understand why no one listened to Superman's father while there was still time enough to save the planet. He was Krypton's top scientist, and even after he had presented clear evidence that the planet was dying, no one believed him. Now I realize that was the most realistic part of Superman's story. The way we're going, people on earth are going to have to blast their kids off into space one day to save them too. I wouldn't mind going first. Right now, in fact."

"You need someone to save you?"

"I need to escape. Anything to get out of Exemplar Academy. If I could somehow get superpowers in the process too, that would be even better."

"Superpowers, huh?" Mr. Gray said, an amused look on his face.

"I'm kidding," Joey said, putting his hands up. "I understand the similarities between my world and Superman's world don't extend quite that far."

"Noted," Mr. Gray said, scribbling intently in Joey's file. "So, what are you doing here, Joey?"

Joey didn't understand the question. "I had to come here. My school wants me to take the PMAP."

"Because of your test results, I know. How'd that happen?" He opened Joey's file and started looking through the pages. "These scores don't line up with your grades at all. I mean, you beat these tests into submission. How'd you do it?"

"I'm just a good test taker."

"So? Tests measure what we know, right? Unless there's some other explanation?"

"I didn't cheat."

"I didn't say anything about cheating. We're talking for two minutes here; already I can tell you're a smart kid. A little cynical maybe, but smart. I'm just trying to understand how you managed to surprise everyone like this."

Joey shook his head. "I don't know what to tell you. I just know how to answer questions the right way. Especially multiple-choice questions."

Mr. Gray looked intrigued. He leaned forward and tented his fingers. "Go on."

Joey took a deep breath. So far he'd been unable to give anyone a satisfactory explanation for his high test scores, but Mr. Gray worked in the testing industry. Maybe he would understand. "Okay, let's say you've got a math question where three of the answer choices are fractions, and the fourth choice is a whole number. I know not to pick the whole number there. It's an outlier. They put that in to make it look inviting, but it's almost always wrong. Or, let's say there's a question involving prime numbers. I know the answer's probably going to have something to do with the fact that two is the only even prime number. Teachers always expect you to forget stuff like that. I don't forget. Or, how about when a question has some absurd equation that looks like it would take an hour to complete? I know there has to be a shortcut somewhere. Why? Because on a test with a hundred questions and a one-hour time limit, you've got less than a minute to spend on each question. That means there has to be a faster way to solve the problem. Once you know that, you just look for a way to cancel things out and simplify the equation. It's always there if you look. There's a million little tricks."

"And you see through the tricks."

"Exactly. That's all it is. Even with subjects I don't know very well, I can at least narrow things down to guess between two answers instead of four. It's not a total guess, though. The answers are all there in the details."

Mr. Gray leaned back in his chair, clearly impressed. "You're a fascinating young man, Joey."

Joey folded his arms. "I was happier back when I was boring."

"Who said you were boring?"

"No one. I'm just not used to being at the top of anyone's list. Before I took these tests, my teachers hardly noticed me. It's like I was invisible."

Mr. Gray raised an eyebrow. "And you liked that better?"

"Sure. I could do what I wanted. Not anymore. Now I have to go to Exemplar Academy and study whatever this ridiculous PMAP test says I should study. No offense."

"None taken. I'm not going to waste your time with the PMAP."

Joey straightened up in his seat. "You're not?"

Mr. Gray shook his head. "Standardized tests are for standardized people. That's what I say. I have more effective ways of gauging your potential."

"For real?"

"For *real* real." Mr. Gray got up and started digging excitedly through the bins on the shelves. Several items fell to the ground, including a large container of plastic building blocks. "When a student displays a talent for architecture, I test them using Legos," he explained as brightly colored bricks spilled across the floor. Still rummaging around, he knocked over a stack of puzzle boxes, sending jigsaw pieces flying everywhere. "Kids who are good at putting puzzles together usually make for good investigative reporters," he said. "Some of them end up becoming detectives," he added with a shrug.

"Is that what you think I should do?" Joey asked.

"No. You're something else entirely." Mr. Gray found what he was looking for, a black trunk the size of a toolbox. He set it down on the desk.

"What's this?" Joey asked.

"Open it up. See for yourself."

Joey ran his fingers over the black trunk case. The leather exterior was soft and smooth, like a well-worn baseball mitt, lined with nickel-plated corners and rivets. It looked like a piece of carry-on luggage that someone had forgotten to bring on board the *Titanic*. He flipped the buckles on the front and lifted the lid.

"This is a magic set," Joey said, confused.

"You like magic, Joey?"

"My dad does tricks sometimes."

"Interesting," Mr. Gray replied. "But you're wrong. It's not a magic set. It's a test. It's *your* test."

The interior of the trunk had thick, red velvet lining and trays that folded up and out like a tackle box. Every little compartment contained a neatly organized magical illusion. "You think I should become a magician? I'll tell you right now, that is not what my parents have in mind."

Mr. Gray laughed. "I don't think people grow up to be magicians anymore, Joey. This is about logic and reasoning. I want to give you a real challenge. I'm measuring a very specific kind of intelligence here—the power to see possibility where other people see limits. The insight to understand how things really work." Mr. Gray unbuttoned a pocket that had been sewn into the lid of the trunk. He reached inside and pulled out a black instruction booklet. "This magic set has one hundred and fifty tricks. If I gave you an hour, how many do you think you could get through?"

Joey made a face. "I have no idea."

"Me neither." Mr. Gray switched on the surveillance camera. The red light glowed steadily. "What do you say we find out?"

Joey looked back and forth between the camera and the magic set. "And I thought the helmets and the plastic suits were weird."

"Not weird. Alternative." Mr. Gray twisted the dial on a timer and set it down on the desk. "Let's do this. One hour, starting now. Good luck."

Joey patted the lucky coin in his pocket instinctively as Mr. Gray excused himself, stepping over Legos and puzzle pieces on his way out.

Alone in the room, Joey picked up the magic set's instruction booklet. The sturdy, cardboard-bound cover was stamped with shiny, silver foil lettering:

REDONDO THE MAGNIFICENT
PROUDLY PRESENTS

THE MYSTERY BOX
150 MAGIC TRICKS TO FOOL YOUR FRIENDS, UNLOCK THE IMPOSSIBLE, AND MAKE REAL THE UNREAL!

Joey scratched his head. In his mind, things were already pretty unreal. He eyed the camera, wondering how Mr. Gray was planning to grade this test. The timer ticked away on the desk, telling him to worry about that later.

Joey opened the book. Inside, he found something that

looked like a warning. Large block letters at the top of the first page declared, ATTENTION PLEASE. Below that was the image of a classic tuxedoed magician, complete with a top hat, a wand, and a thin mustache. Joey assumed this must be Redondo. He had a very serious look on his face. Joey continued reading and discovered that the message was not a warning as much as it was a call to action:

Before you begin, know this: The world is running out of magic. Unless we act, this most precious of natural resources will disappear forever from the earth. I cannot prevent this by myself. No one can. The purest, most powerful form of magic cannot be created alone. That's where you come in.

The wonders contained in this Mystery Box and described in the pages that follow hold the key. Master the tricks in this booklet and join me onstage as my assistant. Together we will perform feats of wonder to dazzle, amaze, and inspire. The world needs us, and we must answer the call. Onward, young magicians! We have work to do!

"We've got work to do, all right," Joey agreed, flipping through the rest of the book and scanning the contents of the case. One hundred and fifty tricks were a lot to get through in an hour. There were interlocking steel rings, boxes with false bottoms, weighted dice, multiplying coins, handkerchiefs that changed color, and several different sets of playing cards. Joey read the labels on each box: a marked deck, a tapered deck, a Svengali deck, and more. He didn't know what any of that meant, but he didn't waste time wondering. Joey turned his attention to the first trick and got down to business.

Most of the tricks came easy. He was able to do them on the first try after merely scanning the directions. Others took more effort. As Joey worked, he was reminded of a magic set he'd had when he was younger. He used to do tricks at family get-togethers, putting on little shows for his aunts and uncles. He'd forgotten how much fun he used to have doing that. Joey had outgrown his interest in magic years ago, but working on the tricks lifted his spirits in a way he didn't expect. For the whole hour, he didn't think about Exemplar Academy or their change-the-world mandate once. The time flew by. Joey finished the one hundred and fiftieth trick with time to spare. He had emptied the case. A cornucopia of magical props covered the desk before him. It was the first time he had ever wished a test wasn't over.

As Joey returned the instruction booklet to the pocket inside the lid, he noticed a key tied to a golden string at the bottom of the case. It was a skeleton key, the kind that looked like it might fit a lock on a very old door. The key had a tag attached, labeled TRICK #151. Joey flipped the tag over to find a faded message, written in elaborate cursive. He leaned in close, squinting to read the lines:

You have come to the end, and a new beginning.
I have one final trick up my sleeve.
Come and find me if you want to learn more.
Pull the string if you believe.

Joey pulled the string. There wasn't any room in his mind for doubt, because there wasn't any time for it.

The string snapped off in his hand. Joey heard a loud *crack*, and all around him the walls dropped away like falling curtains. Joey jumped up, tripped over his chair, and fell down, landing not on the tiled office floor, but on hard concrete. The white-walled office was gone. The entire thirteenth floor of the NATL building was gone. Joey was alone on a foggy city street.

2

Thinking Outside the Box

"Hello?" Joey called out. "Mr. Gray?"

Joey held his breath and listened. He wrapped his arms around himself. It was spring, but the cold bite in the air made it feel like winter. The sun, which had been strong that morning, was now blocked out by a thick blanket of clouds. Joey stood up. He was on the street outside the NATL building, and there wasn't a soul in sight. Joey held up the key, still tied to the severed golden string, and stared at it in a daze.

What the . . . ?

"Hello?!!" Joey shouted again, this time with more urgency in his voice. Fear and confusion swirled inside his brain. He tensed up as if his skin were suddenly too tight for his body. Whatever was happening, it wasn't natural. He was still in New York, but nothing made sense. Day or night, the streets were never this empty or this dark. It looked like someone had cut the power to Manhattan and had evacuated the city. Where was everybody? Joey heard a noise behind him. He spun around with his guard up. There was nothing there. A thin layer of fog hugged the pavement, rising into a murky mist in the distance. He couldn't make out anything beyond the end of the block. What he could see was familiar—identical to the street he had walked that morning with his father, in fact—but that came as no comfort. The buildings were all dark and quiet, their doors all shut. He tried the entrance to the NATL building, pushing hard on the glass revolving doors. They wouldn't budge.

"This isn't right . . . ," Joey mumbled, unconsciously giving himself permission to freak out. "HELLO?" he shouted for the third time, now pounding on the doors with his fist. Giving up on the NATL, he looked up and down the empty street. "IS ANYBODY OUT THERE? SOMEBODY HELP ME!"

His voice echoed in the haze. No one answered. No one came.

"Where am I?" Joey asked himself, pulling out his phone to check his map. "No signal. Of course there's no signal." Joey pocketed the phone and ran his hands through his hair.

He worried that he had suffered some kind of psychotic break. Nothing he was seeing was even remotely possible. How did he get out here?

The fog drifted before him, revealing the answer. The magic set was right there on the sidewalk. Redondo's Mystery Box. Joey froze when he saw it. He stared at the black trunk case for several seconds, making the connection.

The wonders contained in this Mystery Box . . . hold the key.

Lights flickered on across the street, illuminating the marquee of an old theater. The glare was intense in the dark gloom of the ghostlike limbo Joey had found himself in. He didn't remember the theater being there that morning, but then, he hadn't really been paying attention at the time. Joey and his father had passed a dozen theaters on their way through Times Square. They had all blended into the scenery, but this one stood out. Especially here. It seemed to be the only building on the block with working electricity. Joey felt a tinge of relief. Lights turning on outside meant someone might be inside. He hoped that somebody in there could tell him what the heck was going on. In the meantime, the theater itself hinted at an explanation. The marquee was missing too many letters for Joey to read anything on it, but the name of the theater glowed big and bright in the space above:

THE MAJESTIC

Even as Joey read the words, half the lights blinked out and died, but the remaining letters still told a story:

_ _ _ MAJ_ _ _IC

Magic. It didn't make any sense, and yet it was the *only* thing that made sense. Joey was halfway to the theater door before he realized he was moving. He stopped when he saw the man at the end of the street. At least, Joey hoped it was a man. A shadow was lurking out where the fog grew thick: a tall, thin, silhouette with arms and legs that were too long for a human. It was twenty feet away and looking right at him. Joey's mouth went dry. His body temperature plummeted. The creature dove into the fog like it was diving into a pool, swimming beneath the mist like a shark. It covered the distance between them in seconds, bursting out of the fog at Joey's feet—a living shadow, seven feet tall and hissing like a snake. Joey screamed and stumbled, trying to get away. He fell hard on his rear end and dropped the key. Kicking himself backward on the ground, he shouted, "Get away from me!"

The creature kept coming, slowly advancing on Joey. It towered over him, black as pitch, reaching out with an arm that looked like it was made out of dark, solid smoke. Still scuttling away, Joey bumped into the curb. He turned his head and saw the magic set behind him. Fight or flight kicked in, and Joey scrambled to his feet, grabbed the black trunk case by the handle, and swung the Mystery Box around like a weapon. "LEAVE ME ALONE!"

The creature screeched like a pterodactyl as the magic set connected with its midsection. It split apart and stretched wildly, but held together, tethered by a few cotton candy-like strands. "I can't believe that worked," Joey said, looking down at the magic set in his hand. He looked back up. "Then again . . ." His assailant was already knitting itself back together. Fight or flight kicked in again, and this time Joey ran. He tucked the magic set under his arm like a football and barreled through the shadow creature, tearing it apart all over again as he went racing toward the only place that looked the least bit inviting . . . the theater.

Joey flew to the row of glass doors below the marquee, praying they weren't locked. The first one was. Joey couldn't tell if there was anyone inside. The faded poster plastered on the door blocked his view of the lobby. He moved on to the second door. Locked as well. Relentless, the shadow creature closed in behind him, looming over his shoulder. Joey spun around with the magic set, desperate to keep it at bay. The creature shrieked again as Joey defended himself and slid over to the next door. It, too, was locked, but Joey noticed something that could change that—a keyhole large enough to fit an old skeleton key.

Joey's heart sank as he turned around to look at the foggy street behind him. The key was out there somewhere, hidden beneath the rolling mist. With no time to lose, Joey sprinted across the street and fell to the ground, searching frantically for the key. Crawling around on his hands and knees, he heard more hissing. The shadow at the theater door was reconstituting itself yet again, but much to Joey's dismay, it wasn't making a sound. The snakelike noises were coming from elsewhere. Apparently, this thing had friends.

Joey counted six of them standing shoulder to shoulder in the fog at the end of the street. At the other end of the block, there were four more, and that was just the beginning. They were poking their heads out from around the corners of buildings . . . stepping into the intersections . . . rising from the fog . . . They were *everywhere*. Joey looked back over his shoulder at the magic set that, so far, had served him well as both sword and shield. He had foolishly left it outside the theater door some ten feet away. It might as well have been a thousand. He doubled his efforts to find the key, fanning his arms to push away the fog. He was done for unless he found the key in the next few seconds—assuming it was even a match for the lock in the theater door.

As the mist wafted away, Joey spied a glittering thread lying on the curb. He lunged for it, snatching it up like a lifeline. The large metal key dangled at the end of the string. Joey leaped to his feet as the shadows came for him, hissing like vipers. They chased him to the theater. Reaching the door first, he inserted the key into the lock. It was a perfect fit. As he turned it, there was an audible *click*, and the key disintegrated into twinkling dust. Joey's hand shook as he wrenched the door open and dashed inside. The shadows rushed the entrance, eager to follow him in, but Joey pulled the door shut behind him quickly. He was about to turn the dead bolt when he saw the magic set was still outside the door. Again, if Joey had stopped to think, he might have left it behind, but instead he found himself pushing the door back open to grab it like Indiana Jones going back to get his hat. The shadows swooped in, but Joey locked them out just in time. Try as they might, they couldn't get the door open after that. Joey collapsed in a heap as they pulled on the handle from the outside and pounded the glass in vain.

He exhaled, feeling momentarily safe but not mentally sound. Was this really happening? It couldn't be. "This is all in your head," Joey told himself. "You're just under a lot of pressure right now. None of this is real. You're gonna close your eyes, count to ten, and everything's gonna go back to normal."

Ten seconds later, when Joey opened his eyes, things were still very much abnormal. The shadows were still there, pressed up against the glass. Joey pinched his wrist, trying to wake himself up. When that didn't work, he gave himself a good hard slap in the face. Nothing changed. Either hitting himself wasn't the answer, or he needed to hit himself harder. Joey backed away from the doors as the creatures outside gave up and drifted off. He didn't know what those things were, and he didn't want to know. All he wanted to do was to go home. Joey turned his attention to the theater, hoping to find someone in there who could help him.

He wandered through the spacious, empty lobby. The place had clearly not been "majestic" for years. Joey flipped a light switch, and a handful of wall sconces lit up, followed by a few buzzing bulbs in a crystal chandelier overhead. The rest of the fixtures were either burned out or so caked with dust that it didn't matter if they were on or off. A grand staircase, no longer worthy of the name, led up to an uneven balcony with broken spindles on the railing. Joey remained on the ground level, unwilling to trust the platform with any amount of weight. Large mirrors hung throughout the room were spotted with black rustlike stains. The white walls they adorned had all yellowed with age, and the carpet, probably once a rich shade of red, had faded to a frayed, balding pink.

"Anybody in here?" Joey called out. The room was quiet and still. *There has to be someone*, he thought. *Who turned on the lights?*

He spied a series of vintage posters on the back wall advertising a performance by none other than Redondo the Magnificent. "No way . . . ," Joey said, entranced. His picture matched the one in the instruction booklet exactly. Redondo was dressed in a black tuxedo with a crisp white dress shirt, a vest, a bow tie, and gloves. He was a young man with black hair, heavily laden with pomade, who looked like his photo belonged in the dictionary next to the word "magician." One poster depicted him onstage, levitating a beautiful young woman. In another, he stood contemplating a skull with green, ethereal smoke pouring out of its eyes.

Did he bring me here? Joey wondered, staring at the posters. *Is that even possible?*

Joey entered the main house of the theater. The cavernous auditorium was as empty as the lobby and in equally bad shape. Everywhere Joey looked he saw signs of decay. The plush red velvet seat cushions were torn and littered with debris. On the walls, paint peeled off cracked paneling to expose the bare brick and mortar underneath. The decorative molding that seemed to cover every surface with an impossible level of detail had been buried under a layer of dirt and grime. Intricate, gilded designs had grown dull, worn away by age and neglect, but the theater's problems went further than that. Fire damage spread out from the stage like a rash, covering the walls with dirty black streaks. Joey craned his neck up toward the ceiling. Its curved surface was warped and riddled with holes large enough to make him worry about the structural integrity of the building.

"Anybody home?" Joey called out. The acoustics made his voice resound through the theater. "Redondo?" he added, taking a chance. Again no one replied. He climbed up onstage, and looked out on the empty room. It was big enough to hold a few thousand people. *What do I do now?* he wondered.

Joey heard a noise backstage. It was a gurgling sound, like air bubbles rising inside a water cooler. Cautiously, he crept to the rear of the stage and put an ear to the heavy red curtain. He heard the noise again, or something close to it. This time it sounded like water sloshing around in a tub. There was definitely someone back there.

Joey was nervous, but he parted the curtains and slipped between them. On the other side, he took one step and nearly slammed his face into a giant aquarium. Inside the tank, an old man floated upside down, his eyes closed. He was wrapped up tight in a straitjacket with heavy chains tied around his chest. He had a thick head of white hair and a pencil-thin mustache. He shimmied ever so slightly, working to free himself while inverted. The scene was oddly tranquil as the man went about his work with Zen-like calm. Careful not to make a sound, Joey knelt beside the tank to get a closer look.

Joey's face was two inches away from the glass when the old man's eyes flew open. Joey shouted and leaped to his feet. The old man let out a garbled cry that was swallowed up by the water. Joey backpedaled and fell through the curtain, tumbling out onto the stage. By the time he'd scrambled back to the aquarium, it was churning with bubbles as the old man struggled to free himself. His Zen-like calm had vanished. Still floating upside down, the man wrestled with the straitjacket and kicked his legs like a wild horse. "Don't worry!" Joey rushed to the side of the water tank. "I'll get you out of there. I'll . . ." He trailed off, looking around the room for something to help pull the man out of the tank. "I'll be right back!" The man looked pained, desperate. Joey darted off to find something that would save him.

Backstage was a mess of props, costumes, lighting rigs, ladders, ropes, pulleys, and crates. Joey rummaged through a cluttered desk looking for tools, but it was a prep station with nothing to offer but stage makeup, powders, and brushes. He rifled through a series of cardboard boxes filled with magic tricks. There were unbreakable ropes, color-changing gemstones, invisible light bulbs, and waterproof fire . . . all of them very interesting, but nothing useful. Then he saw an iron crowbar lying on top of a wooden shipping crate. *Jackpot.*

"Get back!" Joey yelled as he bounded back to the tank, holding the crowbar like Babe Ruth.

The old man shook his head, writhing in the water. "Mmmmmph!!!"

Joey swung the crowbar. The glass shattered. Water poured

out everywhere, followed by the old man. And more water.

And more.

And more.

An ocean of water—more than the tank could ever hold—gushed out of the aquarium, stronger than a massive wave at the beach. The force of it knocked Joey off his feet. When he got up, he was submerged to the knees and the entire backstage area was flooded, as if some invisible dam had burst. Joey waded over to the old man, who was on his knees, still tied up in the straitjacket and weighed down by heavy iron chains.

"Are you all right?" Joey asked, helping him to his feet. "Don't worry. I've got you."

"You've got me?" the old man repeated. "You've got me?!!" He wrenched a sopping, straitjacketed arm away from Joey. "WHAT ON EARTH DID YOU DO THAT FOR?"

Joey backpedaled, sloshing in the water.

"Who are you?" The old man was soaked to the bone. His hair was matted down, dripping water onto his face. He shook his head like a wet dog and blew sharp bursts of air up to dry out his mustache. His skin was wrinkled at the eyes, with sharp character lines around the nose and mouth. "Well?" he demanded. The old man had a crisp, proper voice, enunciating every word precisely. "Where did you come from? How did you get in here?"

"I, uh . . . I'm Joey? I don't really know about the rest. . . ."

"What did you think you were doing?"

Joey, who'd had a growth spurt during the school year, suddenly felt very small. "Saving you?" he said feebly.

"Saving me! Is that a fact?" The man let out a rueful laugh. "Do you want to know what you've done? Shall I tell you?"

Joey saw something out of the corner of his eye. A splash. Something moved in the water behind him. "What was that?"

"What indeed? Young man, I hope you're a strong swimmer. Because if I can't get out of this straitjacket in the next sixty seconds, you've killed us both."

Joey shook, startled. "Did you just say I killed us?"

The old man smiled brightly. "I did!"

As unsettling as that was to hear, Joey was even more alarmed to find the water he was standing in had a current. A strong undertow was pulling at his legs and feet. "This doesn't make any sense! Where's all this coming from? That tank couldn't hold this much water."

"Do tell." The man nodded to something over Joey's left shoulder. Joey turned. An ominous swell of water rose behind him like a ghost. Glowing sapphire eyes appeared inside the flowing, wraithlike liquid.

"What is THAT?"

"That," said the man, "is Aqua de Vida. Also known as the Water of Life."

"It's alive?" Joey said, backing away from the agitated water.

"It's alive, and it doesn't like you." The old man wriggled in his straitjacket, trying to free his arms.

Joey's stomach writhed. "What's it going to do?"

"Certainly nothing I intended. This water is said to have regenerative properties for those who treat it with respect. For those who hit it with a crowbar, however . . ." He gave Joey an accusatory look. "Quite the opposite."

A mouth opened up below the water creature's eyes. It let out a gargling moan and crashed into Joey and the old man, sending them both flying. When Joey came up for air, he was in the water up to his waist. "What the—" Joey asked, splashing around. "Is this water getting deeper?"

"Nothing gets past you." The old man rolled himself onto the top of the large shipping crate where Joey had found the crowbar. He was still in his straitjacket. Still chained up. "We're in deep, all right."

"Can I help you out of that?" Joey asked.

"Don't you dare." The old man looked at Joey like a water moccasin ready to strike.

"But you said we have less than a minute before—"

"You've done enough. Just hold on to something and try not to drown."

The current started up again, swirling in a circle. Joey latched on to a thick rope connected to the theater curtain as the rushing water pulled him off his feet. Holding on for dear life, Joey looked over his shoulder and saw the floor drop away as a whirlpool took shape all around him. He was trapped in the maelstrom, and down at the bottom, a much larger pair of eyes opened up, turning the watery pit into a wide, hungry mouth. Joey screamed in terror. "HELP!"

"Patience." The old man's voice was calm and even. Somehow, he had managed to shimmy his way into a stable position on top of the crate and stand up, even with his arms bound.

"Patience?!! We're gonna die!" The monster's gargling moan gave way to a roar as it sucked everything in. Its gaping maw devoured whole costume racks, equipment cases, and assorted magical paraphernalia. One of Joey's shoes slipped off and disappeared into the churning bubbles. Joey

48

couldn't see the floor. The pit of the whirlpool was impossibly deep, at least twenty feet below what should have been ground level. "Get me out of here!"

"Quiet, please!" the old man barked. He was balanced on top of the crate, circling the water funnel and trying to free his arms.

Ordinarily, Joey would have been astounded by the old man's ability to ride the crate around the flooded room, but, the circumstances being what they were, he didn't give it a second thought. It was far from the most unbelievable thing that was happening.

"What do we do?"

"I've already told you. If you can't follow simple instructions, you're not worth saving."

Around and around the old man went, using the crate like a surfboard, and sinking lower with each revolution. Even as he descended into the unnatural depths of the water creature's mouth, the determined look on his face never faltered. His hands popped out below the waistline of the straitjacket. He flashed his palms twice. The first time he did it they were empty. The second time, a key appeared in his left hand. Armed with that, he attacked the huge padlock that held his chains in place. It popped open with a loud *click*. The heavy chains splashed into the water.

Joey's hands were slipping, as was his grip on reality. Between the shadow creatures outside and the water monster inside, he could only hope he was losing his mind. The alternative meant all of this was really happening and he was in actual danger. Joey's heart galloped in his chest as the relentless current tugged at him. "I can't hold on!"

"I strongly suggest you do."

The man pulled off the straitjacket and cast it aside. Beneath it, he wore a rumpled tuxedo jacket. He shook out his hands and passed one over the other, producing a red silk handkerchief. Joey lost his hold on the rope and went flying back, carried off by the raging force of the whirlpool. He flailed in the water, certain he was doomed as the vortex whipped him around. Joey sailed into the old man just as he dipped the corner of his handkerchief into the water. They spun violently in the pit of the whirlpool, and Joey felt a powerful whoosh as the water flew away and vanished into thin air. They dropped to the floor with a *whump*. Every piece of backstage equipment came crashing down with them.

"Ow," Joey grunted. He propped himself up onto his

knees and pushed his hair out of his face, looking around in wonder. The floor was back where it belonged, and it was dry. Not even a puddle remained. "What did you do?"

The old man gave Joey an irritated look, hoisted himself off the floor, and took something down off a shelf that was still standing upright. It was a small ornate bottle crafted from brilliant blue glass. Had Joey seen it in a department store, he would have thought it held perfume. He watched as the old man very carefully wrung out the handkerchief, depositing the water creature inside the bottle like a genie in a lamp. The tiny square of silk had absorbed every drop of Aqua de Vida in the shop. The old man closed the bottle up tight, made a loose fist with his left hand, and tucked the handkerchief into his fingers. He blew into his palm, and *voilà!* His hand was empty.

Joey looked around. A scattered mess of boxes and props covered the floor. The old man picked up a chair from the makeup table that had fallen on its side in the flood. He collapsed into the seat and let out a weary sigh. Then he set his sights on Joey. "Well?" he asked. "What do you have to say for yourself?"

3

Redondo the Magnificent

Joey shuffled over to the man, his remaining shoe *sploosh*ing against the floor. "I'm sorry," he said. "I'm so sorry. I didn't mean—"

"That was a disaster," the man said, cutting him off. He ran a hand through his wet hair and glared at Joey, seeming to be simultaneously infuriated and baffled by his presence in the theater. "Who the devil are you? Where did you come from?"

Joey didn't know where to begin. His mind was reeling from the madness of the last few minutes. "I . . . I don't really know."

"You don't know?" the man snapped, incredulous.

Joey pointed back the way he came in. "The door. It was open. I thought—"

"What do you want here?"

"Nothing! I want to go home."

"Then what did you come in here for?"

"Because!" Joey blurted out, flustered. "I was out in the street. Those things out there . . ." He shivered at the thought of the living shadows that had chased him into the theater. "I had to get away. I needed help."

"Help? You attacked me."

"I thought you were going to drown."

"Thanks to you, I nearly did. Good God, what a mess." He huffed and fluttered his fingers, dismissing Joey. "On your way, young man. Show's over."

"What show? Which way? I don't know where to go."

The man pointed impatiently to the gap in the stage curtain, back the way Joey had come. "Try the door. Evidently it's open."

A jolt of fear rattled Joey's spine. "I'm not going out there. Those things will eat me alive!"

"Bah!" The old man waved Joey off. "They can't hurt you. They're not even really there. Not in the sense that you and I are here, anyway." He paused suddenly. "Exactly how did you say you got here again?"

"You're asking me? I don't even know where 'here' is! What is this place? Why is this happening to me?"

"To *you?*" The old man broke into an unexpected coughing fit. He stood up, covering his mouth with a white handkerchief. "I'd like to know what force inflicted you upon me. One doesn't simply walk into this place. Something or someone sent you. What was it? Think."

Joey felt like he might melt under the old man's glare. "The magic set," he said, grasping for an explanation. "The box."

The old man's face contorted. "What?"

"Redondo's Mystery Box. It had to be."

The old man's mouth fell open. He said nothing.

"I'll show you." Joey darted back through the curtain to retrieve the magic set he had left out onstage. Thankfully, the Mystery Box was still there, and still dry. He came running back in holding it. His soggy sneaker squeaked and his mushy sock squished as he ran. "I had a key. It was in here. There was a string with a tag on it down at the bottom of this case. It said it was trick number 151, which was weird, because there's only supposed to be 150 tricks in the set, but it was there, and the note at the end said, 'Pull the string if you believe.' So I grabbed the key, I pulled the string, and *bam!* Next thing I know—"

"Let me see that," the old man cut in, grabbing the case out of Joey's hands. He knelt and examined the magic set with great interest. The expression on his face softened. He was captivated by the Mystery Box, as if he had some special connection to it. "How in the world?" the man whispered to himself. "Where did you get this?" he asked Joey, looking up with penetrating eyes.

"I was taking a test. They had me do all these magic tricks, and—"

"What do you mean you were taking a test? A magic test?"

Joey shook his head. "A logic test. It was supposed to help me figure out what I should be when I grow up."

"Using magic tricks?" The old man looked skeptical. "Where are you from?"

"Hoboken."

"New Jersey?" The old man chortled. "You've got to be kidding me. Is there a less magical place in the world?"

The old man snickered at his own joke. The twinkle in his eye tipped Joey to something he should have realized sooner. "It's your magic set." Joey took out the instruction booklet and turned to the first page. "This picture . . . It's you. Redondo the Magnificent."

The trace of a smile formed on the old man's lips. "You've heard of me?"

"No." Joey shook his head. "Never."

"Never?" Just like that the smile was gone. "You could at least have the decency to lie."

"Never before today, I mean," Joey said, trying to extricate his foot from his mouth. "Obviously, I read this book. And . . . and I recognized you from the posters outside."

Redondo crossed his arms, disappointed. "Not right away."

"You look a lot older than you do in those pictures," Joey said in his defense. Even as the words left his mouth, he couldn't believe he had said them out loud. "Sorry! I don't mean—you look good! I'm just . . . wow. I'm really off my game right now. I'm not trying to insult you. I don't know any magicians. Maybe Houdini. That's about it."

The old man nodded, as if he should have known better. "I knew Houdini too." He inspected the booklet. He had a wistful, nostalgic look as he stared at the image of the young magician printed on the page.

"Didn't Houdini die, like . . . a hundred years ago?" Joey asked.

"It was a long time ago," Redondo admitted.

"A long time since what?"

Redondo rapped his knuckles on the top of the black trunk case. "A long time since someone brought in one of these." He got up and carried the magic set over to the makeup prep station. He set it down in front of a Hollywood-style mirror with light bulbs running around the perimeter of the glass. "Am I to understand you did all the tricks in this magic set by yourself?"

Joey nodded. "That's right."

"No help from anyone? All in less than an hour?"

"That was the test. How did you know that?"

Redondo wagged a finger. "It's part of a test. That is, it used to be." He paused to stroke his mustache. "Have you ever studied magic before?"

"I had a magic set I used to play with when I was younger. Does that count?"

"It might. Were you any good?"

Joey lifted his shoulders half an inch. "I was pretty good with the card tricks."

"I like card tricks too." Redondo rubbed his chin. "What's your name?"

"Kopecky. Joey Kopecky."

"Well, young Kopecky. I wasn't expecting you, but since you're here . . . You might as well show me something."

At first Joey didn't understand what was being asked of him. "You want to see me do magic?"

Redondo held out his arms. "What else?"

"Right now?"

"If you're not too busy." Redondo motioned to the shattered aquarium. "Perhaps there's something else you need to demolish first?"

"No. Of course not. It's just . . ." Joey trailed off, unsure of what to say or do. "Well, for one thing, the magic set's empty." He crossed the floor to Redondo, lifted the lid, and turned the case on its side. All the tricks that came with it were back on Mr. Gray's desk.

"That doesn't matter," Redondo said, undeterred. "If you're telling the truth about how you got here, novelties such as the contents of this case have already served their purpose."

"What purpose? What am I supposed to use?"

"Your imagination." Redondo opened his arms, presenting the expansive backstage area and the random assortment of items present there. "This theater is a treasure trove of magical artifacts and relics. That's why the shadows outside keep trying to force the door open, but they can't get in. Not yet." Redondo broke out coughing, covering his mouth with the handkerchief again. He tucked it away quickly, but not before Joey saw a spot of red on the otherwise clean, white cloth.

"Are you all right?"

"I'm fine. Wonderful, in fact. Don't I look fine?"

Joey shook his head. "I'm so confused right now. I don't know what this is. . . . I don't know what you want me to do. . . ."

Redondo turned the magic set right-side up and closed its lid with a bang. "The Mystery Box exists to spark imagination and to identify children who may be of use to the Order of the Majestic. Maybe that's you. Maybe it isn't. My hopes are not high, but as you are technically here at my invitation, I'll give you the benefit of the doubt. Having said that, I want to see something real. No boxes with false bottoms, trick decks, or double-sided coins. Proper magic only."

Joey's head was swimming. "Something real? The Order of the Majestic? What are you talking about?" Joey thought about all the unbelievable things he had seen so far. They were beyond comprehension and, without question, beyond his ability to reproduce. "I can't do real magic."

Redondo frowned. "One doesn't *do* anything to make magic work. One simply gets out of the way. Isn't that how you ended up here?"

"All I did was pull a string." *And my whole world unraveled.* "I didn't know all this was going to happen. I got here by accident."

Redondo turned up his palms. "If that's all it was, it doesn't matter. A trick you can't repeat is not a trick. It's a fluke. It's meaningless. Not unlike this conversation, I suspect. I should have known better than to get my hopes up. Let's be honest. There's no way a boy growing up in New Jersey, of all places, found his way here to me. I trade in the impossible, not the ridiculous."

"What's your problem with New Jersey?"

"That's your question?" Redondo rolled his eyes. "Fear not, young Kopecky. My quarrel is not with you or your fine Garden State, but rather with a society devoid of magical possibility. You're just a product of that society. It's not your fault. Not entirely. If you'd prefer to go home, I can arrange that."

Redondo went to snap his fingers.

"Wait!" Joey called out, putting up his hands. "Can you please just wait? You're throwing a lot at me here. I need to process. Give me a minute to think."

Redondo took out a pocket watch, checked the time, and regarded Joey impatiently. "Exactly one minute."

"Thank you," Joey said in a keyed-up, testy voice. The situation was wearing on him. It was overwhelming . . . the definition of impossible, but that didn't change the fact that it was happening. He had to accept it. *Magic is real. Okay, that's new information.* There wasn't any point in denying it. What other explanation was there? Did he think this was some kind of hallucination? That he was actually wandering the halls of the NATL building in a delusional state, imagining he had been transported to an old, run-down theater? Joey dismissed that idea out of hand. He had been stressed out about the PMAP test and Exemplar Academy, but not that stressed. Anyway, he could handle stress. That was one of the reasons he was such a good test taker. That was how he got here. This wasn't the test that Joey had expected to take, but he realized it might be the most important test of his life. How many times had he dreamed about an opportunity like this? This moment existed in every book or movie he'd ever escaped into. He had to try. Redondo wanted to see some real magic. The question was, could Joey pull off one more trick?

Redondo snapped shut the lid of his pocket watch. "Time's up." He tucked the watch away and offered his hand, which Joey noticed was splotched with burn scars. "Farewell, young Kopecky. It's been"—Redondo searched his mind for the right words—"an unwelcome intrusion," he said at last.

"Wait!" Joey said. "I've got it."

"Got what?"

"A trick. What else? I can do a trick. Something real." Joey put on a big smile, trying to project confidence. There was one trick he remembered that could be done without any kind of ruse or hidden device. It wasn't magic that made it work. It was math. Cold, hard, boring math. "I need a deck of cards."

Redondo looked dubious, but he went along. "I'm already regretting this." He opened up one of the nearby equipment cases and rummaged through it until he found what Joey had asked for. "A woman in New Orleans told my fortune with these cards a long time ago." He cleared off a space next to the magic set and spread out an old deck of cards, presenting them faceup in an even line. An assortment of faded colors and strange images stared up at Joey.

"What are they?" Joey asked. "Tarot cards?"

"Not exactly. They're something much older."

"I need regular cards."

Redondo was way ahead of him, lifting the last card at one end of the line by its corner. Turning it over, he flipped the entire deck in one fluid motion. The cards rose and fell like a wave. On the other side, the cards displayed standard numbers and suits. Joey gathered up the deck, noting as he did that the unfamiliar images had disappeared from the other side. The cards were now branded with the kind of designs normally found on the backs of playing cards. "All fifty-two cards here?" he asked.

"It's a standard deck. I've seen to that."

"Good." Joey found and discarded the jokers, then started shuffling. "My father taught me this one," he said, stalling as he tried to remember all the steps of the trick.

"Your father? Is he a magician?"

"He's an accountant."

Redondo made a face like he'd just drank spoiled milk. "My condolences."

Joey squared the deck and set it down on the table. Redondo cut the cards to keep him honest. That was fine. Redondo could mix up the deck as much as he wanted. It was a self-working card trick. Joey didn't understand it, but as long as he was playing with a full deck and followed each step to the letter, some kind of algorithm took over, resulting in a specific arrangement of the cards every time. It was one of the first card tricks Joey had learned how to do, and it was by far the easiest to master. He didn't know how it worked and he didn't know why. It just did.

"Get ready for some real magic," Joey said, picking the cards back up. "First, we deal out half the deck, faceup."

"Why?"

Joey paused before dealing the first card. "Because we do." Joey dealt out twenty-six cards and quietly took note of the seventh card in the pile: the three of diamonds. He picked up the stack of cards and placed it back on the bottom of the deck, careful to keep everything in order.

"Next we're going to take three more cards from the top."
He dealt out a jack, a king, and a two. "We need to make
each of these piles add up to ten."

"Make them add up how?"

"By adding more cards to each pile. The jack and the king
are already worth ten. The two here needs some help." Joey
peeled off eight cards and laid them down on top of the two
he had just dealt.

"Why did you do that?"

"It's just the way the trick works."

"Well, as long as you've got a good reason. Your delivery
is flawless, by the way. The way you extinguish doubt and
parry each objection? Masterful."

"Going all in on the sarcasm, I see."

"A keen observer, as well! You'll go far."

"Stay with me here. This is the cool part. Check out the
first three cards I dealt in each of these piles. What do we
have? A jack, a king, and a two. Ten plus ten, plus another
two equals twenty-two."

Redondo suppressed a yawn.

"Which means, the twenty-second card in this deck, is
going to be . . ." Joey made a show of trying to conjure up

the image of a card in his mind. Really, he was thinking back to the seventh card in the pile he had dealt out at the beginning of the trick. "The twenty-second card will be . . ." Joey snapped his fingers. "The three of diamonds."

Redondo inspected his cuticles, disinterested. "Is that a fact?"

"Don't believe me? Watch."

Joey started dealing out the cards. But when the twenty-second card turned over, it was not the three of diamonds. Redondo drew in a sharp breath at the sight of the card that had taken its place. It was solid black and bore the image of a single hand, drawn in a white dotted line. The fingers on the hand were bent in a clawlike grabbing motion. "Huh?" The strange card's appearance took Joey by surprise. He didn't understand. This trick always worked. It couldn't *not* work; it was a mathematical certainty. The seventh card he dealt back at the beginning of the trick should have been there. Instead he got this . . . What *was* this? The grabbing-hand image looked sinister, the kind of symbol an evil army might have stitched on its flag. Joey didn't know what it was supposed to be, but it clearly meant something to Redondo. The old man cautiously picked the card up and turned it over. One word was written on the other side:

Soon.

Redondo dropped the card as if it were hot to the touch. He looked up at Joey with fear in his eyes. "Get out of here."

Joey picked up the card, stunned. "What . . . ? What just happened? Did I do that? Was that me?"

"Leave now."

"Wait a minute. You've got to tell me what this is. Did I just do real magic?"

Redondo pounded the table with his fist. "I SAID NOW!"

There was a loud *crack*, and a disorienting sensation stole through Joey's body. He thought he might fall over, but he spun around, stabilizing himself. Once he had restored his lost balance, he tried to get a fix on Redondo, but all he saw were the plain white walls of Mr. Gray's testing room.

"What the . . . ?" Joey did a double take. "No!"

Joey was right back where he started, which was the last place he wanted to be. "What'd I do?" he asked, hoping Redondo could still hear him. Something told Joey not to hold his breath waiting for an answer.

The timer Mr. Gray had set earlier went off. Joey jerked as if he'd been jolted with electricity. He settled his nerves and patted his clothes and hair. They were bone-dry. The magic tricks were all arranged neatly on the desk, just as he had left them. He looked inside the case. The golden string was back in place, fully restored, key and all. "I don't believe this."

The video camera stared down from its perch near the ceiling. He looked up at it, wondering what the tape would show. For the second time that day Joey worried that the whole experience was the result of an overactive imagination. Then he realized he was still holding the creepy black card he had pulled from Redondo's deck.

Mr. Gray opened the door and poked his head inside. "Time's up! How'd you do?"

"Honestly?" Joey looked down at the strange card in his hand, wondering what it meant. "I have no idea."

4

Strangers in the Night

"What's in the case?" Joey's father asked as they walked through the pristine waiting room to the elevator. All of the kids in plastic suits were off taking their tests, but Mrs. White was still there, giving Joey the evil eye.

"It's a magic set," Joey said, giving the lid a pat, ignoring her.

"A magic set?" Joey's father bunched up his lips. "Why do you have a magic set?"

"They let me keep it after I finished my test."

Joey's father tilted his head to the side, clearly confused.

"Wasn't that nice of them, Dad?"

"Uh . . . yeah. Very nice. Can I take a look?"

Joey passed his father the magic set and hit the call button for the elevator.

"This is a Mystery Box," his father said, looking over the black trunk case, utterly astonished. "I don't believe this . . . Redondo's Mystery Box. I had one of these when I was a kid!"

"Get out of here," Joey said, genuinely surprised. "Really?"

"Really," his father said, looking at the magic set like a long-lost dog that had unexpectedly found its way home. "It's in amazing condition," he added, turning the Mystery Box over in his hands, keenly inspecting every surface. "You could probably get a lot of money for this thing. Not that you should sell it."

"I'm not selling it," Joey said instantly.

"I wouldn't let you," his father replied. "What were they doing with this?"

Joey didn't answer right away. "It's complicated." The elevator doors opened. "I'll tell you on the way down."

But once they got in the elevator, Joey was the one asking the questions—about Redondo. He wanted his father to tell him everything. His father obliged, but there wasn't much to tell beyond the fact that Redondo used to be famous. "Real famous, not Internet famous," his father stressed. It made Joey's father so mad that people could become famous because of things like reality TV shows, having a massive social media following, or by posting videos of themselves playing video games online.

"How come I never heard of him?" Joey asked.

Joey's father gave a shrug. "I guess his fifteen minutes were up. There aren't really any big magicians left, are there? You kids all have your phones and tablets these days. You can find out how everyone's tricks are done online. There's no mystery anymore. Not unless you count this." Joey's father handed him back the Mystery Box, still waiting for Joey to explain its presence.

By the time they made it out the front door of the building, Joey had managed to describe the strangest day of his life in a way that his father could understand, but he had to leave a lot out, as he was having trouble with it himself. Mostly, Joey talked about Mr. Gray and the Department of Alternative Testing. His father found it all very interesting, not to mention terribly confusing.

The first thing Joey did when he got outside was look across the street. The Majestic Theatre wasn't there. In its place was a vacant lot with a restaurant on one side and a hotel on the other. An aged plywood fence, painted blue and papered with advertisements, sealed off the sizable space in

71

between. The ads were for movies that had come out last summer and concerts with show dates well in the past. Joey wondered why the theater still stood in that strange dark world he had visited but was long gone from here. Had he traveled back in time? That didn't seem right. And what were those shadow things that had come after him? What had Redondo meant when he'd said they weren't really there? Where were they? Where was Redondo, for that matter?

"So, they used this magic set to measure what, exactly? Your ability to think creatively?"

Joey snapped back to reality. "What? Oh . . . right. Yeah, I think that was the idea."

"And that takes the place of the PMAP?" his father asked. "How do they grade a test like that?"

"I asked the same thing. Mr. Gray told me not to worry about it. He said he was going to watch the video of me doing the tricks and send his job recommendation to the people at Exemplar Academy tomorrow." Joey gave a disinterested shrug. "It's all good. I'm sure he knows what he's doing."

"You're not worried anymore?"

Joey shook his head. "Not about that." He held the magic

72

case tight in a viselike grip. He was ecstatic that Mr. Gray had offered to let him keep it. He couldn't have known what it was he was giving away.

"I'm glad you're feeling better about all this. I just hope the folks at Exemplar Academy are on board with this Mr. Gray's methods."

"Me too," Joey lied. He didn't really care if they were or not. It was hard to be concerned about things like that after his encounter with Redondo. The world was suddenly bigger and full of more possibility than it had been when he'd gotten out of bed that morning. *Magic is real*, Joey told himself again. He was struggling with the revelation and what it all meant.

The Earth Day marchers were still out in full force, so Joey and his father took the subway back to Penn Station. Later, as they boarded the PATH train to Hoboken, Joey's father tapped him on the shoulder. "I have another question for you."

"Dad, no more quizzes. Please."

"Not that kind of question. I want to know why you're wearing only one shoe."

Joey grimaced. "I was hoping you wouldn't notice that."

His father looked around the train platform, trying to spot the missing shoe. "Did you walk this whole way with just your sock? On New York streets? That's disgusting."

"Don't be such a germophobe," Joey said, trying to downplay the oddness of the situation.

"I'm not a germophobe. This city is filthy. What happened to your other shoe?"

Joey bit his lip. He wanted to tell his father everything. In fact, he was dying to tell him, but how could he do that? The story was too wild to share with anyone. Joey's father liked magic, but he didn't *believe* in it. Joey could hardly believe it himself, and he had seen it up close. His father couldn't handle the truth.

"You're going to laugh, but I actually forgot to put both shoes on before we left the apartment this morning. Funny, right?"

His father stared at him, waiting for the punch line. "You forgot your shoe?"

"I know, it's ridiculous."

"You forgot your *shoe*."

"I was stressed out, okay? All these tests . . . It's a lot of pressure."

"Why didn't you say anything after we got outside?"

"Honestly, I didn't even notice until we got to the city."

"Didn't notice?" His father's eyes bulged. "How could you not notice something like that?"

Joey turned up his palms. "I told you I wasn't a genius. You didn't notice, either."

His father touched a hand to his forehead and let out a weary sigh. "Do me a favor. Don't say anything to your mother about this."

"Don't worry."

Joey's father grunted. "I worry. Believe me, I worry."

That night Joey couldn't sleep. Rain pounded hard against his bedroom window as he sat in bed, scrolling through search results on his phone, determined to learn everything he could about Redondo the Magnificent. He didn't have to look very hard. Joey's father was right. Once upon a time, Redondo had been kind of a big deal. Twenty years ago he'd been touted as the next Houdini. He had toured the world, hosted specials on television, and of course, launched his own successful business—a line of novelty magic tricks bearing his name. According to one article Joey read, Redondo's

Mystery Box had been the must-have toy of the 1984 Christmas season. Children couldn't get enough of them, or him. He was that popular. Critics had hailed Redondo as a master of illusion, going so far as to call seeing him in person a "profound, life-changing experience." *So what happened to this guy?* Joey wondered. *Why'd he stop performing?* The answer was a few clicks away. Redondo's glowing reviews and meteoric rise to fame came to an end after a disastrous performance at the Majestic Theatre in New York.

Joey clicked on old news links with headlines such as LANDMARK MAJESTIC THEATRE DESTROYED IN FIRE and FRIGHTFUL BLAZE TERRORIZES BROADWAY. Apparently, the theater had burned down as a result of an accident during Redondo's grand finale. After that there was nothing. The Majestic Theatre had gone up in smoke twenty years ago, and Redondo's career had gone with it. Joey kept digging, but he couldn't get the full story on what had happened at the theater that night. A headline that read CHILD MISSING AFTER THEATER FIRE caught his eye, but the link went to a dead URL.

The closest Joey got to an answer was a scanned image of an old tabloid newspaper.

DISAPPEARING ACT!

"REDONDO THE MAGNIFICENT" IGNORES SUMMONS, WARRANT ISSUED.

Joey zoomed in on the article and read as much as he could. A twelve-year-old boy named Grayson Manchester had yet to be found a week after the fire. Joey looked a little while longer, but he wasn't able to find out what happened to him. Just the odd fact that the Majestic Theatre lot—a piece of real estate valued in the millions—was still empty twenty years later. It was a detail Joey already knew, having seen the vacant lot himself, but it was only part of the story. Why had no one else ever tried to build on that spot? Joey wondered if the theater might still be there in some strange, mystical way. After all, if magic was involved, anything was possible. The theater could have been invisible from the outside, but Joey dismissed that idea as quickly as it came to him. Not because it was too "out there," but because it wasn't "out there" enough. He had gone *somewhere* that morning; he was sure of it. Some kind of other dimension, or reality . . . someplace cold and dark. Where had he been that he was able to stand in the ruins of a theater that had burned down long before he was born? Was it some kind of ghost world? Was that how Redondo knew Houdini, a man who, according to Joey's online research, died in 1926?

Joey stayed up late into the night, hunched over his phone, googling in vain. He kept at it until his eyes drooped and his vision blurred, but his search seemed to turn up more questions than answers. Outside, a howling wind added its voice to the rain. Joey was tired. His brain was mush. He was about to give up and go to sleep when lightning flashed, flooding the room with flickering light. The momentary strobe effect revealed a man in a top hat sitting at his desk.

Joey flinched. He rubbed his eyes and squinted in the darkness, trying to focus on the figure at the desk. "Redondo?" he asked hopefully.

There was a brief silence, then, "No," an unknown voice replied. "Not Redondo."

The man's eyes lit up with an eerie glow, and Joey's heart lurched. His neck and shoulders tightened and he screamed, but a chorus of thunder followed the lightning just in time to drown out the sound. "Shhhh," the man whispered after the moment had passed. He sat in the darkest corner of the room, where he wasn't much more than a silhouette. "No need to raise your voice, Joey. I can hear you just fine." The stranger had a British accent, soft, sophisticated, menacing. He sounded like a Bond villain.

His hand shaking, Joey turned his phone on the man, shining its weak light in his direction, trying to get a better look at him. The intruder wore a black suit with a black overcoat and top hat. A long green scarf was wrapped high around his neck, covering the lower half of his face like a mask. He made no move against Joey. He just sat there at the desk, staring. The man's calm, reserved demeanor inspired the opposite emotion in Joey. For him the mood was tense and threatening despite the quiet. Joey cleared his throat. "Am I dreaming?" he asked in a fragile voice. "Please tell me I'm dreaming." He was breathing very fast.

"Heh." The man chuckled in his seat. "I thought you might say something like that." He tugged down gently on the scarf as he spoke, but not enough for Joey to see his face. "If you don't want to believe your own eyes, that's fine. Most people don't. When I'm gone, you can tell yourself this was nothing but a dream, but I'm here, Joey. Not like those friends of mine you met outside the theater today. I'm here in the flesh."

Joey scooted back in bed, pulling the blankets up to his chin. "You're with them." A cold feeling churned in the pit of his stomach. The shadows had followed him home. "What do you want?"

"From you? Nothing. Redondo on the other hand . . . He has something that belongs to me. You're going to help me get it back."

Joey clutched his blankets. "Who are you?" he squeaked. He was so scared he could barely get the words out.

"I'm your benefactor," the man said coolly.

Joey backed up all the way to the wall. He felt as if his intestines were tied up in knots. "What does that mean?"

"You know the answer to that, don't you? A bright boy like yourself? It means I make things possible. You didn't see me today, but I was right there with you. Even gave you my card."

The man picked up the creepy playing card that Joey had produced that morning. Joey had left the card on top of the magic set, which was also there on the desk. The man in the top hat and scarf moved the card across his hand, flipping it from pinky to pointer, then snapped his fingers. Just like that, the card was gone. The man stood up, patting the breast pocket of his coat. Joey felt something inside the pocket of the T-shirt he was wearing. The card was there now. He took it out and stared at the strange image printed on its face.

"The Invisible Hand, at your service." The man took a bow. "You never see us coming."

Joey remembered the look on Redondo's face when he saw the card. Like he'd seen a ghost. At the moment Joey felt the same way. "What are you talking about? What is this?"

"I helped you." The man threw Joey a wink. "No need to thank me."

"Right." Joey grimaced. He didn't need to be told that. He would thank the man to leave, but that was about it. There was a darkness about him that chilled Joey to the marrow. He was tall and thin like a skeleton with long, spindly arms and legs. As for his face . . . Joey couldn't see any of it. His top hat cast a shadow over his eyes, and the scarf covered up the rest. He looked like the kind of guy who went on picnics in the graveyard, and that wasn't even the scariest thing about him. He knew Joey's name, where he lived, and apparently, had the power to drop in anytime he felt like it. Joey wasn't sure he'd ever feel safe in his room again. How could he, with this guy out there? Who was he? And his "friends" outside Redondo's theater . . . the shadows . . . What did they want with him?

"Don't be afraid. I'm not going to hurt you," the stranger said soothingly, perhaps sensing the turmoil in Joey. "Provided you do as you're told," he added as a caveat.

Joey swallowed hard. "I'm not doing anything with you." The words took every ounce of courage he had.

The shadowy man tittered at Joey's bravado. "What exactly are you going to do, I wonder?" he asked, clearly amused. "Something heroic, like a character in one of your comic books?" He motioned to the long boxes of comics in the corner of Joey's room and the random issues scattered on the floor. "I don't think so. In the real world, Joey, bad guys win. Not that I'm the bad guy," he added, almost as an afterthought.

"What are you, then?"

The man in the top hat and scarf spread his arms wide. "I am what I am. I want what I deserve. And I'll get what I'm after . . . one way or the other. Tell Redondo if he tries to keep it from me, somebody's going to get hurt."

"Why don't you tell him? Leave me out of it."

"If only I could. We're not on speaking terms, Redondo and I. That's where you come in."

82

"No! I don't come in anywhere! He kicked me out!"

"You'll go back. I know you will. Here's a little something to take with you when you do," the man said, reaching for Joey.

As he leaned in, Joey leaned back, but he had nowhere to go. He was already up against the wall. "Stop! What are you doing?"

"Just planting a seed. Wherever you go, I'm going to be right there with you, Joey. A sinking feeling in the back of your brain . . . something you're not quite sure of but can't quite dismiss, either . . . a reason—a need—to be afraid." The man touched a finger to the center of Joey's forehead. "There. That ought to do it."

Joey pulled away as an ice cream headache hit him right between the eyes. He rubbed his forehead, half expecting to find a layer of frost on his skin. He felt violated, like his brain had just been infected with something terrible. "What did you do to me?"

The man in the scarf snickered. "Maybe nothing, but you'll always wonder." The snicker grew into a laugh that was so icy, so full of evil delight, Joey felt a strong desire to hide under his covers. "You've got your work cut out for you, Joey. Don't disappoint me, or history might repeat itself."

"What are you talking about? What history?"

"Redondo's final performance," the man replied. He picked up Joey's phone. The story about Grayson Manchester and the theater fire was still up on its screen. "Would you like to know what happened at the Majestic Theatre all those years ago? What really happened?"

Joey turned away from the stranger's glowing eyes. "I just want you to leave."

"Don't worry. I'm not staying." The man waved a hand. "In fact, I'm already gone."

Joey blinked, and suddenly he wasn't lying in his bed anymore. He was standing upright in a large wooden box—the kind a magician might place his assistant inside for a trick.

"What the—where'd you go? Hey!" Joey pounded on the walls. They were not only solid, but also hot to the touch. Flames appeared at his feet and climbed up the walls like burning ivy. Joey pressed himself against the back wall of the box. Outside, the man in the scarf cackled. More flames rose up behind Joey. He shuffled forward, but there was nowhere to go. "Let me out!" he screamed. "LET ME OUT!" Joey threw a kick into the wall before him. It gave way. He fell forward . . .

. . . and woke with a jolt.

There was no fire. No flaming coffin. He was safe in his bed, and most important, he was alone. The room was quiet and empty. Joey wiped his brow. He was drenched with sweat. Yesterday he would have been grateful that the nightmare was over. Tonight he was afraid it was only just beginning.

5

The Order of
the Majestic

Joey's fascination with Redondo had now moved beyond curiosity and intrigue. He needed answers. More than that, he needed protection. There was only one place he could hope to find either. Joey threw back the covers and got out of bed. He emptied the contents of the magic set onto his desk and looked inside the case. The golden string and key twinkled up at him.

"Let's try this again."

Joey gripped the key tight in his fist. He pulled the string, and the walls fell away, just as they had done in Mr. Gray's office. Once again Joey was transported to Redondo's strange Bizarro World and deposited in front of the Majestic Theatre. The streets were just as dark and foggy as he remembered them. The Majestic's marquee was still partially lit up.

Joey hustled to the theater door before the shadow creatures had a chance to come back out. He had been told by Redondo that they weren't really there, and Joey's mysterious visitor had hinted at the same, but that didn't change anything as far as he was concerned. They were real enough for Joey, and he had no desire to see them again. He turned the key in the lock, transforming it once more into dust, and darted into the lobby. Safely inside, he pressed his face up against the glass and waited. One of the shadows drifted by a few seconds later, gliding through the haze in the middle of the street. As Joey backed away from the door, he heard someone coughing inside the theater.

Redondo, Joey thought. *Good. He's awake.*

Joey followed the coughs. The noise led him all the way into the theater, where he found Redondo sitting in the front row, staring up at the stage by himself. He was holding something in his right hand. When Joey got close enough, he saw it was the strange deck of cards he had used that morning.

"You again," Redondo said without turning.

Joey came around the end of the aisle. "Me again," he agreed. Joey took stock of Redondo with a more careful eye than he had that morning. He looked old and tired. Worn out. He still had on the same wrinkled tux with the bow tie hanging loose around his collar. With his tousled white hair and mustache, he looked like the Monopoly Man fallen on hard times.

"What time is it?" Redondo asked, barely looking up.

"It's late. I had a little trouble sleeping."

Redondo cleared his throat, somewhat painfully, judging by the expression on his face. "I often have trouble sleeping myself. That doesn't mean I want company. Why are you back?"

"I was hoping we could put our cards on the table." Joey took out the Invisible Hand's calling card, the one that had gotten him thrown out of the theater that morning. He set it down on the armrest of Redondo's chair. Redondo eyed the card with distaste, but he picked it up, slid it back into his deck, and mixed the cards up, hiding it in the pack. He then pulled three cards from the top: the Collector, the Traveler, and the Unknown.

"What's that there?" Joey asked.

Redondo frowned and put the cards away. "It's hard to say."

"What about the Invisible Hand? Is that hard to talk about too?"

Redondo's eyes narrowed. "Where did you hear that name? Who've you been talking to?"

"That's what I'd like to know. This guy showed up in my room tonight. He said he was with them."

"Someone came into your home?" Redondo asked, the edge in his voice lifting. "They were actually there?"

Joey nodded. "He made a special point of telling me that. Even poked me in the head to make sure I got it. I'm lucky that's all he did."

"What did he look like? Can you describe him?"

Joey shook his head. "He had a top hat and scarf on. I couldn't see his face. He said you had something that belongs to him, and people were going to get hurt if you didn't give it back. I got the feeling he was talking about me."

Redondo made a face like he'd been forced to swallow a spoonful of foul-tasting medicine. He let out a troubled sigh and got up out of his seat. His joints made popping noises as he moved. Joey didn't know who was in worse shape, Redondo or the theater.

"What are you doing in here?" Joey asked.

Redondo cast a sideways glance at Joey. "Why shouldn't I be here? This is my theater."

Joey looked around, wrinkling his nose at the dusty, depressing space. "Feels more like a hideout. Do you live here? All by yourself?" Redondo didn't answer. The question seemed to annoy him. Joey figured he had about two seconds before the old man sent him packing again. "What happened to you?"

Redondo turned around, scowling. "Nothing happened to me," he said, getting defensive.

"Something did," Joey replied, not buying it for a second. "This place burned down twenty years ago. The newspaper said a kid died in the fire."

"The theater didn't burn down. You're standing in it."

"I don't know *where* I'm standing. We're not in New York. I know that much. I was there today, where the theater's supposed to be. It's just an empty lot. Where are we, some kind of ghost world? Are you dead?" Joey hoped Redondo wasn't dead. After the night he'd had, he didn't think he could handle that.

Redondo barked out a short laugh. "No. I'm not dead. I'm retired. There's a difference. It's subtle but not inconsequential." Picking up on Joey's anxiety, he sought to ease his concerns. "Relax. This isn't the afterlife. You haven't traveled quite that far. This is just another realm. A redoubt in between realities," he added by way of explanation.

"In between realities?" Joey repeated. His mouth hung open when he was done speaking. In truth, Joey had already guessed that much, but to hear the words actually spoken out loud . . . for Redondo to confirm the impossible truth about the theater's location and to do it so casually . . . it boggled the mind.

"There used to be enough magic in the world to open doors to all kinds of different realms," Redondo continued. "Faerie, Asgard, the Thrice-Tenth Kingdom, Tír na nÓg . . ." Redondo smiled, reflecting briefly on the list of magical destinations, but the smile faded quickly. "I couldn't reach those high heights, but I was able to plant my flag here. Beyond space and time. Short of any real substance. I call it Off-Broadway. It's seen better days, I know." He motioned to the fire damage all around the stage. "But it's safe. It's still safe."

"From them?" Joey asked. "The Invisible Hand?"

"For now, yes."

"Who are they? What do they want?"

Redondo clammed up again. He was extremely reticent

on the subject of the Invisible Hand, but Joey would not be dissuaded.

"I think I deserve an explanation. I've got a creepy dude showing up in my bedroom in the middle of the night, threatening to burn me alive. I know magicians never reveal their secrets, but you've got to let me in on this one. . . . What did I walk into the middle of?"

"Nothing."

"Don't give me that."

"It's the truth. This isn't the middle of anything. It's the end."

"Of what?"

"Magic. My life's work. Any purpose I served. Take your pick."

"What are you talking about?"

"I'm talking about the bitter conflict between two secret societies of magicians. The Order of the Majestic, which aims to keep magic alive and free, and the nefarious Invisible Hand, which seeks to hoard magic and control it. The two sides have been at it for centuries—rivals since the days of Merlin. The Order of the Majestic was founded to ensure the world remains a magical place, fighting the influence of dark, evil magic wherever it rears its ugly head."

"Fighting evil . . . ," Joey whispered. "Like a superhero team?"

Redondo cast his eyes upward. "If that helps you . . ."

"Why is that ending? What's going to happen if the Invisible Hand gets their way?"

Redondo seemed resigned to defeat. "I'm afraid they've been getting their way for some time now. That's why the world is how it is. No magic. No wonder. No hope. They've wrapped an invisible hand around the world and are slowly squeezing the life out of it." Redondo balled a fist and clenched it tight, as if crushing an orange. "Most people don't even notice. They don't know what they're missing."

"How's that work? This stuff is pretty hard to miss."

"It's easier than you think. Most people your age ignore magic. Your generation in particular finds it on TV, online . . . in their phones. The world is full of magic, but no one believes it. They choose not to."

"I believe in magic."

"Since when?"

Joey looked down. "This morning," he muttered.

Redondo smirked. "That's what I thought. Too little, too

late. Best to put all this out of your mind. Forget you ever came here. Ignorance is bliss."

Joey scrunched up his face. "I don't want that."

"In my experience, the world doesn't care very much about what we want." Redondo patted Joey on the shoulder. "Nothing lasts forever, young Kopecky. This . . ." He gestured around at the theater in all its degradation. "All of this . . . It's over."

Joey looked around the run-down theater, trying to follow along with what Redondo was telling him. "What do you mean it's over? If it's over, why are people breaking into my house at night to tell me you better play ball? Why am I here?"

"You're here because you passed my test, and the Invisible Hand doesn't want me getting any ideas. They can't follow you in here, but every time you show up, they slip a note under the door." Redondo drew the card with the hand on it from the deck, inexplicably plucking it right out of the middle. He flipped it over to the side that read, *Soon*. He handed it back to Joey. "Message received."

Joey looked over the card. "Is that why you kicked me out before? You thought I was with them?" Redondo nodded in the affirmative. "I'm not, you know," Joey said, taking umbrage at the notion.

"I know. You dropped this earlier." Redondo went inside his jacket pocket and took something out. It was the Save the Planet pamphlet that the girl on the train had given Joey that morning. He scanned it, amused. "Not exactly the Invisible Hand's agenda. Too optimistic."

Joey took the pamphlet back from Redondo, realizing it must have fallen out of his pocket during the magical flash flood with the Water of Life. He hadn't bothered to read it on the train, but seeing it again now got him thinking . . . not about clean air and clean water, but something rare and precious just the same. He remembered Redondo had put his own call to action inside the Mystery Box:

> *The world is running out of magic. Unless we act,*
> *this most precious of natural resources will disap-*
> *pear forever. . . . That's where you come in. . . .*

An idea took root in Joey's mind.

"Can you teach me magic?" he asked Redondo out of the blue.

"What?" Redondo looked at Joey as if he'd asked if he could borrow a million dollars. "Don't be ridiculous."

"Why is that ridiculous?"

"Because it is," he said flatly. "I don't have the time. I don't have the energy. I don't have the temperament. I'm not a teacher. I'm a magician. And I work alone."

"Doing what?" Joey asked. "You haven't worked in years."

Redondo stiffened, affronted by Joey's bluntness. He pushed past him, heading up the aisle toward the exit. "I don't have to listen to this."

"Where are you going?" Joey called after him. He took the instruction booklet out of the Mystery Box and read aloud, at the top of his voice. "'Master the tricks in this booklet and join me onstage as my assistant.' What do you call that?"

"Ancient history," Redondo said, still walking away. "And I never *taught* anyone magic even then. Read that page again, the part about mastering the tricks. Have you mastered anything?"

"I did the tricks!" Joey shouted. "Isn't that enough?" He hustled after Redondo. "Hey! You said the Mystery Box was there to kick-start imagination and find kids who have what it takes to join the Order of the Majestic."

96

"I'm certain I never used the word 'kick-start.'"

"So they weren't your exact words. Whatever," Joey said, catching up to Redondo outside the doors that led to the lobby. "The point is, I passed your test. You said so yourself."

Redondo slowed to a halt. Putting one hand on the door, he turned to face Joey. "You passed the first part of a very old test. One I didn't even know was still out there."

"Who cares? Any way you slice it, I passed. What's next?"

Redondo shook his head. "Nothing. There is no Order of the Majestic. Not anymore."

"Can there be one?" Joey asked.

"Can there be—" Redondo cut himself off, exasperated. He pressed his fingers to his temples and made a noise like Joey was giving him a headache. "What does it matter to you? Why do you care?"

"Are you kidding? This is the most amazing thing that's ever happened to me in my life. You can't expect me to just forget about it. This is my shot. My Hogwarts letter!"

"Your *what?*"

"My dream come true! Being here is like finding Narnia in the back of the wardrobe. It's Luke Skywalker meeting

Obi-Wan Kenobi or Dr. Strange tracking down the Ancient One. This is an origin story right here!"

Redondo stared at Joey, dumbfounded. "Who do you think you are?" He shook a finger at Joey, adding, "I'm fifty-five years old, by the way. That's hardly ancient!"

"Come on," Joey pleaded. "Put yourself in my position. It's not every day you find out magic is real."

"It's only real if you believe in it."

"I do believe in it."

"Because you've seen it. You have proof, not faith. It's all well and good to believe in someone else's magic. If you want to make your own, you have to believe in yourself. I can't teach you how to do that."

"You don't have to. I did magic. I did enough to get here. Twice in one day! You've got to give me that."

"You did . . . a little," Redondo said grudgingly. "Very little." He held his thumb and forefinger close together. "This much."

"Thank you! That's something, isn't it? Please. I'm begging you. Out there they want to plan my life out for me. In here anything's possible. This is what I want to learn. I want to learn it all. Teach me."

Redondo exhaled loudly. He touched a hand to his forehead and then slid it down his cheek to rub his chin, giving the matter serious consideration. After much hemming and hawing, he locked eyes with Joey.

"No."

The matter settled, he pushed through the doors into the lobby, leaving Joey alone in the auditorium.

Joey stared at the swinging lobby door, too stunned to speak. He thought for sure he was getting through to Redondo. Why was the old man being so thick? Didn't he realize Joey needed this?

Joey gave the doors a good hard shove and stormed into the lobby. "You could at least show me how to protect myself if that guy in the top hat comes back. Or is that too much to ask? Do you even care if I get caught in the cross fire of your stupid fight?"

"It's not stupid," Redondo said matter-of-factly. "By the way, that's a very hurtful word. I was under the impression children were being taught not to call things 'stupid' these days. And I do care. I care enough to keep you safely removed from it. You don't have to worry about the Invisible Hand."

"How do you know?"

"Becau—" His reply was interrupted by a coughing fit that he was hard-pressed to stop. He put up a finger, signaling for Joey to wait as he turned away and doubled over, violently hacking into a handkerchief. When the coughing finally subsided, Redondo looked back, red faced and teary eyed. "Because they're only coming after you to get to me . . . and I won't be here much longer." He folded up his handkerchief and put it away. This time the bloodred stain on the cloth was unmistakable.

Suddenly Joey understood something he had completely missed during his first trip to the Majestic Theatre. One of the little details he was so good at noticing had escaped his watchful eye. Redondo had said the Water of Life contained regenerative properties. He hadn't been practicing a trick. He'd been practicing medicine—on himself.

"You're sick?"

Redondo gave a grim nod. "Cancer."

The fuse on Joey's temper was snuffed out instantly. "I'm sorry," he said, unsure of the right thing to say in that moment. "Is it . . . bad?" he added awkwardly.

Redondo considered the question a moment before answering. "I'll put it to you this way. You know the kind of cancer people eventually triumph over?"

"Yeah," Joey said hopefully.

"I've got the other kind." A rogue's smile formed on Redondo's lips. As he found comfort in his own gallows humor, a horrible realization struck Joey:

"I smashed your aquarium," Joey said, feeling heat rise to his face. "You were using that to get better. Did I ruin that? Your—your chance? I didn't realize—I didn't know!"

"Stop. Stop right there," Redondo said, but not unkindly. "That was just meant to give me a boost. A magical shot in the arm, if you will. It wasn't a cure. What I've got . . . the stage I'm at . . . there is no cure."

"Are you positive? Isn't there some treatment you could try? What did your doctor say?"

"It doesn't matter what she says. It won't be the cancer that gets me. It'll be them." Redondo pointed at the door to the street. Joey jumped when he saw the shadow creatures gathering outside. He'd been so focused on Redondo, he hadn't noticed them creeping up. Joey cringed as they hissed and rattled the door, trying to get in. Redondo eyed them with the cool detachment of a nanny waiting out a child's tantrum. "Don't worry," he told Joey. "They're not here . . . not yet," he added quietly. As the shadows pounded the walls outside, the lobby lights dimmed and flickered. Dust fell from the chandelier overhead, but the doors held.

"What are they?"

"Magicians," Redondo said matter-of-factly. "Dark magicians," he added, just to be clear. "Agents of the Invisible Hand. This is how they appear in this place. Only those who pose no threat can physically enter this realm. All they can do is lurk in the shadows."

"If they can't get in here, why did you think I was with them?"

One of the dark magicians beat a defiant fist against the door, and a light fixture fell off the wall, crashing to the floor with a bang. Redondo grimaced. "Things are changing. I'm not as strong as I used to be. The walls I put up around this place . . . they're crumbling. I give it about a week. Maybe less."

"What happens then?"

Redondo scowled, facing the dire future. "They'll come in. And they'll take everything. All the secrets . . . all the knowledge . . . every magical item I've managed to save over the years. All of it."

"What about you?"

"Oh, I expect they'll make short work of me. People like

you will be hard-pressed to find any magic in this world after that. They'll control it all."

"No . . . ," Joey said, struggling with Redondo's bombshell.

"On the plus side, the Invisible Hand will leave you alone. As I said, you don't have anything to worry about."

"No!" Joey said again, this time more forcefully, refusing to accept the situation. This was terrible news. Not just Redondo's condition, but the condition of the world at large . . . Joey had just found out that a magical light he'd never known existed was real, and it was about to be extinguished. "Can't you stop them?"

"What do you think I've been trying to do all these years?"

Not much, judging by the looks of this place, Joey thought. This time he had the good sense not to voice that opinion. Instead he said, "You can't give up. You used to be a great magician."

"Great?" Redondo was offended. "First of all, I was never merely 'great.' I was magnificent."

"Sorry. Magnificent."

"Second, I thought you said you've never heard of me."

"That was this morning. I've been up all night reading about you on my phone."

"On your phone." Redondo rolled his eyes. "Saints preserve us."

"What's wrong with that?"

"Everything. I'm surprised you could find any mention of me using one of those things. They've done their best to erase me from memory."

"But I did find you. And I found this place. Coming from 'the least magical place in the world,' I believed enough to find my way here! That should count for something."

Redondo stroked his mustache, thinking. "It should. You're right; it should."

"Of course it should! Don't let whatever's in here die with you. Don't let them win. You can't!" Joey waved at the posters of Redondo's glory days, hung throughout the lobby. "Look at you up there. What happened to that guy? Where'd he go?"

"He was diagnosed with lung cancer."

"You're not dead yet, are you?" Joey knew he was being harsh, but he was too desperate to care. "What about your legacy? Don't you want to leave something behind. If magic was your life's work, keep it going. Pass the torch."

Redondo cast about, struggling with the decision. "You

don't know what you're asking." He had a pained expression on his face. "I swore I wouldn't . . . I can't."

"You *can*," Joey implored Redondo. "My dad told me something this morning. He said, 'Whether you think you can or you can't . . . you're right.' What do *you* think? It's your decision."

Redondo nodded ever so slightly. He let out a sigh. "Shamed by an accountant. What's the world coming to?"

"Teach me what you know. I promise, you won't regret it."

Redondo's eyes fell upon a poster where he was depicted onstage working alongside an assistant, a young boy he was about to saw in half. "You might," he said, a note of foreboding in his voice.

Joey studied Redondo. "Is that a yes?" His chest inflated. His eyes lit up with hope. "What are you—what are you saying right now?"

"I'm saying . . ." Redondo took a breath, possibly second-guessing himself. Joey couldn't read his expression, but this was it. Redondo was either going to send him home or invite him in. This was the moment. Joey held his breath and waited.

"I'm saying, onward, young magician. We have work to do."

6

The Nature of Magic

"I should warn you, this isn't going to go the way you think," Redondo told Joey as he led him back into the main house of the theater.

"Nothing has so far," Joey replied. "I'm getting used to it."

"Good. Don't expect that to change. In fact, from this point on, expect only the unexpected."

"Got it."

"The first thing you need to learn is I won't be teaching you anything."

Joey stopped dead in his tracks. "Okay, I wasn't expecting that. Didn't we just agree that you were going to teach me magic?"

"When did I say that?" Redondo continued down the aisle without breaking his stride. "If you recall, my exact words were 'we have work to do.' Work, young Kopecky. I'm not going to teach you; I'm going to test you. This isn't an apprenticeship. I'm not running a school of witchcraft and wizardry here."

Joey pointed. "I knew you got the Hogwarts reference!" he said, hustling after Redondo.

Redondo grunted. "Of course I got the reference. I've been living off the grid, not under a rock. The fact remains, if you're expecting a magical education, you're going to be disappointed. That's the stuff of storybooks and movies. This is the real world. If you want to learn magic, you'll do it by watching and absorbing. By picking up whatever you're able to pick up. You figure it out as you go; that's how I did it. That's how it's always been. Do you understand what I am saying?"

"Are you sure we've got that kind of time?" Joey asked, trying to make his point delicately. Surely Redondo didn't need to be reminded that he only had a week to live.

"Don't worry about time. If you're successful, there will be plenty of time later."

"How? You mean you might beat the cancer after all?"

Now it was Redondo's turn to stop dead in his tracks. He

turned around to face Joey, looking like he smelled something he didn't care for. "No. I told you that already. Please don't keep bringing up my condition. It's depressing. That's not the kind of energy we need right now."

"Right. Sorry," Joey said, hopelessly confused.

"Follow me." Redondo marched down the aisle past the front row. He turned before he reached the stage, heading for a hidden door in the wall. He paused before opening it. "Bring the Mystery Box," he told Joey.

"I thought you said we didn't need that anymore."

"It's not the box we need, but what's inside it."

"It's empty."

"Is it?" Redondo cocked an eyebrow and waited. Joey gave in and climbed up onstage to retrieve the magic set. He gave it a good shake as he picked it up by the handle. It felt empty to him. Coming back, he caught Redondo rubbing the burned portion of his hand as he stood facing the burned-out stage. He had a haunted look in his eyes. Joey wanted to ask him about the fire, but he decided to hold off on it. He didn't want to put out any more bad energy. Upon his return, Redondo clicked his tongue and pushed the door open. "Through here."

From there they went downstairs to a storage area filled with props: a man-size safe, a guillotine, and in the corner, a birdcage with three perfectly folded origami birds perched inside. Redondo threw a sheet over the cage, then pulled it away to reveal three white doves flapping their wings. Redondo took one bird out of the cage, held it close, and released it in Joey's face, shouting, "Hassan!"

Joey threw his hands up to keep the bird from hitting him, but it disappeared en route, and he was left waving at empty air. Redondo tittered, reaching back into the cage for another dove. "What was that about?" Joey asked.

In lieu of a response, Redondo tossed a fresh bird at Joey, this time shouting, "Valkov!" Joey flinched again, but his reaction was less pronounced the second time around. Once again the bird vanished after leaving Redondo's hands.

"Not bad," Joey said, looking around for the doves. They were both gone. "Were those magic words?"

"No," said Redondo. "Magic *birds*."

"Okay," Joey said, not really understanding. He was impressed by the trick, but he wasn't sure what, if anything, he was supposed to have learned by watching Redondo perform it. He wasn't even ready for it when it happened. Each bird vanished too fast for him to see how Redondo had done it, but there was one more left in the cage. "Can you do that again? I totally missed—"

"This way," Redondo said, already moving on. "We're nearly there."

"Where are we going?"

Down another level, they pressed on through an underground library. Weaving their way through the labyrinthine stacks, they eventually arrived at a black door with a sign that read THEATER MANAGER. Behind that door was the kind of mess that made the rest of the theater look clean. It was overflowing with ideas, plans, random thoughts, and distractions. There were papers piled high on a desk and towers of books on the floor. A mosaic of multicolored Post-it notes and index cards papered the walls.

"This is some office," Joey said, trying not to sound critical.

"This is where I've been planning my comeback for the last twenty years." Redondo paused to tap at a dying bulb, trying to coax more light out of it. "It's a process. At least, it was. As you said, it's time to pass the torch."

"I'm ready."

"You're not ready," Redondo said, taking a seat behind the desk. "You don't know the first thing about magic."

"I know you have to believe."

"There's more to it than that."

"Tell me. Whatever it is, I'm in." Joey pulled up a chair across from Redondo, accidentally knocking over a sprawling house of cards in the middle of the floor. It was like a mansion of cards, it was so big. Joey started to apologize, but cut himself off midsentence as the card sculpture flew apart, then re-formed, bigger and better in the shape of the Statue of Liberty. "Okay, how does that work?" Joey asked. "Magic cards?"

"Not exactly." Redondo held up his deck of fortune-telling cards. "This is a deck of magic cards." He pointed to the sculpture. "Those are merely enchanted."

"What's the difference?"

"I'm getting to that." Redondo settled into his chair. He seemed to be wondering where to begin. Joey said nothing. Redondo looked like he was finally getting ready to drop some knowledge. Joey waited him out, and was rewarded for his patience. "If you're going to understand what magic is, you first need to understand what it was."

Joey scooted forward, eager to learn. "I'm listening."

"It used to be everywhere," Redondo began. "Magic. It was a part of life. Part of nature. Everyone believed. Ages ago, long before your time—or mine—magic flowed through the air like the breeze . . . an unseen energy touching everything . . . connecting everything."

"Like Wi-Fi," Joey said.

Redondo pursed his lips. His eyes were cold. "Not like Wi-Fi."

"I'm going to shut up now," Joey said. He mimed locking his lips and tossing away the key, then waited for Redondo to pick up where he had left off. Redondo grumbled, but he went on with the tutorial.

"People today believe it was just the stuff of legends, but in Merlin's day—what? Why are you looking at me like that?"

Joey didn't even realize he'd been making a face, but it was the second time Redondo had mentioned Merlin. He couldn't contain his surprise. "Merlin was real?"

"You don't believe me?"

"No, I do!" Joey said quickly. "Trust me, I'm ready to believe anything at this point. I just didn't expect . . ." He trailed off and touched a hand to his forehead, trying to order his thoughts. "I guess I'm just one of the people who always thought those stories were legends. Also, I thought that was a whole other kind of magic. People like you and Houdini . . . Aren't you different from wizards like Gandalf and Merlin?"

"Actually, Gandalf *was* fictional, but otherwise, no, we're not. Magic is magic, young Kopecky. The only difference between Houdini and Merlin was the fashion of the era in which they lived."

"Really? So, they were like . . . the same power level?"

"I believe so." Redondo bunched up his lips. "I suppose it's debatable. It's not as though we can check the back of their baseball cards and compare statistics, but I assure you, the answer to your question has nothing to do with their wardrobe. Would you think me to be a more capable magician if I were to wear a funny hat or grow a long bushy beard? I don't think so. This isn't medieval times; nor is it Brooklyn."

"Got it. No beards necessary. Should I be writing this down?"

Redondo stared at Joey for several seconds, looking like he was debating whether or not to continue. "Moving on," he said gruffly. "After Merlin's death things changed. Magic was cut off. Locked away. We don't know how. We don't know why. There are, of course, stories. There are always stories, but little is known. We do, however, know magic is still out there. It exists as an elemental force, but the world somehow has less of it. Less access. Today we rely on magical objects. Relics. Unique artifacts and places that were infused with magic back during the lost golden age. Ancient castles, secluded forests . . . Even the ground upon which this theater was first built is one such place. The Majestic itself is full of rare and powerful relics. Some are more powerful than others. This . . ." Redondo pressed his palms together as if in prayer, and then slowly drew them apart. A classic magician's wand, black with a white tip, appeared and hovered between his hands. "This is the most powerful of them all." The room brightened with a warm, golden light. "What you see before you once belonged to Harry Houdini."

"You knew him?" Joey ogled the floating wand before him. Redondo nodded. "He taught you?" Joey asked.

Redondo shook his head. "I learned from him."

"How?"

"After I inherited the wand, the ghost of him lingered inside it. For a time."

Joey's eyes widened. Redondo had learned magic from the ghost of Houdini! It was almost too much for his brain to handle. "This is what they're after, isn't it? The Invisible Hand . . . This is what that guy in the top hat wants."

"You catch on fast. Perhaps there's hope for you yet." Redondo plucked the wand out of the air and held it aloft. "After the death of Merlin, the Order of the Majestic was formed to preserve any magic worth saving. The Invisible Hand rose up in opposition. They've spent centuries collecting and stealing magic-infused items. Consolidating power. Nothing that once belonged to Merlin remains intact, but his wand . . . This is the prize. The most coveted magical artifact in the world."

"What makes it so special? What's it do?"

"Almost anything. You have to understand, the majority of magical objects do very specific things. Most of them were created long ago for singular, extraordinary purposes. Whips that leave behind gold coins when you crack them, boots that let you walk across water, hourglasses that slow time to a crawl . . . All quite miraculous, yes, but ultimately limited. It's only a select few relics, like this one, that are able to act as conduits, tapping into the world's dwindling supply of magic—harnessing it to bring imagination to life." Redondo aimed the wand at the enchanted playing cards. They disassembled and reassembled themselves in the form of a scale model of the Eiffel tower. "To enchant nonmagical objects." He flicked his wand again, and they rose into the air, taking the shape of a snowflake. "To make new magic." One last, tight circular motion with the wand had the snowflake rotating in midair as the cards flipped and turned like a kaleidoscope image. "It takes a lifetime to learn how, but for those who know how to use it, this wand can do nearly anything. Its connection to magical energy is stronger than any other known artifact. Are you still with me?" Redondo asked, snapping his fingers to draw Joey's attention back from the floating cards.

"I'm with you." So far it was easy enough to follow. The majority of the world's magical objects worked with a spotty Wi-Fi magic signal, but Houdini's wand had a hard-line fiber-optic connection to the source. Joey declined to share this analogy with Redondo.

Redondo brought his hands together with a clap, and the

wand vanished between them. The cards continued to turn in the air like a Ferris wheel.

Joey blinked. "This is unbelievable."

"Not for a magician. Magic requires belief. Also focus. Clarity of thought. Absence of fear. The relics aren't enough by themselves. You can't simply pick up a wand and say 'Abracadabra.' It takes more than that."

"You need a wand or a relic . . . ," Joey said, the wheels in his head turning along with the cards.

"You need all of it."

"How did I get here, then? To this place? Wasn't that magic? I didn't have a relic. I didn't have anything."

Redondo smiled. "Of course you did. Open the Mystery Box." Joey picked up the empty magic set, only it wasn't empty after all. When he opened it, the skeleton key was back inside the case, once more attached to the golden string. Redondo untied the knot around it. "I enchanted this key using Houdini's wand a long time ago. Anyone who displayed the proper zeal for magic . . . this key would bring them to me, wherever I was—provided they believed. That was the first part of the test," Redondo added. He handed the key to Joey. "From now on this is how you get here. Use it on any door. Unless you'd rather keep running the gaunt-let outside?"

"Definitely not," Joey said, happy to know he would be able to avoid future run-ins with the shadows of the Invisible Hand. He took the key as if he were being handed a priceless diamond. "My own magical object. This is so cool."

"There's a small bit of magic in there, but enough. Treat it with the respect it deserves, prove you can handle it, and maybe one day I'll trust you with more. For twenty years I've kept Houdini's wand safe from the Invisible Hand. If I bequeath it to you, that would become your responsibility. You think you're ready for that?"

Joey looked up with a start. He hesitated for a second, then said, "Yes." Mainly because it felt like what he was expected to say. Redondo didn't seem convinced.

"We'll see." An unpleasant cough rattled out of Redondo. "As you continue to remind me, time is not on my side. I thought it was enough to keep this wand away from the Invisible Hand, but I see now I was wrong. Someone has to use it. I'm just not sure that someone is you."

"Who else is there?" Joey asked.

Before Redondo could reply, they were interrupted.

Someone was calling Redondo's name. The voice was coming from outside the office. It sounded like it belonged to a young girl. Redondo checked his pocket watch, his expression casual and unconcerned. "That was fast."

"What was fast? Who is that?"

Redondo gestured to a window on the wall. "See for yourself."

Joey knew that opening the window was pointless since they were down in the subbasement, but he got up and threw the shutters open just the same. He was surprised to find Redondo's office was actually on the back wall of the theater, high up above the balcony, facing the stage. Looking down, he was even more surprised to find two sleepy-eyed children waiting below. "What the . . . ? How?" Joey asked, unable to form a complete sentence. "Who are they?" he finally managed.

Redondo joined him at the window, looking out. "They're your competition." He turned to Joey with a devilish wink. "Welcome to the second part of your test."

7

May the Best
Magician Win

"Competition? Since when is this a competition?"

"Since about . . ." Redondo checked his pocket watch. "Five minutes ago."

Joey nearly fell over. "I was with you five minutes ago!"

"Why are you acting so surprised? You saw me send out the birds."

"The birds?" Joey didn't see what that had to do with anything. Then he realized Redondo must have been using the paper doves like messenger pigeons. "I thought you were showing me a trick. I didn't expect—"

"I told you, 'expect the unexpected.' To be honest, I'm not even sure this qualifies. Surely you don't think you're the first person to show up here looking to claim Houdini's wand."

"I didn't come here to claim Houdini's wand. I didn't even know it existed." Joey leaned out over the windowsill, trying to get a better look at the other two children. "How did they know? Where did they come from?"

"Over the years great magicians from around the world—my peers—have urged me to take on a protégé. I haven't been in the market for an assistant in quite some time, but still they've sought me out, asking me to train their children and pass on Houdini's legacy. Up until now I've refused them all. I'm sure these two were surprised to hear from me tonight, but they didn't waste time getting here, did they?" He patted Joey's shoulder. "They're going to hate you, young Kopecky. Shall we join them?"

Joey's head whipped around toward Redondo. "Did you just say they're going to hate me?"

"Trust me, they hate you already. You're in their way." Joey felt a lump in his throat. He didn't like this. "If I could offer you some advice, stop repeating everything I say in the form of a question. It makes you seem terribly dim. I'm telling you this for your own good. You don't want to embarrass yourself down there, do you?"

Redondo lifted a long black cane out of an umbrella stand

by the door. Passing the cane to his other hand, he twirled it with a theatrical flourish. The fancy walking stick had a shining silver handle in the shape of a perched raven. Reaching up with the cane, Redondo hooked the silver bird through a steel ring in the ceiling and pulled open an attic door. The rectangular hatch above their heads swung down, and a wooden stepladder folded out and locked neatly into place. Redondo gave it a shake, testing its sturdiness. "That'll do," he said, satisfied with the ladder's durability. "Up you go."

"Up?" Joey repeated, staring into the pitch-black attic space. Redondo sighed. Joey was doing the question thing again. "Sorry." Joey didn't understand how climbing up the ladder would lead him down to the stage, but he did as he was told, ascending into darkness.

Redondo clapped his hands. "Chop, chop, young Kopecky. The hour is already late. No more questions. Climb."

Joey picked up the pace, his stomach clenching tighter with each step. Before he reached the top, his head bumped on a low ceiling. There was nowhere to go.

"That's it; you're nearly there," Redondo said, urging him on from below.

Joey pushed on the ceiling, which gave way, rising on a hinge. Light poured in through the opening, and Joey saw the footlights of the stage, along with two pairs of illuminated feet. Somehow, the attic door in the office ceiling doubled as a trapdoor in the stage floor below. It made sense in a roundabout sort of way. They had gone down to go up, so naturally they had to go up in order to get back down. Even so, as Joey pushed the door open the rest of the way, he gawked at the main house of the theater with eyes as wide as billiard balls.

Joey crawled out of the door in the floor and gave a nod to the boy and girl who stood there waiting patiently. They both looked to be about Joey's age and had identical "Who the heck are you?" looks on their faces. The boy was at least a foot taller than Joey. He had a linebacker's body, light brown skin, and a judgmental scowl. Joey felt the boy looking down on him both literally and figuratively. He wore black pants, a bright red shirt, and a cape that went down to his waist—Lando Calrissian style. The cape was black to match his pants, with a shiny gold interior lining. Joey almost joked that he didn't know this was a costume party, but something told him the boy wouldn't find it funny. Standing next to him was a young girl who had wavy black hair with a bright red streak in it. Several pendants and medallions hung around her neck, and she wore a folk dress with embroidered patterns and beaded fringes. The girl studied Joey with a curious expression. She was very pretty. So much so that Joey shied away from looking her in the eye. It was an awkward moment. He didn't know what to say. "Hey" was all he could muster. The other two children said nothing. Their dead stares made Joey uncomfortable, and he struggled to fill the silence between them. "Hi. I'm, uh . . . My name's—"

"Excuse me," Redondo broke in. "One side please." Joey realized he was blocking the trapdoor exit.

"Sorry." He scuttled back a few steps to make way for Redondo.

Joey felt relief as the spotlight shifted away from him. Once Redondo took the stage, he was no longer the center of attention. Redondo stood tall, all eyes on him, which seemed to suit the old man just fine. Taking his moment, he circled the trapdoor and tapped it shut with his cane. A cloud of dust puffed up as the door slammed down, causing Redondo to lapse into another one of his coughing fits. "Pardon me," he said, frowning, once he regained his composure. Not exactly the entrance he had hoped to make, if Joey had to guess. Redondo turned to face the three children. "Let's get the introductions out of the way. You know who I am?" Everyone nodded. "Good. You're Hassan's boy, I take it?" he said, addressing the boy in the cape.

The boy stepped forward. "I am indeed," he replied in what sounded like a Middle Eastern accent. "Shazad Hassan of Jorako."

"And how are things in Jorako?" Redondo asked. "Well, I hope?"

Shazad smiled. "Always."

Redondo gave a nod. "Welcome to the Majestic Theatre, Shazad." He continued on to greet the young girl. "You can only be—"

She stepped forward. "Leanora Valkov, formerly of Freedonya, presently of the traveling Nomadik clan of magicians. Why are we here?"

Joey's eyebrows went up. This Leanora was a bold one. She spoke with a tone that commanded respect—and got it. Her tough Russian accent was part of the reason, but there was more to it than that. She was confident and direct. The way she kept her chin up, looked Redondo square in the eye, and held his gaze was more than impressive; it was down-right intimidating.

Redondo smiled. "Why do you think you're here, Leanora?"

"I take it you're looking for an assistant?"

"More than that," Redondo said behind a tiny cough. "A successor."

Leanora's eyes widened, appreciating the opportunity before her. "In that case, I have a different question. Why are we *all* here?"

"I'd like to know that as well," Shazad chimed in. "Surely, you don't need—"

"Anyone but me," Leanora cut in, raising her voice to be heard over Shazad.

Shazad and Leanora eyed each other competitively, sizing each other up with standoffish looks. Each of them was clearly of the opinion that they were the most talented young magician on the stage. Joey wished he had some of that same fire in his belly, but there in that moment, his stomach felt cold as ice. He was still reeling from the news that it wouldn't just be him learning magic with Redondo. Even worse, he might not get the chance to learn anything at all. Instead of teaching Joey, Redondo had decided to turn the whole affair into a reality show competition. *Welcome to America's Next Top Magician!* Joey worried that his origin story was going to be over before it began. Already out of his element, he suddenly felt way out of his league. Where did these two come from? Freedonya? Jorako? Joey had never heard of any of these places. "I'm sorry, what does that mean?" he asked, trying to keep up. "The traveling Nomadik clan? What's that?"

"It's a nice way of saying her people are too reckless with their magic to ever stay in one place very long. A Nomadik's only home is the road," Shazad said with a detached air about him.

"At least we use our magic to do more than hide," Leonora replied, getting defensive. "What's the use of having magic artifacts if you're afraid to do anything with them?"

"My family keeps magic artifacts safe," Shazad countered. "We don't put them at risk by going out and playing hero."

Leonora smirked. "You're the only one here wearing a cape. Where's your mask, Boy Wonder?"

Joey snickered. Shazad shot him a stern look and he stopped laughing immediately.

"This cape is a priceless relic, cut from an ancient cloak of transfiguration," Shazad told Leonora, reaching for the hem of the shiny fabric. "I promise you, I'm not afraid to use it."

Leanora set her jaw and fixed Shazad with a hard stare. Joey watched as she clutched at one of the medallions that was strung around her neck. At the same time, she made a fist with her other hand. It lit up red and orange, like burning embers in a fire. Joey saw the bones inside her hand, silhouetted in black. His mouth fell open. Shazad didn't bat an eye.

"Is that supposed to scare me?" he asked.

"It should," Leanora told him. "It's a firestone. With this I could punch a hole in a mountain. What do you think it would do to you?"

Joey took a couple of steps back. He was afraid of what was in Leonora's hand, even if Shazad wasn't. She drew her fist back, ready to throw a fiery punch.

"Ah, ah, ah . . . ," Redondo said, intervening. "We'll have none of that." He waved Houdini's wand in the air, drawing light and power away from Leanora's hand until the wand lit up like a magnesium flare. It hurt Joey's eyes to look at it, but Redondo extinguished the light simply by covering the tip with his fingers. It made a hissing noise, like a red-hot poker being plunged into ice water. "We're all friends here," Redondo said. Everyone stared at the wand as smoke drifted up and away from it. "Well, perhaps not *friends*," Redondo allowed, "but this *is* a friendly competition. Which means you are not to threaten, endanger, or otherwise end the lives of any of your rivals in this theater. Do I make myself clear?"

Joey gulped. *Did he just say "end the lives"?*

Joey tried to gauge Leanora's and Shazad's reactions to that, but it didn't look like they had heard a word Redondo had said. They were staring at the wand as if in a trance. On the plus side, Redondo inserting the wand into the situation had quelled the bourgeoning unrest between them. "Do I have your attention now? Good. You want to know why you're all here? This is why," Redondo said, brandishing the wand. "To prove yourselves worthy of inheriting Houdini's legacy. Go ahead. Have a look." He handed the wand to Shazad, surprising him. Shazad took the wand carefully, as if it were a sleeping baby he was trying not to wake. He felt its weight in his hands and studied it in awe before passing the wand to Leanora. She accepted the wand with care and examined it like a museum curator inspecting a priceless work of art. Next, it was Joey's turn. He knew from Redondo and the other children's reactions that the wand was a one-of-a-kind treasure, but it didn't feel like anything special. He held it aloft as if ready to cast a spell. Houdini's wand didn't strike him as any more substantial than the wand he had purchased at Universal Studios the summer before last.

"Nothing happened," he said.

"Of course nothing happened," Redondo said, taking the wand back. "What did you expect? Swirling winds? A choir of angels serenading you as heavenly light shined down from above? You're getting ahead of yourself."

"I don't understand. Why are we here now?" Shazad asked. "My parents asked you to take me on more than a year ago."

"Mine as well," Leanora added. "With all due respect, why are we called here out of the blue, and at such an hour?" She put her hands up. "Don't misunderstand. I'm grateful for the opportunity. My parents thank you. I thank you. . . . I came running, of course. But what is different? What has changed?"

"Two things. Number one, I'm dying." This information elicited the appropriate expressions of alarm, concern, and sympathy from Leanora and Shazad. "As for difference number two . . ." Redondo waved a hand, presenting Joey, whom no one had paid any attention to so far. "It's him. This boy. Joey Kopecky of Hoboken, New Jersey. He changed everything."

Joey froze as all eyes turned once more to him.

"Him?" Shazad asked, incredulous.

"Hoboken?" Leanora said, equally disbelieving.

"That's correct." Redondo stepped aside to give Joey the floor. "Say hello."

Joey gave an awkward wave. "Nice to meet you." Shazad and Leanora greeted him with standoffish, unfriendly looks.

"Thanks for that intro, Redondo. That was awesome."

"It's true. Before tonight I was going to destroy the wand rather than let the Invisible Hand get it. Young Kopecky here reminded me that people like him can still find magic in this world, and that means someone has to carry on the fight once I shuffle off this mortal coil. It's going to be one of you."

"Why only one?" Joey asked. "I don't mind sharing."

"This wand does," Redondo replied. "It obeys only one master at a time, forging a special bond between wand and magician. As long as I'm alive, this is just a piece of wood

131

to you. . . . But once I'm gone, it will become a wish engine of infinite possibility. One of you will wield it. May the best magician win."

The three children looked at one another as the weight of Redondo's words sank in. Joey thought the others took the news remarkably well considering they'd had no time to prepare for it. Redondo aimed the wand at the rear of the stage.

"Now, if there are no more questions . . . let's make some magic."

A rumbling noise erupted inside the theater. Joey looked up. It sounded like thunder, but he saw no rain coming in through the holes in the ceiling. There was no lightning outside either, just the pitch-black sky.

Boom!

The noise grew louder. It was coming from behind the walls.

Boom! Boom!

Something large and heavy was banging around backstage. If the jump in volume was any indication, it was getting closer. It sounded like a raging bull had been let loose deep inside the Majestic. Maybe more than one.

Joey looked to the others, trying to read from their reactions some sense of what was happening. They seemed remarkably unaffected. *Do they know what's coming?* Joey wondered. *Is this kind of thing normal for them?* It probably was. Their parents were both magicians. For all he knew, they had been studying magic since kindergarten. Maybe earlier.

Joey turned back to Redondo. He was no help, with his eyes fixed firmly on the backstage wall, waving his free hand as if directing the movements of something only he could see. The thunderous noise grew louder and closer until it was just backstage, and then suddenly it arrived.

Two large boxes the size of coffins flew out from behind the musty old stage curtain. Joey and the others ducked down as they zoomed by, narrowly missing them.

"Watch your heads," Redondo said after the boxes had already passed. He swept the wand out in a wide arc, and the boxes went soaring over the empty seats in the audience. Redondo turned with them and brought the wand back around. The boxes mirrored his movements and lapped the theater before returning to the stage. Rather than set the boxes down, Redondo twirled the wand and they swirled around, ten feet in the air. Up close, Joey saw they were crafted from smooth, polished black wood. Each box had three handles on its front panel. Soon after spotting that detail, Joey found out why. The two boxes were actually six.

Redondo flared the fingertips on his empty hand, and each coffin split in three. Six wooden cubes floated in the air above everyone's heads, rotating in place. Joey clapped his hands, an action he regretted almost immediately, as he was the only one applauding. Leanora and Shazad stood motionless, tracking the boxes with their eyes. This was nothing to them. They looked at Joey like he was a farm boy gawking at tall buildings his first time in the big city. Joey dropped his hands to his sides and fell in line with them, resolving to play it cool from that point on. *Act like you've been here before,* he told himself. *Act like you belong.*

Fortunately, Joey's lack of cool went unnoticed by Redondo, whose only concern was the heavy wooden boxes that were held aloft by his wand and magical willpower. They must have weighed a hundred pounds each. Working with intense focus, he waved the boxes away from the space over Joey and the others and lowered them gently toward the stage. As they neared the ground, more dust billowed up and Redondo was seized by another violent coughing episode. The boxes all came crashing down in a heap.

Joey let out a yelp, but this time, at least, he wasn't alone. Everyone reacted with their own startled cry. Even Redondo cringed when he saw the result of his momentary lapse in concentration. The boxes had all been broken into pieces, their splintered, ruined remains spread out across the stage. Shazad, Leanora, and Joey surveyed the wreckage, and Redondo, with dubious looks.

"You should know I let them drop on purpose," Redondo said, straightening out his tuxedo jacket and composing himself. "Just trying to see what the lot of you are made of. For the record, every one of you flinched."

So did you, Joey thought.

"No harm done," Redondo said. He flicked his wand, and the boxes started putting themselves back together. It was a neat trick, but Joey wasn't ready to believe it was all part of the show. He had seen Redondo's face after he had dropped the boxes. Even as the boxes repaired themselves in miraculous fashion, Joey wondered how rusty the old man was after twenty years out of the spotlight.

Once every chip and crack was mended and the boxes had been reassembled good as new, Redondo arranged two stacks of three, side by side, in the center of the stage. A light swish with the wand was all it took to move them into place.

"Does anyone know what these are?" Everyone raised their hand except Joey, but Redondo wasn't really looking for an answer. He just liked to hear himself talk. The hands went back down as Redondo pontificated. "What you see before you are Waywayandan Separating Boxes. Some of the first magic I ever learned involved these wondrous devices, handcrafted from wood grown in an ancient forest long since paved over. This trick is a simple but powerful statement on the impermanence of all things, not to mention a fine place to start taking the measure of your abilities." He patted one of the boxes. "Who wants to go first?"

Shazad and Leanora's hands shot back up like lightning.

"Good. Step forward, both of you."

Joey felt the pang of a missed opportunity. He should have been ready to volunteer. That would have shown some initiative. Then again, he didn't know what Leanora and Shazad had just volunteered for, so it was probably for the best that he didn't go first. He had a better chance of doing whatever he had to do properly if he knew what he was supposed to do going in.

Watch and learn, young Kopecky. Watch and learn.

Redondo opened up the doors on all the boxes. Each stack of three was tall enough for a child to fit inside while standing upright. Redondo motioned to the open doors. "In you go." Leanora and Shazad faced off like two boxers tapping gloves before a fight and got into position. "Any questions?" Redondo asked as they entered.

"Not from me," Leanora replied.

"Are you ready?" he asked Shazad.

The boy nodded. "Whenever you are."

Redondo nodded. "Good answer."

He closed the boxes and began to move them around, starting with the ones on top that contained Shazad's and Leanora's heads. Using his wand, he pulled them up and away from the stack and held them there, suspended in midair. Next he did the same with the other boxes. They parted from one another with a light, airy motion—feathers on a breeze. Redondo shuffled them around and put them back together in order. Or so Joey thought. Redondo opened the top-left box and Shazad's feet were inside. Redondo took a step back, examined the stacks, and opened the middle box on the right-hand side. Leanora's head was there, in the place where her stomach was supposed to be.

"Still with us, my dear?" Redondo asked.

Leanora nodded. "I'm fi—"

Redondo closed the door in Leanora's face, cutting her off. He knelt down to the bottom-left box and knocked on the door. "Yes?" Shazad's voice asked from the other side. Redondo opened the door and there Shazad was. Part of him, anyway. Redondo checked the top-right box, the one over Leanora's head, and found Shazad's torso. With three box doors now open, his full body was present and accounted for, albeit completely out of order. Joey was more than impressed, but he managed to keep his poker face intact. Redondo didn't ask Shazad how he felt. Instead, he gave him a sharp jab in the ribs with the end of his wand. Down on the floor, Shazad's head let out a painful, surprised cough. Redondo gave a satisfied nod and shut the door in his face too.

Waiting in the on-deck circle, Joey watched as Shazad massaged his side. As far as he could tell, Redondo hadn't poked him in the stomach to be mean. It was more like the magical equivalent of a doctor testing someone's reflexes by hitting their knee with a little hammer. Redondo just didn't have any bedside manner, that was his problem. Doing the impossible, however, that was no problem at all.

Joey's poker face cracked, and he watched in wide-eyed wonder as Redondo went about his business. Redondo made the boxes fly as he rearranged them again, putting Shazad's head on Leanora's body and vice versa. It was an amazing spectacle, but Joey couldn't help feeling that something was missing. There was no heart. No style or panache. No master showman. He was running a routine with preset moves, and Shazad and Leanora might as well have been mannequins in those boxes. Redondo didn't speak to either of them again until it was time to let them out.

"Next!" he called, beckoning Joey to come forth without bothering to turn his head and look at him.

Joey passed Leanora and Shazad on his way to the boxes. They were both working out kinks in their necks. Joey wanted to ask them if it felt weird being taken apart like that, but the competitive atmosphere got in the way. "Child's play," Shazad said to Leanora as they went by.

"At best," she replied.

Joey was thrown off by the exchange. What were they bragging about? Shazad and Leanora hadn't done anything except stand inside their respective boxes. Redondo was the one who had done all the work.

Joey's heart sped up as he neared the box. Was there more to this than he realized? There was so much he didn't know, but only one way to learn. Joey told himself Shazad and Leanora were just trying to psych him out. He had seen this trick already. There was nothing to it. But as soon as Joey turned his back to get in the box, he heard a sound like a sword being drawn across a whetstone.

Shing!

He spun around to see Redondo holding two blades—large, flat razors with sharp, slanted edges. "What are those?" he blurted out.

Redondo scraped one blade against the other, making the noise again. "Spare blades from the guillotine you saw backstage," he said lazily. "You'd be surprised what I have lying around this place."

"What are they for?"

"My next trick. What else?" Redondo paused his sharpening and looked up. "Is there a problem?"

"These boxes are magic boxes, right?" Joey asked, his voice cracking a little. "They count as relics?"

Redondo answered with a condescending smile and nod that made Joey feel foolish for having asked the question. He forced out a smile of his own as Redondo closed the door, leaving him completely in the dark. Blindly, Joey ran his fingers along the smooth wooden interior, not knowing what to do next. Did he have to do something special, or was he just supposed to stand there and wait for Redondo to chop him up? He wanted to ask, but his throat tightened up on him. His mouth went dry. He couldn't seem to form a sentence. Joey's heart, which was already beating fast, kicked into overdrive as a creepy sense of déjà vu took hold of him. He had been here before—in his "dream." The man in the scarf had shut him up in a box and set it on fire. All of a sudden questions filled Joey's head. Alarms went off in his brain. What had happened to the kid who went missing after the theater fire? What had gone wrong in this place twenty years ago? What was so bad that it had caused Redondo to go into hiding? Joey thought about Redondo coughing and dropping the boxes. What if it happened again? What about the dust? There was so much dust!

There was a rustling sound on the side of the box, and Redondo pushed the blade in. Joey felt a pain in his side and that was it. He bailed. He didn't mean to do it, but instinct took over and he flew out the door. Just like in his bedroom, he kicked his way out of the box and fell forward. Only this time he didn't land in his bed. He dropped five feet out of the air and landed hard on the floorboards of the stage. Everything came to a crashing halt.

Joey rolled over painfully on his side, trying to get his bearings. He hadn't even felt Redondo raise the box into the air. He'd had no idea he was up there. "What was that?" Redondo asked, positively aghast. Joey caught a glimpse of his face and had to turn away. His expression was pure, weaponized disappointment. Leanora looked at Joey like someone who had crashed a wedding and thrown up on the bride.

"So much for the boy who changed everything," Shazad said quietly to Leanora.

"Someone might want to go back to Hoboken," she agreed.

Joey's fortunes did not improve as the evening wore on. Redondo trotted out relic after relic, testing the group's magical acumen, but for a child who normally ate tests for breakfast, Joey came up short at every turn. Redondo challenged the children to walk through a freestanding wall of rocks that had been taken from the foundation of an ancient castle. They were mortared together with hard cement, but

Leanora and Shazad passed through them without a care. Meanwhile, Joey succeeded only in flattening his nose against the stones.

Next Redondo borrowed Shazad's cape of transfiguration and shook it out until it was the size of a picnic blanket. He threw the magic cloth over Shazad and proceeded to fold it up until both the blanket and the boy inside were small enough to fit inside his pocket. When he shook it out again, the cape unfurled like a sail. Shazad tumbled out, flying across the floorboards, turning handsprings, and launching himself into a flip. He stuck the landing at the lip of the stage, finishing strong like an Olympic gymnast. Even Leanora looked impressed.

When Joey's turn came, he had a twist of his own, but one that was far less elegant. After Redondo had finished folding him up inside the blanket, he dumped him out onto the floor. Joey landed in an ungraceful heap and stood up looking like Quasimodo. He was hunched over, unable to straighten out. His elbows bent back the wrong way, and his neck was crooked to the side. Joey hobbled around like a human question mark until Redondo straightened him out, and that wasn't even the freakiest thing that happened to him that night.

When it came to messing with Joey's mind, nothing beat the Russian nesting doll trick. Redondo had a life-size matryoshka doll large enough for a person to fit inside. He said it was originally the property of the first Russian czar. Redondo closed Leanora inside the doll, and when he reopened it, there was a smaller version of the doll there in her place. Inside of that doll was another smaller doll, followed by another and another, until Redondo reached the smallest doll in the center, which did not open. Redondo reassembled everything in order, and when he opened the outermost doll shell a second time, Leanora emerged unharmed.

Approaching the task with some trepidation, Joey crouched down inside the bottom half of the doll. Redondo lowered the top half over him, and when he opened it up again, Joey had found a new and exciting way to fail. He was still there, but he had been transformed into a living matryoshka doll, pear-shaped and made of wood. Joey's likeness was captured perfectly, painted on the outside of the doll in his precise image, right down to the pajamas he was wearing. He had no way of knowing what was happening at the time, but after Redondo changed him back again, Leanora

144

told him how he had sat there in doll form . . . his eyes blinking . . . a look of terror frozen on his face. She had to be the one to tell him, because for thirty minutes after the trick, Joey was incapable of speaking anything but Russian.

When it was time to go home, Joey was afraid he had failed to make it past the first cut, and rightfully so. He asked Redondo if he could come back and try again tomorrow, but the old man shook his head and said he'd have to think about it. Joey asked how he would know when Redondo made up his mind.

"A little bird will tell you," Redondo replied.

Joey hoped his wasn't a vulture.

8

Exemplary Students

The next morning Joey was back in the city for a tour of Exemplar Academy. This time his mom and dad both came with him. Everybody was excited to get a look at Joey's new school. Everybody but Joey, of course. Everything that had happened the night before only made him dread Exemplar Academy even more. How could he possibly be expected to handle school—especially *that* school—now that he knew the world was full of magic? How was he supposed to spend his days locked up in a classroom when he could be out there learning so much more? Doing so much more? Joey's mind ran around in circles as he struggled with everything he had learned in the last twenty-four hours, while trying to pretend that anything else mattered.

When Joey returned home from the theater, he couldn't

sleep. He tossed and turned all night, still processing the fact that any of this was real and reliving each failure, wondering why the tricks didn't work for him the way they had for the other children. It wasn't that hard to figure out. After all, hadn't Redondo told him the relics alone weren't enough? That magic required focus? Clarity of thought? Absence of fear? He didn't have any of that. Not the way the other kids did. He kicked himself for not getting his head right and cursed Redondo for rigging the game against him. The other kids had all grown up with magic. Joey had learned about it only that day. How could he keep up with them? Was he even going to get the opportunity to try? He hoped he hadn't already ruined his chances.

"We'll get out here," Joey heard his father tell the cabdriver. They were stuck at a red light behind a long line of cars, and the school was up on the next block.

"This is so exciting," Joey's mom said in a singsong voice as they exited the cab.

"Wait until you see this place," Joey's father told him. "I have a feeling actually being there is going to change everything for you."

Joey's expression told his parents what he thought of that theory.

"I mean it. I was reading up on the school's notable alumni last night. It's amazing what some of these students have accomplished. Last year one of Exemplar's seniors sold a social media company she started in her freshman year, for eight hundred million dollars."

"I saw that too," his mother said. "They're not all tech wizards, either. Back in the eighties, a sixteen-year-old boy from Exemplar was confirmed as a federal judge!"

"Yeah," Joey said, looking sideways at his mother. "In Florida."

"It still counts!" his mother said, not giving an inch.

The school was on the Upper West Side, across the street from Central Park. Exemplar Academy cut an impressive figure, taking up a full city block. Joey stayed cool and detached as they approached, determined not to marvel at the giant building's stately facade. Boxcar-size foundation stones at the sidewalk level gave way to subtle brickwork tastefully arranged in shades of brown and tan. The many rows of flat, rectangular windows, intersected by columns of turret windows, were all bordered with decorative stone molding. The roof was a mountain range of peaks, steeples, and cupolas that were layered beneath slate shingles and accented with copper highlights that had turned green with age. Joey's father whistled in admiration. "Wow. They don't make 'em like this anymore, do they?"

"No, they don't," his mother agreed.

Joey said nothing. He was not prepared to endorse the school in any way, shape, or form. Even offering a harmless compliment about the building's architecture was a bridge too far, but he did appreciate its old-school vibe, no pun intended. He knew a bit of the building's history from reading the Exemplar Academy website. It had once been the private residence of an old-money New York family, constructed during the city's horse-and-carriage days, back when a harsh-toned "Good day, sir!" was still considered a sick burn. Old buildings like this usually got knocked down to make room for condos and corporate headquarters, but sometimes people stepped in to save them by turning them into museums, libraries, or in the case of Exemplar Academy, schools.

They arrived at a massive arch in the center of the building, right in the middle of the block. There was a gated entrance there, and beyond that, a courtyard filled with manicured hedges. Thick, black, wrought-iron bars, twenty feet high, separated the honking bustle of city traffic from an academic oasis. The bars twisted into ornate patterns throughout the gate, and gilded touches of flair added an extra layer of sophistication. Joey's parents were visibly impressed, but Joey wouldn't allow himself to be taken in so easily. He saw what was really going on. They had made the iron bars look pretty so that people would forget they were iron bars. The gate wasn't there to keep people out; it was there to keep people in. To Joey, the whole school was one big fancy jail cell. His father hit the call button, and someone on the inside buzzed them through.

They were greeted in the courtyard by a middle-aged woman with toned arms, perfect skin, and a big smile. She waved with one hand, and in the other held a leather folio, presumably filled with information about the school, Joey, or both. Next to her was a young girl wearing a plaid skirt, a jacket with the Exemplar Academy crest, and a white button-down shirt underneath. She made the school uniform look cool with her striped tie knotted loosely around her neck and several buttons pinned on her lapels. She had dark brown skin and her hair was done up in short, natural curls. Sunglasses shielded her eyes as she stood there, typing away on her phone. Once Joey got close enough, he was able to read the buttons on her jacket: HAN SHOT FIRST! MARCH FOR OUR LIVES, GREEN IS THE NEW BLACK, EVIL GENIUS, and more. She looked up to smile at Joey and put the phone away.

"You must be the Kopecky family," said the older woman as Joey crossed the flagstone path with his parents.

"That's us," Joey's father replied. "I'm John, this is my wife, Helen, and this, of course, is Joey."

"The boy I've heard so much about! So nice to meet you! Welcome!" She made a point of shaking Joey's hand first. "I'm Dr. Cho, dean of students, but please don't call me that. We're very casual here. My first name is Julianna. Feel free to call me Jules."

"Okay," Joey said, a little flustered.

"It's wonderful to finally make your acquaintance. I feel like I know you already, but of course, there's only so much one can learn from looking at someone's test scores, isn't there? I'm excited to get to know you in real life."

"Yeah, it's . . . nice to meet you too." Dr. Cho was not at all what he had expected. She was welcoming and warm. He had anticipated some kind of educational drill sergeant. *Only so much you can learn from test scores?* Joey had assumed the people here cared about test scores and nothing else.

"We'll have plenty of time to get acquainted later on. Today I'm just going to let you wander around and explore. You get the fun part of orientation day. Your parents and I will deal with the more tedious aspects of getting you enrolled." Dr. Cho made a queasy face. "Registration forms, permission slips, liability waivers . . . yuck."

"Liability waivers?" Joey asked.

"All part of the process." Dr. Cho smiled. "I don't want to waste your time with every boring detail. I think you'll get a lot more out of speaking with a fellow student. But I do want to explain to your parents how we, as administrators, view our role here at Exemplar, which is to put every conceivable resource at your disposal and help you unlock your potential in a relatively risk-free environment."

"Sounds great," Joey's father said.

"What does that mean, *relatively* risk free?" his mother asked.

"That's what we're here to find out today. It really depends on Joey. We're going to go through his file together." Dr. Cho patted the leather folio she was holding and smiled at Joey. "It's all in here: academic history, psych profile, medical records . . . everything we need, from favorite foods, to phobias, allergies, and more."

"Bees," Joey's mother said.

"I'm sorry?" Dr. Cho asked.

"He's allergic to bees," she repeated.

"Oh. Let's keep him away from Sandy's project, then," Dr. Cho told the young girl next to her.

The girl nodded and removed her sunglasses. "My friend Sandy is running experiments to reverse the decimation of the bee population," she explained. "She has forty-seven hives in her lab—thousands of bees—all genetically engineered to resist the effects of climate change. In fact, they're completely indestructible, which presents another problem altogether. She can't release them into the wild. You need to wear a suit and everything on that floor until she figures out what to do with them."

Joey's eyes widened. "Right, let's stay away from that. Please."

"Joey, this is Janelle Thomas. She's going to be taking you around today. You're here just in time. Janelle is going to be leaving us soon." Dr. Cho gave her a little one-armed hug, her eyes at once sad and beaming. "We're going to miss her terribly."

"Don't tell me you're off to college already," Joey's dad said to Janelle.

"It's only for a month," she replied. "I'm going to help lead a renewable energy project at Caltech."

"Wow." Joey's mother was impressed. "That's fantastic. Good for you."

"They wanted her to matriculate in the fall, but she's opted to stay with us a little while longer," Dr. Cho said, full of pride. "Janelle is too modest to tell you, but she's one of our greatest young minds in the field of physics. And when I say 'our,' I don't mean 'our school.' I mean 'our planet.'"

"I believe it," Joey's father said.

"Okay . . ." Janelle tucked her sunglasses into a jacket pocket and picked up her backpack off a nearby bench. "Joey, we should head out before it gets any more embarrassing. Come on, I'll show you around." She tugged on his sleeve and waved to the others. "It was nice meeting all of you!"

"You too!" Joey's parents replied in unison.

"Janelle, we'll be in the visitors' lounge if you need us," Dr. Cho said. "Joey, have fun—you're in good hands!"

"Thanks," Joey replied as he followed Janelle into the school. He thought he knew what to expect going in. The former mansion had been built in the late 1800s, so he had envisioned a refined, classical interior: dimly lit oak-paneled halls lined with oil paintings of hundred-year-old men and an oversize portrait in the lobby depicting a crotchety old headmaster with a book in one hand and a switch in the other. Joey had imagined a plaque that read OUR FOUNDER, TOBIAS EXEMPLAR, or some other such thing, but none of that was there. Instead, it was like stepping into the future. The lobby was bright and thoroughly modern, a large, empty space with a clean, streamlined look and feel. The wall to Joey's left curved around to meet the one on his right, creating a room shaped like the upper-left quadrant of a circle. The contoured wall doubled as a high-definition video screen, which was displaying a sort of digital motion mural. Streaks of white light set against a field of brilliant blue drifted across the room from left to right like slow-moving comets, briefly hypnotizing Joey.

"So, how's it going?" Janelle asked Joey.

"It's going," Joey said, gawking at the lobby. It felt more like the office of a trendy tech company than it did an exclusive prep school. "I'm actually kind of overwhelmed, to tell you the truth. I feel like my whole world just got turned upside down this week, and it's only Tuesday."

Janelle nodded. "I guess that means you haven't gotten started yet."

Joey turned. "Started on what?"

"Don't you remember? Hang on." She dug around in her backpack and pulled out a pamphlet that read SAVE THE PLANET. She handed it to him, grinning. "You told me you were going to get right on that. What's up? No progress?"

Joey scanned the pamphlet, putting two and two together. "That was you on the train?"

"Good to see you again. I didn't expect it to be here."

Joey looked up at Janelle and felt embarrassed. "Holy cow. I didn't even recognize . . . I don't know what it is. . . . My head's all over the place right now. . . . I'm sorry."

"It's all right," Janelle said. "I didn't recognize you at first, either."

"I mean, I'm sorry for yesterday. I was kind of rude, wasn't I?"

"You were," Janelle confirmed casually. "Don't worry. I won't judge," she added with a smile. "I remember when I started here too. This place . . . It's *a lot.* You've got some stuff on your mind. I know how it is."

"I've got some stuff, all right," Joey agreed. "How long have you been going to school here?" he asked, trying to work out how old Janelle was. She looked like she was his age, but she seemed so much more confident and mature.

"I've been here two years. Trust me, it's cooler than you think."

"No kidding," Joey said, unable to suppress a skeptical half smile. He was going to say it would have to be, but he didn't want to be rude again.

"I mean it," Janelle reassured him. "When I first came here, I heard about the year-round classes and I thought this school was going to be a prison. It took a little while before I realized the inmates run the asylum here."

"You mean the kids are in charge?"

"One hundred percent. Exemplar is all about giving us free rein. The last thing they want to do is stifle a young creative mind that might be on the verge of some monumental breakthrough. Whatever you're into, you get to do that thing here. That and nothing else. You follow your passion. Isn't that the way it's supposed to be?"

"In a perfect world," Joey agreed. "Dr. Cho . . . um, Jules . . . said you study physics? That's your passion?"

Janelle smiled enthusiastically. "Oh yeah. Physics, quantum physics, theoretical physics, string theory . . . you name it. I *love* physics. Love it all."

Joey smiled along with her. Physics was the study of matter and energy . . . the way the world worked. He wondered how Janelle would feel if she knew what he knew. That the world didn't work the way she thought it did and there were mysteries science could never explain. He looked around the lobby, wondering where they went from here. The room was completely empty. There was no elevator bank, no check-in desk, and apparently no way in or out except for the door they had just walked through. Janelle went to the center of the room, and a thin, clear glass kiosk rose out of the floor to meet her. She touched her phone to it, eliciting a pleasing chime, followed by an automated voice that spoke her name: "Thomas, Janelle."

"Elevator please," Janelle told the disembodied voice, and the kiosk descended.

"I feel like I'm on the bridge of the *Enterprise*," Joey said.

"What'd I tell you? Kids come here from all over the world for a reason."

"Where are you from?" Joey asked.

"Hoboken."

Joey staggered a step. "*I'm* from Hoboken!"

"I know. We met on the PATH train, remember?" Janelle laughed as the elevator arrived, or more accurately, appeared, opening up inside the digital mural. "Why do you think Jules wanted me to show you around? She's awesome, by the way. You'll love her." She motioned for Joey to follow her into the elevator car and pushed the button for the fourth floor. "Two geniuses from 'Boken. What are the odds?" She put up her fist for Joey to bump.

Joey gave her some reluctant knuckles. "Pretty unlikely," he said, thinking he didn't qualify.

Janelle didn't catch his real meaning. "How about that? The birthplace of baseball, Sinatra, and the two of us. What kind of genius are you?"

Joey shook his head. "Not much of one," he said, still anxious that he didn't belong.

"The modest kind!" Janelle said, surprised. "That's refreshing. We don't see a lot of that around here." Her phone beeped. "Excuse me one second." She took a quick time-out to respond to a text. The elevator bell *dinged*, and she put the phone away. "Here we are! Fourth floor:

sportswear, appliances, robotics labs, holographic imaging, laser science . . ."

"Lasers?"

"You keep repeating everything I say as a question," Janelle observed.

"Sorry. It's a habit. I do it when things get weird."

"It's only weird until it becomes the new normal." Janelle nudged Joey out the door. "Have a look around. Get used to it."

Joey stepped off the elevator. The hallway was quiet. Just like downstairs, everything looked brand-new and curiously empty. He wandered down the hall, peeking through the window in every closed door he passed. They were not classrooms, but state-of-the-art labs. He had to go halfway down the corridor before he found one that was occupied. Inside, a boy younger than him was fixing goggles over his eyes. He was getting ready to do something. Maybe fire a laser? A mess of wires, tubes, and high-tech hardware was bolted to a workstation in front of him. The boy flipped a few switches on a nearby control panel, and a circle of thin, emerald beams of light materialized, converging on a central point. A second later their combined energy formed a single, much stronger laser beam that shot out like a blast from the Death Star. The next thing Joey knew, a blinding light filled the lab, pouring out into the hallway. Joey threw his hands up over his eyes and turned away. There was an electric crackle followed by a loud *bang*, and the light show stopped.

Seeing spots, Joey went back to the window and found that the boy's project had exploded. The workstation was on fire, and the boy in the goggles was pounding the desk in frustration. Joey felt like he might as well have been watching himself at the Majestic Theatre last night. His own experiments there had been less explosive but also far less impressive.

"That's Suhash, our resident expert in optical amplification," Janelle said, looking over Joey's shoulder. "Ooh," she added sympathetically, surveying the damage to his lab. "Not a good time. We'll come back." She urged Joey on, but he lingered at the window, staring at the fiery mess on the other side of the glass. It occurred to him that once upon a time, people would have believed such a device to be a form of sorcery or witchcraft. Joey couldn't imagine putting something like that together. Somehow, mastering Redondo's impossible style of magic felt like a much more attainable goal. They continued down the hall, but the other labs were all empty.

"Where is everyone?"

"They're around. Don't expect a big crowd when the bell rings, though. There's only twenty-five students in the whole school."

Joey was about to repeat "Only twenty-five?" but he stopped himself before the words slipped out. Instead he asked, "Why so few?"

"What do you expect? Exemplar is hyperexclusive. The top one percent of the one percent. Academically speaking, not economically. Tuition is free."

"I think that's my parents' favorite part of this."

Janelle's phone beeped again. She checked it quickly. "I'm sure they're excited about the quality of the education you're going to get. Class size is as small as small can be here. It's just you. That's how they can be so super focused and play to everyone's specific strengths."

Joey grunted. Janelle said that like it was a good thing. And maybe it was for her, but Joey saw it as a detriment to his preferred method of getting through the school day. A school with only twenty-five students that was big on individual attention was not at all good for him. You can't hide in the back of the class when there is no back of the class.

Continuing the tour, they took the stairs up to the next floor, exiting the stairwell into a spacious gymnasium. "This is the athletics level," Janelle explained. The room was bare except for some gymnastics equipment arranged on the floor: padded mats, a pommel horse, uneven parallel bars, and a set of rings that hung from the ceiling. Joey noticed a boy wearing a warm-up suit stretching in the corner. A tiny woman in a matching tracksuit was directing him.

"You guys have sports here? I thought this school was all work, no play."

"That's what I've been trying to tell you. Work *is* play when you do what you love. And, depending on your job, play *is* work. This school is for the best of the best—in every field. The next LeBron James, Tom Brady, Serena Williams . . . you'll find them here too."

"Come on . . ."

"I mean it."

"How do you put together a team with only twenty-five kids in the school? You telling me you have five LeBrons in the house?"

"No. I'm just making a point using names you're likely to recognize. Mainly we focus on individual sports. Esteban over there is training for the Olympics." The boy shed his warm-up suit and got up on the rings, where he quickly moved into the iron cross position. The kid must have been nine years old and he looked like he could bend steel bars with his hands. Joey could see his muscle definition from across the room. His hyperfocus on gymnastics must have started in preschool.

"Personally, I think it's a waste of space. I wanted to use this room to build a particle accelerator like the Large Hadron Collider at CERN."

"Yeah, right." Joey laughed. He actually knew what that was. He remembered his science teacher had once told the class about a massive machine that smashed subatomic particles together in an effort to literally unlock the secrets of the universe. Joey didn't have the first clue how it worked or why, but it had stuck in his memory because it sounded like something a supervillain would build in a secret volcano base. Janelle wasn't laughing. Once again Joey's eyes went to her EVIL GENIUS pin. "For real?"

Janelle just shrugged. Sure she was for real. Why not?

Joey looked at her. "A supercollider?" he repeated in disbelief. "Like the one in Switzerland? Doesn't that thing go on for miles?"

"I solved for that. I had a design that could fit in this room without sacrificing power or productivity. Why does it have to be so big when the particles are so small? They should have given me the space. There are more important things in life than winning gold medals. I'm talking major questions we can answer. Are there parallel dimensions out there? Can we detect them? What can we learn about dark matter, which, by the way, appears to account for twenty-seven percent of the mass energy of the universe? Real-life science-fiction, Joey. The school was going to work with me to find a place for the project, but I made a mistake."

Joey shook his head. Keeping up with Janelle wasn't easy. "You don't want to make any mistakes with something like that. My old science teacher said there was an outside chance it could create a black hole that would swallow up the whole world."

"A microscopic black hole," Janelle corrected. "And that was my mistake—telling the school about that. It's more like an infinitesimal chance. Statistically insignificant. The nerds at CERN didn't suck the world into a black hole, did they?"

"Not that I know of."

"Exactly. Any black holes would have shrunk away to nothing in twenty-four hours—if they even lasted that long."

"So much for not stifling inquisitive young minds," Joey said, trying to sympathize but secretly agreeing with the school that some limits were a good thing.

Janelle's phone beeped again. She looked at it and furrowed her brow.

"Everything okay?" Joey asked.

Janelle typed at the screen with her thumbs, then pocketed the phone again. "Everything's fine. Let's talk about you. What are you going to study here?"

"I don't know. They haven't told me."

"They haven't? Most kids show up knowing exactly what they want to do."

"Not me."

"What did your PMAP say?"

"I, uh . . . didn't get it back yet." Joey decided not to go into detail about the strange alternative test he'd taken in place of the PMAP. He felt silly trying to explain it. Exactly how was Mr. Gray supposed to come up with a job recommendation by watching him perform magic tricks? Joey had no idea. He

166

added it to the growing list of things that defied explanation.

"Forget the PMAP, then," Janelle told him. "What do *you* say?" She sat down on the bleachers and tapped the seat next to her. "Tell me about yourself. What are you into? If you could study anything in the world—and you can, by the way—what would it be?"

"I don't know," Joey lied.

"Don't do that. Really think about it. What do you want to get good at? What do you want to learn? Tell me."

Joey grimaced. Only one subject came to mind, but it wasn't something they taught at Exemplar Academy. "What if I told you I want to learn magic?"

"I'd tell you, join the club."

"Huh?"

"What do you think I do here every day? What do you think Suhash is doing in his lab? Magic is just science people don't understand yet. What's your brand of magic?"

Joey smiled to himself. Janelle didn't get it. The people at Exemplar Academy liked to think they were doing the impossible, but they didn't understand the meaning of the word. He imagined Janelle's response if he told her he wanted to study *real* magic. She would probably understand that as well as he understood quantum physics. "I honestly couldn't tell you," he said quite truthfully.

Janelle was persistent. "You have to have some idea. How else are you going to change the world?" she asked, quoting the school motto.

Joey chuckled. "Good one."

Janelle didn't crack a smile. "I'm serious. Don't you want a better world than the one the grown-ups keep messing up for us? I read this morning that we had an oil spill on Earth Day! How wrong is that?"

"Pretty wrong," Joey replied, a little sad that he wasn't more surprised by the news.

"What are you going to do about it?"

Joey stared at her. "What am *I* going to do?" At first he thought Janelle was messing with him. Then he remembered she had thought building a particle collider in the gymnasium was a good idea. Janelle was clearly a type A, go-big-or-go-home kind of person—perfect for this school, unlike himself. "Look, Janelle," Joey began. "I'm sure you're going to take what you learn here and go create some kind of clean, alternative energy that transforms society one day. You could be the next Stephen Hawking—in fact, you probably are—but that's you. Not me. I'm not going to change the world. I shouldn't even be here."

Janelle leaned back, reevaluating Joey. "I see how it is. . . . You weren't being humble before. You don't believe in yourself."

"That's not what I'm saying."

"It kind of is, but that's okay. I told you, I'm not judging. Back in the day I was worried about coming here too. Why don't you talk to Jules about it? She's not just the dean; she's also our school counselor."

"I don't need counseling."

"There's nothing wrong with talking to somebody if you're having a problem, Joey. You should—"

"I'm not having a problem. I believe in myself plenty. I'm just being realistic, that's all."

"Define realistic," Janelle said. "Better yet, redefine it. That's what I did. Before I came here I had all kinds of ideas in my head that I was afraid to say out loud. They weren't realistic. They weren't possible. People wouldn't let me try. What I didn't understand was, people like us . . . we get to decide what's possible. You'll see. If you want to make magic, you've got to believe in yourself. It's a prerequisite."

Joey straightened up with a start. "Who told you that?"

"I don't know if anyone ever told me," Janelle said. "Maybe I heard someone say it in a movie one time. Or maybe I put it together for myself just being around this place." She thought for a second, then got up off the bleachers. "Let me show you what I mean." Janelle led Joey out of the gym and into the hall. Once she was satisfied the coast was clear, she took her phone back out. "That supercollider they told me I couldn't build? I did it anyway."

Joey's eyes bugged. "What?"

"I miniaturized everything and set it up in the basement. It's running right now."

She turned the screen toward Joey. He saw a webcam image of what he assumed was a homemade particle accelerator, but he had to take Janelle's word for it. To him it was just a ring of metal tubing the size of a Frisbee, attached to a mini-generator and circuit board with a tangle of wires and a series of flashing lights. The table it was on vibrated as the device emitted a steady hum.

"This is what you've been doing on your phone? I thought you were texting someone."

"No. I'm looking for Higgs boson particles," Janelle said with a smile. "Been doing it all morning." She swiped to another app, opening a program she used to monitor the experiment. There were numbers running, energy wavelengths spiking, and power levels pulsating, none of which Joey understood.

"That's incredible."

"I know, right?" Janelle's phone *ping*ed again, and a notification flashed on the screen in red. "Hmm." She frowned and tapped a few buttons. "That's interesting."

Before Joey could ask if it was interesting good or interesting bad, they were interrupted by Janelle's phone again. Joey had a hunch it would be the latter because of the sound it made when the alarm went off. This wasn't the soft chime of a notification. Janelle's phone was blowing up. "Okay, this is a little embarrassing." She fiddled with the screen, trying to fix the problem, whatever it was. Another series of beeps came out of the phone, and Janelle made a concerned face. "That's not good."

Joey's eyebrows went up. "What's not good?"

Janelle blanched as she read the numbers on the screen. She put up a finger. "I'm sorry. Will you excuse me for one second?" Without waiting for an answer, she hustled down the hall to the elevator and hit the call button.

"Is there a problem?" Joey called after her.

"No problem!" she said brightly, hitting the button again.

Joey caught up with her outside the elevator. Her eyes were suddenly frantic. Her cool, confident veneer rattled. "Janelle, should I be worried about a black hole in the basement that could swallow up the known universe?"

"*Pssshh.*" Janelle smiled, playing it off. "You're funny." She hit the down button a third time. "Maybe a little one," she admitted a second later. She put her fingers close together. "Teeny-tiny," she stressed. She hit the button a fourth time and stared at the numbers above the door. "I mean, it's probably nothing. Definitely not big enough to swallow the *universe*. The building maybe, but I really don't think . . . I just need to . . . I mean, I want to have a look at . . ." She trailed off and hit the down button over and over. "Come on, come on, come on . . ." The elevator finally arrived, and Janelle smiled with relief. "There we go! Just wait here, okay?" she said, stepping inside. "I'll be right back. Don't go anywhere. And whatever you do, don't tell—"

The elevator doors closed, cutting her off. She was gone.

Joey stared at the elevator doors, grappling with the fact that so far life at Exemplar Academy was almost as out there as anything he'd seen at Redondo's theater. He thought about what to do next. Running seemed like the most sensible option, but how do you outrun a black hole? (Assuming there was a black hole, and further assuming Janelle couldn't handle it if there was.) Joey scratched at an itch on the back of his neck, nearly hitting the ceiling when a white dove flew out of his collar.

"KOPECKY!"

Redondo's voice echoed down the hall as the bird took off, flying in an erratic, confused pattern. Once Joey's heart resumed beating, adrenaline surged through his body like super-soldier serum.

A little bird will tell you. . . .

Redondo was calling him back!

For the moment, Joey forgot all about Janelle and the cosmic incident brewing in the basement. The dove flew into the gym, surprising Esteban and his trainer. Joey grabbed his magic key and ran to the nearest door. It was a broom closet. Unsure of how to proceed, he held the key up in front of the doorknob. A keyhole appeared in the wood beneath it, with bright blue light pouring out of the opening. Joey pressed the key into place. He was going to take Janelle's advice. It was time to redefine reality.

9

Through the Looking Glass

Joey was very happy to step into Redondo's Off-Broadway realm *inside* the Majestic for a change. Thanks to his magic key, the Exemplar Academy broom closet door opened directly into the theater lobby, which looked a little brighter than it had the day before. Redondo had apparently replaced some of the bulbs in the chandelier and he had repaired the fallen sconce on the wall. The added light made the faded carpet appear more red than pink. As Joey walked across the lobby floor, it felt thicker and softer beneath his feet. Maybe it was just his imagination, but the plants by the theater door seemed to be "less dead" too. Joey touched a leaf on his way into the main auditorium. It was still brown and wilting, but it was more substantial than he remembered. Joey was sure that the same leaf would have crackled into dust at the slightest touch yesterday.

He wondered if the theater looked any better from the outside, but he wasn't about to go check. The shadows of the Invisible Hand were still out there. They watched him from the door, talking to each other using screeching noises that sounded almost curious. Joey hurried out of the lobby, eager to leave them behind. When he entered the main house of the theater, it looked as though they were already inside.

Shazad and Leanora were both onstage, tied up from head to toe in thick ropes—the kind sailors might use to secure a ship to a dock. It was as if they were each stuck in the center of a giant knot. Only their heads were visible as they struggled to free themselves. Redondo was nowhere in sight.

"Oh my God!" Joey exclaimed, shocked to find them in such peril. They looked up, equally surprised to see him enter.

"You're back?" Shazad asked, momentarily pausing his efforts to escape the ropes as Joey ran down the aisle. "I thought after yesterday Redondo would have gotten rid of you."

"Not yet, he didn't," Joey said, joining them onstage. "Lucky for you. Hang on. I'll get you out of there . . . somehow," he added, searching the ropes for a weak point. He didn't find one. The ropes were moving too much for that. They slithered around Shazad and Leanora like snakes, actively countering

175

their efforts to try and slip out. Joey got too close and nearly got pulled into the massive knot with them. He jumped back just in time. "What do I do?"

"Don't do anything," Leanora said. "We're kind of in the middle of something here."

"What are you talking about?" Joey asked. "Who did this to you?"

"We did," she replied. "And we're going to undo it."

"What? Where's Redondo?"

"Not here yet," Shazad said, squirming in place. "Don't worry, it's all part of the show." His fingers emerged from in between the mess of ropes covering his midsection. "I've nearly got my right hand out. It won't be long now."

"You haven't won anything yet," Leanora said, looking very determined.

"What is this, another competition?" Joey asked. "You did this to yourselves on purpose?"

"Just a little something to pass the time," Shazad said in a nonchalant voice. "We found the rope backstage. You might want to keep your distance." But it was too late. Joey gasped as the ropes lashed out at his ankles and climbed up his legs like fast-growing vines. Before he knew it, they had wound their way around his torso and cinched his arms tight.

"What the—hey!"

Joey's words were cut off as rope lines crept over his shoulders and ran over his mouth, gagging him. He gave a garbled, helpless cry and fell to his knees. The rope made several more passes around him, continuing to grow until it covered nearly every inch of his body.

"I guess Joey's playing now too," Leanora said. As she and Shazad worked to extricate themselves from the enchanted entanglement, they explained that they were conducting their own Houdini-style escape challenge. So far, Shazad was winning. Every time Leanora got a hand free, fresh restraints wrapped around her wrist and tied it back down. Joey couldn't even get that far. He squirmed around in the ropes, trying to break out, but it was no use. He had zero leverage, and the more he struggled, the tighter the ropes constricted. He might as well have been encased in cement.

"How are you doing that?" Leanora asked Shazad, frustrated as he stretched his right arm up, clearing the ropes around his collar.

"That's the wrong question," Shazad said matter-of-factly. "The wrong frame of mind. You can't worry about what

I'm doing, or how far ahead I am. You have to focus what you're doing. What you can do." Completely immobile, Joey watched as Shazad got his other arm free and pushed down on the ropes around his neck and shoulders. "If you want to be free, you can't see yourself as trapped." He squeezed his way out of his bonds and alighted gracefully on the stage. "That's all there is to it." The rope made no move to recapture him, but still, it refused to let Leanora and Joey go. "It's a magic problem," Shazad said, crossing the stage to where they were. "It needs a magical solution. You have to visualize the way out, or it won't be there." Shazad dove his arm into the shifting mass of ropes. "Keep still."

Like I have a choice, Joey thought.

Shazad extracted his arm and walked across the stage with a line of rope in tow. He pulled it taut and gave the rope a good hard yank. Just like that, the knot came undone. Leanora and Joey stepped out of the lifeless coils and kicked them off. The ropes fell away and piled up on the stage. "That's how you untie the un-untieable knot." Shazad dropped the rope like he was dropping a microphone.

Leanora muttered a grudging thank-you and congratulations. Much like Joey, it appeared that only her pride had

178

been injured, but Joey felt doubly foolish. It was the second time he had rushed onto the stage to rescue someone who didn't need his help, only to end up being the one who needed saving. "Thanks for showing me the ropes," he quipped, trying to cover his embarrassment with a little humor. "When I came in here, I was afraid the Invisible Hand had tied you two up."

"You know about the Invisible Hand?" Shazad asked.

Joey's stomach churned as he thought about his conversation with the Invisible Hand's sinister agent, the man in the top hat and scarf. "We've met," he said, determined not to let his unease register on his face. "They dropped in on me last night."

"I'm surprised you came back after last night," Leanora told Joey. "I would have quit if I were you."

Joey grimaced. "Thanks for sharing."

"No offense," Leanora said. "I'm just saying, you didn't exactly distinguish yourself. Are you sure you're up to this?"

Joey thought about Redondo's warning. *They're going to hate you. . . . They hate you already. . . . You're in their way. . . .* "I know what you're doing," he said.

"What am I doing?" Leanora asked innocently.

"Trying to psych me out. Get me to quit."

"You *should* quit," Shazad chimed in. "For your own good," he added hastily. "I know this isn't what you want to hear, but she's right. You're not ready for this, and you don't have time to play catch-up. It's obvious you can't do magic. There's no shame in bowing out."

Shazad spoke as if he were more concerned about Joey's well-being than anything else, and maybe he was. Joey certainly hadn't given Shazad any reason to be worried about him as competition. During the brief time they had spent together, Joey's magic record had been an unbroken string of failures. Whether Joey liked it or not, Shazad was making sense.

"You're right," Joey said. "That isn't what I want to hear. And I can do magic," he added, stubbornly trying to convince himself as much as Shazad and Leanora. "Don't forget, Redondo said he was going to destroy the wand before I found this place. I convinced him to pass it on to one of us. You should be thanking me, not playing games, trying to get inside my head."

"That's not what we're doing," Leanora said gently. "I don't think you understand what you're getting into, Joey.

This is serious business. Whoever wins Houdini's wand from Redondo inherits a solemn duty."

"And gets a target painted on their back," Shazad said. "The Invisible Hand is outside the theater right now, trying to get in. Look at this place. It's falling apart. How long do we have before the shadows beat down the front door and take the wand by force? We don't have time to waste dragging out this competition. We need to get Houdini's wand out of here. Now."

"You keep saying *we*," Joey observed. "I get the feeling what you really mean is *you*."

Shazad shrugged. "Of course I think it should be me. Don't we all? The difference is, the wand would be safe with me. Can either of you say the same?"

"I can," Leanora said.

"You don't know that," Shazad countered. "Your people don't know where they're going to be from one week to the next. And you . . ." Shazad looked to Joey. "You're a norm. From the normal world." He said "normal world" as if the idea of the wand ending up there was completely ridiculous.

"But you could hide the wand away in Jorako with the rest of your treasures. Is that it?" Leanora asked.

"That *is* the Order of the Majestic's mission, isn't it? To preserve magic and keep it alive?"

"Staying alive isn't the same thing as living," Leanora said. "It's not enough to preserve magic. The Order needs to take the fight to the Invisible Hand."

"I thought the Order of the Majestic didn't exist anymore," Joey interjected.

"They don't," Shazad confirmed. "You can thank Redondo for that. He pushed things too far."

"Too far?" Leanora said, raising her voice slightly. "When Redondo led the Order, he scored the kind of victories we haven't seen since the days of Houdini."

"If this is what victory looks like, it didn't work out very well for him, did it?" Shazad gestured to the run-down theater. "Redondo poked the bear and paid the price. Just like Houdini."

"What?" Joey and Leanora exclaimed together, both of them surprised to hear the memory of Harry Houdini evoked in anything less than reverent tones.

"You heard me," Shazad said matter-of-factly. "All those performances for the norms . . . always drawing attention to himself . . . Houdini practically dared the Invisible Hand to come after him. For what? Tell me, what did he actually accomplish? Other than nearly losing the most powerful magical artifact in the world, that is . . . For all the hype around that man, he never did anything that mattered."

"If that's what you think," Leanora began, "then you don't deserve his wand. He inspired people. Houdini hid magic in plain sight and filled the world with wonder."

"Right up until the point when they killed him."

"Maybe so, but his legend never died," Leanora said. "Even he knows Houdini's name," she added, indicating Joey. "In his day, Houdini was the most famous magician—the most famous person—in the world. That made him more powerful than the Invisible Hand. More influential. You're wrong about him. He made people care about magic. He made them believe."

"Hang on. Are you saying the Invisible Hand killed Harry Houdini?" Joey said, struggling to keep up.

"Of course they killed him," Leanora replied, as if Joey had interrupted the conversation to confirm that two plus two equaled four. "What exactly do you know about the Invisible Hand?" she asked, scrutinizing Joey.

The truth was, Joey didn't know very much at all, but he

wasn't about to admit that. Instead, he folded his arms and said, "I know the Order of the Majestic fought them over the world's remaining magic."

"Exactly. Fought. Past tense," Shazad said. "The fight's over. They won. Houdini's wand is the only thing that stands between them and total control."

"Of magic?" Joey asked.

"Of the world!" Shazad said, astounded by Joey's cluelessness.

Joey's eyes bulged. *"What?"* Shazad had to be exaggerating.

"This is what I'm talking about," Shazad said. "You don't know. The Invisible Hand is a bigger superpower than any country or corporation. They control the world's magic—most of it anyway. They decide what's possible out there, and they make the world a very hard place to live in."

"What for?" Joey asked. "What do they get out of that?"

"Isn't it obvious? They get to keep you down. If people like you don't recognize magic when you see it, chances are you won't go looking for it either. Less for you, more for them."

"I went looking for it," Joey said.

"I'm glad you did. I admit it. You got Redondo going again, and we're all grateful, but I'm sorry. It's not enough."

Shazad looked at Joey with compassion, trying to let him down easy. "I understand this is difficult for you. You got a taste of magic and you want more. I would too if I were you. Your world is filled with war, pollution, corruption, and things are getting worse, not better. Don't you see? That's the reason you can't do magic. You can't solve the problem when you're part of the problem."

"The problem isn't the world. It's the Invisible Hand," Leanora said. "The wand is the solution."

"They're too strong," Shazad told Leanora. "We can't defeat them. The most we can do is try to hold the line."

"You guys are messing with me," Joey said, still hoping they were trying to psych him out. "Houdini died of natural causes. It was appendicitis." Joey had read as much online the night before.

"Appendicitis brought about by a punch to the stomach," Shazad replied. "Does that sound natural to you?" Shazad shook his head no. "But imagine if he was hit with one of these . . ." He trailed off, reaching for Leanora's firestone pendant.

"Don't touch that," Leanora said, pulling the necklace away.

"Have you ever used it on another person?" Shazad asked her. "I'll bet you haven't. You like to say my family stays hidden, but yours is always on the run. Why? Because you're smart enough not to take on the Invisible Hand directly. At least, your parents must be. Otherwise you wouldn't be here. You may want to fight, but I have a feeling that's only because you've never been in one. It's one thing to do magic onstage. It's quite another to do it under real pressure. Look what happened here with the rope. You think you could master the wand if push came to shove? Against the Invisible Hand?" Leanora had no answer for that. Shazad looked sideways at Joey. "If they tried to get the wand away from you, I doubt you'd be able to give it to them fast enough."

"But you'd keep the wand safe in Jorako," Leanora said again. "You don't think it would be wasted there? What's the point if you're just going to play keep-away and never use it?"

"There's nothing more important than keeping that wand away from the Invisible Hand," Shazad said. "It's more power than anyone should have. If you lost it to them, they could use it to remake the world any way they want."

"If it's that dangerous, maybe Redondo had the right idea after all," Joey said.

"You mean destroying it?" Shazad scoffed at the notion. "That's not what we do."

"What do we do, then?" Joey asked, legitimately curious. "If the Invisible Hand is such a threat to the world, why didn't Redondo use the wand against them? Twenty years ago everyone said he was going to become the next Houdini."

"Take a look around," Shazad said. "He did."

Joey examined the ruined theater, wondering what had happened to make Redondo hole up here and stop performing. "How did he end up—"

"Here we are!" Redondo announced, stepping out onto the stage. He was holding Houdini's wand at his side, aiming it at a full-length mirror that trailed behind him, floating an inch off the floor. With its ornate, extravagant golden frame, the mirror looked like it dated back to the Renaissance. "Sorry to keep you all waiting. This mirror was in deep storage. Getting at it took some doing, and obviously, it's the kind of thing you want to be careful moving." Redondo stopped short when he saw the tangled lines that had very recently held Joey and the others sprawled out onstage like a dead boa constrictor. "I see you found the Gordian rope." With his free hand, he picked up the end that was closest to him and examined it. "Perhaps you've heard the story about how Alexander the Great unraveled an impossible knot by slicing it in half? Let's just say there is more to that story than is widely known." Redondo gave the rope a light shake, and the lengthy coils shrunk inward like a tape measure retracting back into its container. Once the stage was clear, he tossed the short rope away and brought the mirror down with a wave of his wand. "I'll tell you about it some other time. Right now, we have work to do. Who wants to go first?"

"Me," Joey called out, eager to redeem himself and prove he belonged.

Redondo turned to face Joey. "Young Kopecky. I wasn't sure you'd come. Your performance last night was abysmal, but here you are. Back again. That counts for something. Just like yesterday, it's not much, but it is something. You can have the first crack at today's little test." He tapped on the reflective surface of the mirror. "Just try not to crack it."

Joey stepped forward. "This is a magic mirror?" he guessed.

"I'm interested to see if you can find your way through to the other side and back."

"Okay." Joey took a breath, steeling his nerves. "Let's do it."

Joey stood in front of the mirror, sizing up his reflection. The person staring back at him looked nervous. Unsure. This was neither the time nor the place for such feelings. Using the mirror, he looked at Redondo, who was standing with his arms crossed and an expectant look on his face. Behind him, Shazad whispered something to Leanora. It was obvious they didn't like his chances. Joey focused on himself. It wasn't about Redondo, Shazad, or anybody else. It was about him. Just him and the mirror. That was the key. Yesterday Redondo had told him, "One doesn't do anything to make magic work. One simply gets out of the way." The mirror was a magical object. As Joey stared down his reflection, he understood it wasn't the mirror he had to get past, but rather, the person inside it. It was him. If Joey wanted to do this, he just had to decide he could. But he had to mean it.

You can do this, he told himself. *Believe in yourself. Redefine reality.*

Joey reached for the mirror. His fingers touched the glass. The surface rippled as if the frame contained a vertical plane of water.

Instinctively, Joey retracted his hand slightly. As the

189

ripples settled, he saw Redondo over his shoulder, his face betraying neither encouragement nor concern. The latter was not his style, and the former had to come from within. Joey screwed up his courage. What was he waiting for? He plunged his hand forward. It sank into the mirror as if the glass were not glass at all, but a thick, cool, silvery gel. He broke into a fascinated laugh, smiling as little droplets of mirror fell to the floor and pooled up like mercury at his feet. *I'm doing it*, he thought. *I'm going in!* Already in up to his elbow, Joey kept moving forward. Lifting his foot, he plunged it through the mirror without any thought as to what was waiting on the other side.

His foot touched down on soft, powdery sand. As Joey came out of the magic mirror, the silvery gel slipped off his body and re-formed into glass behind him. Not so much as a droplet clung to his clothes. Joey felt like Neil Armstrong stepping off the lunar module for the very first time, only better. This was way beyond a trip to the moon. This was another reality. Another dimension. This was magic—real magic—and he'd done it on command.

"YES!" Joey shouted, exploding with excitement as he broke into what would have been an incredibly embarrassing happy dance had anybody been there to see it. He fell to his knees, grabbing up handfuls of white sand, giggling uncontrollably. The sand had a smooth, flourlike consistency as it slipped through his fingers. He turned around, smiling at his reflection in the mirror, which was an exact replica of the one he had just walked through. "Who can't do magic now, huh?"

Joey wiped his hands on his shirt and looked around, checking out the alien landscape. It was calm and serene, a pristine white sand beach under an endless lavender sky. Crystal-clear waves lapped gently against the shore, making hardly any noise at all. The water had an iridescent, glimmering quality that for all he knew was pure, liquid magic. The beach went on for miles with no one in sight. There was nothing on the horizon and nothing in the sky. Only sand, water, and mirrors. There were hundreds of them, all in varying shapes and sizes, stuck in the sand up and down the beach.

Joey got to his feet, completely in awe of his surroundings. He walked to the edge of the water. Little compact mirrors washed up on the shore there like seashells. "This is wild," he said to himself, practically glowing from his achievement. He picked up one of the compacts and threw it sidearm into the water, trying to skip it across the waves. The mirror skipped seventeen times. Joey picked up another one, looking around the beach for someone to share this wonder with.

"Well done, Joey," said the man in the top hat and scarf. He tipped his cap. "Very well done indeed."

10

The Man in the Mirror

Joey's euphoric delight at having successfully used a mirror to travel to another dimension bottomed out quickly. The man in the top hat and scarf looked every inch as creepy and evil in the daylight as he had that first night in Joey's room. "How did you get here?" he asked, backing up to the edge of the water.

"This place is open to anyone with the means to travel." The man gestured to the mirrors all around. "On this beach you'll find the other side of every magic mirror in the world. They're the doors to everywhere. We control most of them."

"How did you know I was here?"

"Joey, we're everywhere. You can't escape us. Besides, you're easy to find." The man tapped his own forehead, right in the center, where he had touched Joey's head with an icy finger the night before. "Come here," he said, motioning for Joey to join him. "It's time."

"Time for what?"

"Don't tell me you've forgotten already. I told you, Redondo has something I want. You're going to help me get it, remember?"

"It doesn't belong to you," Joey said, looking around for a way out.

"What's that?"

"The wand. It doesn't belong to you."

The man lifted his chin, peering down at Joey with his glowing eyes. "What do you know about it?"

"I know you—you'll never get your hands on it," Joey stuttered, trying to sound brave. "He'll destroy it before he lets you have it."

"Then we haven't a moment to lose." The man held out his hand. "I don't like repeating myself, but I'm going to say this again. Come. Here." Joey stood his ground, partly defiant, partly paralyzed by fear. The man in the top hat and scarf sighed impatiently. "Joey, I said I wouldn't hurt you provided you do as you're told. Please don't make me do this the hard way."

"It doesn't matter what you do. You can't get into the

Majestic. Only people who don't pose a threat can enter."

"Heh." The man chuckled. "You don't have to tell me that. I know Redondo sealed up all the entrances long ago. Why do you think we're having this conversation?"

"We're not. I've got nothing to say to you."

"Then let me do the talking." The man in the top hat and scarf rested one hand on the frame of the mirror Joey had just come out of and knocked twice on the glass. "I can't pass through this mirror; that's true enough. But you can. Redondo's given you the run of the theater, and I'm willing to bet you can put me on the guest list. Metaphorically speaking, of course. For example, imagine if some unforeseen injury were to befall you while you were here and some Good Samaritan tried to carry you home to safety. Would Redondo deny such a person entry when they were only trying to help? No. He would have allowed for that contingency. Or what if you came across someone in your travels who needed your aid? What then?"

"I was only supposed to go here and back."

"And you will. I'll wager anyone traveling with you can make use of this portal, just as long as you go along for the ride. Let's find out, shall we?"

Waves licked at Joey's heels as he stood with his back to the ocean. He was cornered and totally defenseless against the man in the top hat and scarf. What could he do to get away? He still had the key that led back to the theater whenever it was placed in front of a door, but there weren't any doors in this place. Not unless you counted the mirror that the man in the top hat and scarf was blocking. How could Joey escape without letting the Invisible Hand hitch a ride? He couldn't. He was trapped. Joey thought about what Shazad had said to him earlier . . . how if the Invisible Hand were to threaten him, he would surrender in a heartbeat. The words gnawed at him. As frightened as he was, the last thing he wanted to do was prove Shazad right about that.

Joey looked down at the small compact mirror in his hand, the only weapon he had. It was set in a decorative metal case that opened and shut like a clamshell. Joey threw it, hard as he could, just missing the man in the top hat and scarf. That was all right. He wasn't aiming for him.

"NO!" the man shouted as the projectile struck the magic mirror, hitting it hard right in the center of the glass. A spiderweb crack spiraled out from the point of impact, and the glass shattered, then exploded outward with a force Joey did not expect. Shards flew through the air, pelting the man in the top hat and scarf. He fell to the ground, his hat tumbling from his head, but Joey didn't get a look at his face. He was too busy running in the opposite direction.

By the time the man got back up, Joey had put a significant distance between the two of them and was safely hidden behind one of the larger mirrors. Careful not to be seen, he watched from afar as the man collected himself and brushed the glass from his coat. "Joey, Joey, Joey . . . ," he said, resetting his hat upon his head. "That was a very foolish thing to do." He whirled around, scanning the horizon.

Joey pulled himself back out of sight but kept his eye on the man, watching his reflection in the countless other mirrors on the beach. The man began his search, starting with the mirrors closest to him. He checked behind them one by one, hunting for Joey.

The mirror that Joey had shattered rumbled in place and started to sink into the ground. "You see that? I hope you're proud of yourself. That's a waste of a perfectly good magic mirror. Isn't the Order of the Majestic supposed to preserve magical relics like these?" The ground beneath the mirror turned to quicksand, and within seconds the top of the frame disappeared into the growing sinkhole. "It'll be seven years before that grows back. Seven years of bad luck for you. Think you can hide here that long?" Joey's chest tightened as a seed of dread took root inside him. What had he done? That mirror was his only way home! Now he was stranded here, and Redondo couldn't even come to his rescue. He hadn't thought this through very well.

The man in the top hat and scarf laughed. "Don't worry. We can speed things along, you and I. Redondo has more than one magic mirror in that theater of his. I remember what they look like. I'll find their counterparts here, I'll find you, and if you won't behave, I'll carry your lifeless body into the theater. I promise you I'll do it if I have to. It's up to you how this ends."

Joey stayed quiet and still. He didn't dare move. The man in the top hat and scarf stood motionless as well. He was staring at something. Viewing him as he was from many different angles reflected in multiple mirrors, Joey couldn't tell which direction the man was looking. The tips of Joey's sneakers were sticking out from behind the mirror. Did the man see them?

"This is pointless," said the man. "You can't hide from

me, Joey. We're on a beach. You leave tracks everywhere you go, and what's more . . . you have very distinctive footwear." The man leaped around a mirror, diving at Joey's sneakers. "Got you!"

Joey smirked from the other end of the beach as the man snatched up Joey's empty sneakers. He had slipped them off and tucked them behind a mirror as a decoy while the man was still on the ground, covered in shattered glass. After that he had run in the opposite direction along the water's edge so the waves would erase his footprints.

The man in the top hat and scarf threw the sneakers down in a furious motion. He looked up and down the hundreds of mirrors on the beach. At this point he had to know Joey could be hiding behind any one of them. "Very good," he said. "You're a clever boy, Joey."

That's what they tell me.

"But how clever can you be, really? What are you going to do next? I expect you're wondering the same thing," he added with a confident laugh. "Out of ideas yet?"

Joey hated to admit it, but he was. The move with the sneakers was a good trick, but it was the only one he had. *Now what?*

"This comes to nothing, Joey. You can't avoid me forever, but the longer you delay the inevitable, the more irritated I become. You don't want to see me lose my temper."

I don't want to see you period, Joey thought, falling back a few mirrors while the man looked the other way.

"You know what your problem is?" the man called out, picking up the pace of his search. "You still think I'm the bad guy here. I'm sure by now you've heard all about the Invisible Hand. Believe me, you don't know who the real bad guy is. You're so eager to jump through hoops for Redondo. . . . Where is he now? I'll tell you where. He's in the same place he's been for the last twenty years. Hiding! He doesn't care about you. Is he teaching you anything? Surely not. Has he ever given you a single word of encouragement? I doubt it. He's not interested in any of that. He's just playing games with your life, throwing you into situations you're not ready for." Joey watched as the man in the top hat and scarf turned on his heel, then stepped into a mirror, just as he had done back in the theater. "It's irresponsible, really," he said, emerging from a mirror right behind Joey.

"Ahh!" Joey leaped up and ran, but there was nowhere to go now that the man had eyes on him. Joey tore down the beach, but the man kept stepping in and out of mirrors, cutting him off at every turn. Through it all, he never stopped talking. "What you fail to realize is that magic is dangerous, Joey. The more it goes unchecked, the more chaos there is. Someone has to control magic. That's why we do what we do. The world needs order."

He stepped directly into Joey's path, and they collided. Joey bounced off him, falling back and landing in the sand. "Not your order," Joey said, defiant.

"I suppose you'd prefer the Order of the Majestic?" The man in the top hat and scarf barked out a laugh. "What did they ever do? Redondo . . . Houdini . . . the lot of them with their magic shows . . . ." He kicked sand in Joey's face. "That's what I think of them. Performing for strangers . . . putting on a song and dance . . . I ask you, what does that accomplish? They don't make a difference in the world. We do."

He grabbed Joey's wrist and pulled him to his feet. "Let me go!" Joey said, still struggling to get away. "Redondo! HELP!"

"You are joking," the man said, amused. "He can't hear you. Even if he could, he never leaves that blasted theater . . . that twisted realm of his. Did you know he created that place? It's an alternate reality born entirely out of his depression. That's the most he ever did with the wand. It's pathetic. Redondo cracked up twenty years ago, and he's been there, dying a slow death ever since. Would you like to know why?"

"Because you wouldn't stop talking?" Joey reached up to grab the frame of a nearby mirror and pulled it down with all the strength he could muster. It connected with a satisfying crack, the glass breaking against the man's head. He staggered a step, loosening his grip on Joey's arm. Joey broke into a run. The man threw off the broken mirror and watched him go.

"All right, then, enough talk." He took hold of one of the mirrors and angled it so that his reflection appeared in several others at the same time. He snapped his fingers and every reflected image of him came to life. Dozens of them stepped out of mirrors all along the beach. Joey spun away from one of them just in time, but he tripped over his own feet and went tumbling into the sand. He felt fingers on his ankle and, looking closely, saw a gloved hand reaching out of a nearby mirror, clutching at him. He kicked it away and sprang up, desperate to escape. They were everywhere.

His heart sped up and he ran, zigzagging between mirrors.

Random, unpredictable movement was his only defense, which meant he was pretty much helpless. They had him surrounded and completely outnumbered. No matter where he turned, another figure blocked his path. He kept changing directions, ducking and dodging their grasp.

Eventually he was forced to run for the only place they weren't coming from. The water. Joey charged into the surf and waded out until he was in up to his knees. Then he stopped. The water was icy cold, but that wasn't why he froze in place. It was the view that got him. The ocean stretched out before him in all its vast emptiness. What was he going to do? Where was he going to go? He couldn't swim to freedom. For one thing, he wasn't that strong a swimmer. For another, he didn't have the first clue what was out there. Was there a land, some magical country, for him to escape to, or just an endless sea? He had no way of knowing. The water could have been teeming with mirror monsters for all he knew. Joey turned to face the music. It was hard to tell exact numbers, but it looked like fifty men in top hats and scarves lined the edge of the beach. One of them near the center, most likely the genuine article, stepped forward.

"You've got heart, Joey, I'll give you that. You're wasted in the theater. Stop fighting me. Help me get the wand and I'll teach you real magic."

"Not interested," Joey said.

"That's the best offer you're going to get. I'd hate for you to make a decision of this magnitude without giving it a proper think. Take it from me, Redondo's not very good at holding on to his people. Ask him what happened to Grayson Manchester! See what he says!"

The name got Joey's attention. *The boy who was lost in the fire?* He was about to ask the man in the top hat and scarf exactly what *did* happen to Grayson Manchester, when a streak of lightning split the sky. A blinding light flickered like the flash of a planet-size camera, and then it got dark. Clouds rushed in, filling the violet sky, which rapidly deepened to a shade of indigo that bordered on black. Set against a gray cloud, Joey saw something high in the air. It was far away, just a speck, but it looked like it might be in the shape of a person. Joey raised a hand to his brow, trying to draw focus on the object. "Is that . . . ?"

The men in the top hats and scarves spoke as one. "Redondo."

Thunder followed the lightning. An explosive sound, like

mountains crumbling, rocked the beach, and a giant wave rose up in the ocean. Its shadow fell on Joey as it climbed ten feet in the air, then twenty. It continued to swell. Joey stopped waiting to see how high it would go and ran. The man in the top hat and scarf ran too, as did his reflections. None of them could outrun the tsunami. It crashed down onto the beach, like a meteor falling to the earth, but at the last minute, Redondo swooped in to shield Joey from the impact. Joey's feet had just hit dry sand when suddenly the old man was right there next to him. He touched the wand to Joey's shoulder, said, "Encapsulato," and a protective bubble formed around them. The wave still knocked them around like a pinball inside the churning water, but it was nothing compared to the beating their enemies took. The tidal wave pulverized them, scattering their forces and the mirrors.

The next thing Joey knew, the water had receded, and Redondo was helping him get up. "Are you all right?" Dazed and confused, Joey grunted something unintelligible. "You're fine." Redondo gave Joey's cheek a light slap and pointed down the beach at the mess of mirrors. "There. The mirror with the jewel-encrusted frame. You see it?" Joey looked. A mirror matching Redondo's description had managed to stay upright, rooted in quartzlike stone. "Get there. Quickly."

The path to the mirror was clear—for now. All over the beach, men in top hats and scarves were rising to their feet. They didn't give up easy.

"What about you?" asked Joey.

"Don't worry about me."

"Redondo . . ."

"Go *now*," Redondo said as a throng of attackers, now coated in white sand, charged at him. He turned to face them with all the confidence of Superman staring down a runaway train. Redondo was not threatened in the least. "Volare," he said, waving his wand in their direction. Just like that, they went flying back, knocking down mirrors, and one another, like bowling pins.

Another gang of sand-covered reflections came barreling in from Redondo's right. He pointed his wand at them. "Detonata." A series of explosions ruptured the beach. Sand and broken glass filled the air, dropping them before they got anywhere near him.

"Okay, you got this," Joey said. He set off running for the jewel-encrusted mirror. Several top-hat-and-scarf-clad figures sprinted past Joey and dove headfirst into mirrors, vanishing from sight. They were giving up. *That's right; you better run,* Joey thought. Redondo wasn't playing around. Joey reached the mirror. Before he went in, he paused for one last look at the action. The man in the top hat and scarf (again Joey had a feeling it was the original), stood across from Redondo at the center of his dwindling forces.

"You seem to be running out of cannon fodder." Redondo smirked.

The man grabbed a mirror and spun it around to face Redondo. The glass rippled and the many reflections that Joey thought had fled were unleashed on Redondo in a single burst. "You were saying?"

An endless stream of attackers flew at Redondo as if shot from a cannon. Suddenly on defense, he jumped back. "Quixote!" he shouted, waving his arm in a big circle. His assailants spun away, turning hard, ugly cartwheels headfirst into the sand, but only the frontline went down. The blitz continued, and Redondo was overrun.

The man in the top hat and scarf laughed out loud, pacing around the scrum as reflections of himself piled on top of Redondo. "There you go again, Redondo, tilting at windmills. Why do you do this to yourself? If you don't have the will to use the wand to its full potential, give it to someone who does."

Over at the mirror with the jewel-encrusted frame, Joey's knees buckled. He had one foot in the glass and one on the beach, but he couldn't move. He couldn't leave Redondo like this. They might kill him. Not only that, but they'd take the wand! Joey thought about what Shazad had said about the Invisible Hand seizing control of the world. He watched in terror as they heaped on top of Redondo like football players fighting to recover a fumble. Redondo was at the bottom of the mound, curled up, trying to hold on to the ball, or in this case, the wand.

"Stop fighting us," the man in the top hat and scarf told Redondo. "It's over. *You're* over."

Joey was horrified. It couldn't end like this. Could it? He wanted to help, but he was useless in a fight—especially this fight. He couldn't do anything against odds like these, but he couldn't just bug out and save himself, either. A prisoner of his own indecision, all he could do was watch. He watched as Redondo struggled fruitlessly, buried under a growing mountain of people. He watched as a shadow loomed over them, expanding to cover most of the beach. He watched as another tidal wave fell crashing to the shore. It was taller than the last one, and this time, when it hit, Redondo had no magic shield to protect him.

The raging water knocked Joey off his feet and away from the mirror, but he was far enough from the shore to feel only a fraction of its force. Everyone else got leveled. When the wave receded, Joey was the only one standing upright. The man in the top hat and scarf and his army of reflections were all down for the count. Redondo, too, appeared unconscious. His wand was sticking out of the sand, a good five feet away from his open palm. Joey went for it. As soon as his fingers touched the wand, he understood why the Invisible Hand wanted it so badly.

Whoa.

It was like picking up Thor's hammer. In his mind's eye, he saw a vision of Redondo. Then of Houdini himself, followed by the images of several other magicians he didn't recognize . . . a long line of people who had once wielded the wand, going all the way back to a man with a thick white beard and brilliant blue robes. Suddenly filled with power, Joey felt ten feet tall. Able to leap small buildings in a single bound. The world around him became wrapped in a golden hue. All his senses were hypercharged. Joey's vision was sharper. Everything was moving in slow motion. He could see his enemies recovering one by one. They would soon be all over him, but he wasn't afraid. A word appeared in his head. He waved the wand in a big, sweeping motion and cast the spell with confidence:

"Excelsior!"

Joey didn't know where the idea to say that had come from, but when he spoke the magic words, every agent of the Invisible Hand on the beach floated up into the air, as if gravity had ceased to have any hold on them. They clawed at the sand in futile attempts to anchor their bodies to the beach. The man in the top hat and scarf screamed at Joey as he and his other selves drifted skyward. "How did you . . . ? You can't—you shouldn't have been able to . . . You just made the biggest mistake of your life!" he railed. "Do you hear me? Of your life!" Joey just smiled, watching him drift away until he was so high up he no longer mattered.

Once the beach was clear of all hostiles, Joey turned his attention to Redondo. Shouldering his weight as best he could, he helped him stand up, and together they limped back to the mirror with the jewel-encrusted frame.

"That was fun," said Redondo, coming around with a hint of irony in his voice.

"Yeah, let's do it again tomorrow," Joey said.

Redondo started to laugh, but it was broken up by his cough. He wiped blood from his mouth and massaged his ribs, clearly in pain. "Let's get out of here."

"Right." Joey looked into the mirror, seeing not his reflection, but where he wanted to go in his mind. He dragged Redondo into the mirror. Once again, it was like stepping into liquid, and the two of them were spirited away.

11

The Choice

Joey and Redondo fell forward out of the mirror and collapsed onto the stage. Leanora and Shazad were waiting beside the mirror with the baroque golden frame—the one Joey had originally used to enter the mirror world. When they saw the shape Redondo was in, they were bursting with questions, asking if he was all right, what had happened, and specifically, what had Joey done? Clearly, they had expected to see Redondo helping Joey back through the portal, not the other way around.

Ignoring them both for the time being, Joey set Redondo down gently and turned his attention to the mirror they had just come out of—the one with the jewel-encrusted frame. Knowing that its counterpart in the mirror world was still intact, Joey tipped it back and let it crash down. It hit the stage hard, shattering the glass inside the frame.

"No!" Leanora exclaimed.

"What are you doing?" Shazad demanded.

"You might want to back up," Joey said, turning away from the mirror.

Just like in the mirror world, the glass exploded outward with tremendous force. Perhaps it was the magical energy leaving the broken mirror that did it. Shards of glass shot up into the air and showered the stage. Another relic lost.

When the dust settled, Leanora and Shazad were flabbergasted. "Why would you do that?" Leanora asked.

"Just in case," Joey said. "Don't want anybody following us."

"Can't be too careful," Redondo agreed in a weary voice.

"Following you? What happened over there?" Shazad asked.

"*Bozhe moi!*" Leanora exclaimed. "Why does he have the wand?" she asked, pointing at Joey.

"Oh yeah." Joey looked down at his own hand. He had forgotten he was still holding Houdini's wand. "It's a long story."

Shazad looked at Joey, astonished. "I've got time."

"Not now," Redondo said, his voice exhausted. "Right

now I need to . . ." He struggled to stand, coughing and clutching at a pain in his side. "I need to rest." He turned to Joey. "Take me to my office."

"Right." Joey nodded and carefully swept glass off the trapdoor in the middle of the stage with his foot. Once again he was without shoes, having left his sneakers back in the mirror world. Joey opened the door in the floor and helped Redondo down the steps. "There's a good lad. Leanora, Shazad . . . if you wouldn't mind waiting here. I need to talk to young Kopecky. Alone."

"Alone?" Shazad repeated, taken aback.

"Thank you," Redondo replied as he disappeared down the steps.

Joey read the expressions on Leanora's and Shazad's faces. They couldn't believe they were being left out of this. Joey didn't take any pleasure in the momentary reversal of fortune. His head was still spinning from what had just happened in the mirror world. "Just hang out," he told them. "I'll fill you in when I come back." He followed Redondo down and closed the trapdoor behind him.

Joey and Redondo came out in Redondo's messy office, high up on the back wall of the theater. With Joey shouldering most of Redondo's weight, they descended the attic ladder steps slowly and shuffled over to a sofa that had been buried under an abundance of boxes, papers, and files. Joey pushed everything to the floor and set Redondo down. The old man sighed with relief, but didn't relax. "Help me get this off." Still sitting upright, he turned away from Joey and held his arms behind him so that Joey could help pull off his tuxedo jacket. Joey gripped the cuffs and tugged back gently. Redondo grunted in pain as the jacket came off. "That's better," he said, easing himself down into the couch cushions. "I told you . . . you might regret this," he added with a weak smile. "Sorry to keep you waiting in there. I would have arrived sooner, but the mirror's link to the mirror world was broken. I had to pull another mirror out of storage before I could reach you."

"Never mind that," Joey said, concerned. The man in the top hat and scarf had given Redondo quite a beating. "Are you going to be okay?"

"I'll live," Redondo said. "Another day at least. I'll take that back now."

"What?"

"The wand." Redondo motioned for him to fork it over. "If you would be so kind."

"Of course. Here you go."

"Thank you." Redondo studied Joey as he took the wand back from him, almost as if he was surprised to see him give it up so easy. "Are you feeling all right?"

Joey shook his head. When he'd given Redondo the wand, he had gotten a healthy dose of reality back in return. The feeling of raw power and magical might that had swelled Joey's heart while holding the wand now flew from his body. Suddenly deflated, the magnitude of what had just happened hit him fully. "Redondo, that was close. That was way too close. Who was that guy?"

"An old friend."

"Some friend," Joey said. "That was the second time he came after me. He was the one who showed up in my room last night. He's after the wand."

"Believe it or not, I managed to figure that out on my own," Redondo said, wincing as he gingerly felt at a pain in his side. "The Invisible Hand has obviously chosen a very motivated enforcer to deal with me."

"You think?" Shock was setting in now that the danger had passed. The Invisible Hand was still coming after him. The first time they had met, the man in the top hat and scarf had been content to give him a bad dream, but this time around he had actually intended to hurt him. Joey realized his hands were shaking. "Redondo, I'm—I'm scared."

"Don't be scared."

"I can't help it."

"Of course you can. You just proved that. You weren't scared over there, were you?"

"I was terrified over there!"

"Really?" Redondo tapped the wand lightly in his hand. "I thought you handled yourself remarkably well. Don't you?"

"Redondo, I don't know what you're talking about. I ran away from him. He chased me into the ocean. He would have killed me if not for you!"

"Don't get hysterical. He wouldn't have killed . . ." Redondo paused, clutching his side as he succumbed to an excruciating cough. "He gets nothing out of killing you. He needs to kill me," Redondo stressed, gritting his teeth. "Now stop it. This is what he wants. He wants you scared so you'll give up . . . so you'll quit all this."

"He doesn't want me to quit. He wants to use me to get in here. He told me to take him back through the mirror, but I wouldn't do it. I smashed the mirror on the other side so he couldn't make me try."

The corners of Redondo's mouth twitched. "Smashing things is getting to be habit with you."

"I don't know what I was thinking. I could have been stuck there for good."

"You were thinking on your feet, like a good magician should."

Joey frowned. He wasn't so sure he wanted to be a good magician if this was what it was going to be like. "I don't know if I can do this, Redondo."

Redondo cocked his head to the side. "Don't tell me you want to give up. Not when you've just taken the lead in the competition for the wand."

"I gotta tell you, I'm not really feeling this competition. Can't you just teach me some magic in whatever time you've got left instead?"

Redondo wagged a finger. "What you need to learn can't be taught. This wand . . ."

"I told you, I didn't come here because I wanted the wand."

"But you keep coming back."

"Yes, because I want to learn magic!"

"Why?"

"What do you mean, why? Who wouldn't want to learn magic? It's amazing. . . . It's exciting. . . . It's special."

"And you want those things."

"I want my life to be all those things! That doesn't mean I have to be the world's greatest magician, and it definitely doesn't mean I want to fight some magical Legion of Doom. I don't need to be better at this than Leanora or Shazad. They're way ahead of me already! Let them have the wand and worry about the Invisible Hand. That's fine by me."

"I see." Redondo grimaced. "You want the power but not the responsibility." He gave a little cough and made a face like someone had stabbed him. "I'm afraid it doesn't work that way."

"It doesn't have to be *that* much power," Joey specified. "This place is full of relics, right? Maybe you could just leave me a couple cool things that the Invisible Hand doesn't want so bad. Things that aren't worth going after. I'm not picky about it, really."

Redondo made a sound that was part cough, part chuckle. He had an amused look on his face. "There is nothing I have here . . . nothing I could give you . . . so trivial that the Invisible Hand does not wish to obtain it. There's no halfway in this world, young Kopecky. You're either in or you're out. That's the reason for this competition. Part of the reason, anyway. If I'm going to leave this behind—any of it—I need to know it's in the care of someone with the strength to look after it."

He went back to his fortune-telling cards and once again pulled out three cards from the deck. This time he got the Shield, the Sword, and the Escape Artist.

"What's that about?" Joey asked him.

"Decisions, decisions . . . ," Redondo muttered, putting the cards away. "We've all got choices to make."

Redondo hiked up his shirt on his left side to inspect his wounds. Splotchy reddish-purple bruises covered his body from his waist to his ribs, parting gifts from the man in the top hat and scarf. "That doesn't look good," Joey said.

"No? Because it feels wonderful."

"I'm sorry."

"It's all right. It could have been worse," Redondo said, smoothing his shirt back into place. "And it was worth it to find out what you're capable of. Tell me, how did you get us out of there?"

"What do you mean? I used the mirror. You told me which one led back here."

"But how did we reach the mirror? What did you do to make everyone float away? How did you do that?"

Joey scratched his head. His memory of picking up the wand and putting it to use was a blur, but after some thought the word jumped out at him. "Excelsior. I said, 'excelsior.' It means 'ever upward.'"

Redondo stared at Joey, mystified. "Where did that come from?"

"Marvel Comics," Joey said instantly. "You know Stan Lee? The guy who made up all those superheroes? He says it all the time. It's like his catchphrase. I didn't know what it would do, but it seemed like the right thing to say for some reason."

"Amazing," Redondo marveled. "Who would have thought a lifetime of comic books and superhero movies would come in handy?"

"I got lucky."

"What's luck but a touch of magic? With the right tools, we make our own luck. Do you have any idea what you did? This isn't like the mirror or the key. . . . You didn't just believe enough to *use* a magical object. You cast a spell of your own design and actually made *new magic*. You used the wand!" Redondo shook his head, staring at the wand in disbelief. "That shouldn't be possible. Not while I'm alive."

Joey felt sick. Yesterday he would have been thrilled to achieve something so extraordinary, but today he felt more dread than pride. "I don't know about this, Redondo. I don't want a life where I have to look over my shoulder for the Invisible Hand all the time."

"If you want to use magic, they're going to be there whether you watch for them or not."

"Just how powerful are they?" Joey asked. "Leanora and Shazad made it sound like the Invisible Hand is secretly running the world."

"Manipulating the world would be more accurate. That is, after all, what magicians do. The Invisible Hand believes that only they deserve to use magic. They've filled the world with things that manipulate and deceive audiences, with results that are anything but magical: isolating technology, social media, cable news channels . . . The list goes on."

"Wait a minute . . . social media?" Joey said. "What's that got to do with magic?"

"More than you think. The Invisible Hand has been hoarding magic for centuries. What do you think people replace it with? What fills the void? Technology. The opposite of magic. Things that work whether or not you believe in them. Things that make people lazy and do their thinking for them. People see the world through screens these days. Is it any wonder they can't see magic when it's right in front of their face?"

"What are you telling me?" Joey asked. "The Invisible Hand is hypnotizing people through their phones?"

"It wouldn't surprise me. The world's become a dark and angry place. Maybe you've noticed? People are depressed, distracted, and divided . . . trapped in lives where possibility exists only for the few . . . and yet no one does anything about it. No one thinks they have a chance. The Invisible Hand has had great success turning the public into sheep. People today will believe anything except that which is truly extraordinary."

Joey was quiet for a moment. He thought about Shazad's argument that it was no use trying to fight the Invisible Hand and knew that he was guilty of the same bleak outlook. His own reaction to the Earth Day rally in Times

Square was proof enough of that. He had actually equated the event with the doomed efforts to save Planet Krypton. Joey thought about his attitude toward Exemplar Academy and Janelle telling him he didn't believe in himself. When had he become so cynical? Had the Invisible Hand cast its spell over him, too?

"I still don't get it. How do you fight the Invisible Hand doing magic tricks in a theater, pretending it's all an act? Couldn't you just use the wand to wish them away and change the world into something better? Or are you not strong enough for that?" Joey asked, thinking about Redondo's terminal illness.

"I'm strong enough not to do it," Redondo said. "There is such a thing as free will, young Kopecky. It's not for me to play God with this wand. If I were to cross that line, where would I stop? Would I stop?"

"Free will, then . . . fine. Give people the choice. If you want to keep the Invisible Hand from rounding up all the magic in the world, show people what they're doing. Can't you just tell people the truth about magic? About everything?"

Redondo shook his head. "It wouldn't do any good."

"How do you know?"

"Because people are predisposed *not* to believe what they are told when it comes to such things," Redondo said patiently. "There's a reason we don't share secrets. It's the same reason I won't train you and the other children in magic. Not formally. Magicians don't pull back the curtain and show people how their tricks are done. That is not the path to *belief* in magic. The Invisible Hand can only be defeated when people are willing to believe—when they have faith—that the impossible is possible. You have to get in people's heads. Inspire them. It takes showmanship and stage presence to make that happen. If a magician does his or her job well enough, the magic can last long after the curtain falls. It might even stop being 'magic' and just become part of the way the world works. But people need to think it's their idea. They need to be moved, not pushed. You can't spoon-feed magic to people. They won't swallow it. You've heard the expression 'I'll believe it when I see it?' With magic it's the opposite. They'll see it when they believe it."

With a grunt Redondo forced himself to stand. He walked to the window and looked out on the theater.

"Magic is a noble profession, young Kopecky. Don't ever let

anyone tell you otherwise. People these days . . . they forget how much they need magic in their lives. That's why it's so important people believe in what we do. That kind of belief brings wonder and amazement to the mundane. Great magicians ignite a sense of childlike enthusiasm in their audience, reminding people, both young and old, that the world is a grand and wonderful place filled with potential and promise. We follow Houdini's tradition, inspiring people to make their own brand of magic. It could be anything . . . art, science, simple acts of kindness . . . It doesn't matter what form it takes. That kind of thinking got lost somewhere. We need to get it back. Sometimes it feels impossible. I know that better than most. But that's the whole point of magic—to show people nothing is impossible. You want your life to be better. Special." Redondo shook his head. "The Invisible Hand wants the same thing. We have to choose. If I leave the wand in your care, you have to decide what kind of show you want to put on. You have to pick a side. Will you inspire wonder . . . or terror?"

"What if I choose door number three?"

Redondo raised an eyebrow. "What's that?"

"No offense, but you haven't inspired anything in a long time."

Redondo huffed and looked away. "I hate to think of what you'd say if you were trying to offend me."

"I'm serious. You tell me I can't quit, but you've been gone twenty years. The guy in the top hat . . . He said you gave up. That this place"—Joey motioned to the theater—"was your depression."

Redondo frowned and looked out the window for several seconds. It was a bitter pill to swallow, but he took it. "He's not wrong," he said at last. "This place . . . It's part of me. A reflection of what I became. But I'm trying. I'm trying to see things differently while there's still time. If you want proof, just look around. There's hope for me yet. Maybe for all of us."

Looking out the window, Joey saw that the Majestic was making an inexplicable comeback. Like the once-dead plants in the lobby that were now clinging to life, the theater was repairing itself and restoring its lost splendor. The changes were not drastic, but they were a start. Joey watched as cracks in the walls healed themselves and burn marks around the stage retreated.

"I'm glad you're feeling better, but how did things get like this to begin with? Why did you go away?"

Redondo grimaced. "I had my reasons."

"Grayson Manchester?" Joey asked.

Redondo didn't answer except to give Joey a hard, side-eyed stare, silently warning him not to pursue this subject, but Joey would not be dissuaded.

"It was because of him, wasn't it? Who was he?"

Redondo let out a reluctant sigh. "My assistant."

"The guy in the top hat told me to ask what happened to him."

"I'll bet he did."

"And?"

There was a loud crack as new fissures emerged in the theater walls. Paint peeled, lights faded, and the burn marks around the stage returned. They spread out as if an invisible giant were smearing ink on the wall with oversize fingers. Redondo surveyed the fresh damage to the theater, or rather, the return of the old damage, and hung his head. "I'm tired," he said, his voice turning cold. "I need to rest. Let yourself out please."

Redondo returned to the couch without giving Joey another look. He was done talking. This time, rather than push the matter any further, Joey let it go. *Magicians never reveal their secrets*, he thought. Redondo clearly wanted to hold on to this one, but Joey could guess what had happened and it didn't bode well for the future. He went up the attic stairs. By the time he reached the top step, Redondo was already out cold. Somewhat shaken, Joey left the room, coming out on the stage down below. Leanora and Shazad were on him the second he exited the trapdoor.

"All right, let's hear it," Shazad said. "What happened over there? Why did you break the mirror?"

"Why did you have the wand?" Leanora added, more urgently. "Did someone come after you? Was it the Invisible Hand?"

Joey said nothing. He was lost in thought.

"What did Redondo want to talk to you about?" Leanora pressed. Taking note of Joey's bewildered state, she guided him to a chair backstage and sat him down. "What is it? What did he say? What's wrong?"

Joey looked up at the window to Redondo's office. He thought about the newspaper headlines he had read about Grayson Manchester, the boy lost in the fire. He thought about the burn marks on the stage and Redondo's scarred hand. What could have made Redondo hang up his tuxedo for twenty long years? Only one thing made sense.

"I think Redondo might have gotten his old assistant killed."

12

Journey into Mystery

Shazad and Leanora were shocked. "What are you talking about?" Shazad snapped.

"That can't be true," Leanora said.

"I think it can," Joey replied, looking grim. "I'm not saying I *want* it to be true. I'm just saying it's possible. You don't think it might explain why Redondo's been living here like a hermit all this time?"

Shazad's and Leanora's expressions cycled through a mix of emotions ranging from confusion, to uneasiness, to skepticism. "Where's all this coming from?" Shazad asked. "We asked you what happened over there. This is what you tell us?"

"Joey, focus," Leanora said. She took him by the shoulders. "Go back to the beginning. What happened in the mirror world? Start there. We're in the dark right now. Fill us in."

"Right." Joey took a breath. "Sorry," he said, settling down a bit. He wasn't used to being the one dispensing information. Joey backed up and went through the whole story, trying to stay calm. He told Leanora and Shazad how the Invisible Hand had ambushed him on the other side of the mirror and how Redondo had saved him but needed help getting out of there. Shazad balked at Joey's account of using Houdini's wand to defend himself.

"I'm sorry, this is too much," Shazad said in a huff. "That didn't happen."

"He did come out of the mirror holding the wand," Leanora reminded Shazad.

"I know. I saw," Shazad said, a hard edge to his voice. "I also know no one else can use the wand while Redondo's alive. How do you explain that?"

"I can't," Joey admitted. "Even Redondo couldn't figure that out. You think I know?"

"Do the rules change when the wand's master is dying?" Leanora asked. "Maybe it's testing the waters. Trying new people out."

"It doesn't work like that," Shazad said. His voice was firm. Certain. "The wand obeys one person at a time. Everyone knows that. We all held it yesterday. Nothing happened."

"I'm telling you what happened today," Joey said. "You don't have to believe me, but it's true."

Shazad looked concerned. "Why would the wand pick *you?*"

"Why would you say Redondo got his old assistant killed?" Leanora asked.

Joey went back into his tale, repeating what the man in the top hat and scarf had said about Redondo not being able to take care of his people. He followed that up with the story of the first time the two of them had crossed paths. The late-night threats . . . the death-by-fire illusion . . . It all lined up with the articles Joey had read about the Majestic Theatre burning down and the child who was lost in the blaze.

"What did you say his name was?" Leanora asked.

"The boy? Grayson Manchester."

Leanora's eye twitched. Joey noticed.

"What is it?"

She shook him off. "Just go on."

"Redondo told me the kid was his assistant," Joey continued. "He seemed pretty broken up about it. I'm guessing he must have died in the fire. Look around. The burn marks are right here on the stage. You're standing on them."

Leanora nodded, looking down. "They seem to come and go," she observed.

"I know. It's weird," Joey agreed. "This whole theater is tied to Redondo's mood. He's the only thing keeping it together. That's one of the reasons why I think this is for real. I asked him about Manchester up there in his office, and the burn marks came back! Something happened here. Whatever it was, I can tell it haunts him. Big-time. Everyone back in New York thinks this place burned down, but only because Redondo brought the theater here after the fire. Why would he do that? And why did he refuse your parents when they asked him to take you on as his assistant before this? What could have happened at his last show that was so bad he had to go into hiding for twenty years?" Joey leaned back and let Leanora and Shazad draw their own conclusions. "I can think of only one thing."

"I don't like this," Shazad said.

"I like it even less," Leanora replied. "Grayson Manchester . . . I've heard that name before."

"What?" Joey and Shazad asked at the same time.

Leanora had the look of somebody contemplating a reality she didn't want to face. Joey and Shazad both shut up and waited on her explanation. When she finally spoke, it was clear she took no pleasure in doing so.

"Years ago, when I was much younger . . . I remember hearing some of my people . . . elders . . . They were talking about Redondo and someone called Grayson Manchester. I don't remember the details. I'm not sure I ever knew them. I wasn't old enough to understand, but . . . I do remember the name. And I remember the way they sounded when they were talking . . . the looks on their faces."

Shazad's eyes narrowed. "What are you saying?"

"I'm saying . . . whatever happened with Redondo and his assistant, it ended badly. I'm sure of that much at least." Leanora had a grave expression on her face. "It's possible Joey is right about this. If it's true, it changes everything."

"How do we find out for sure?" Joey asked her. "Redondo doesn't want to talk about it."

"He doesn't have to," Leanora said. "I know someone who can show us what happened that night."

Joey leaned forward. "Did you say *show* us?"

Leanora nodded. She paused to check her watch and do some quick math in her head. "We can go see him now. He should still be awake, even with the time difference."

"Time difference?" Joey asked. "Where is he?"

"Siberia."

"Siberia?" Joey laughed. "You want to go to Siberia? Now?"

"Why not?"

Joey stared at Leanora. "Are you serious?"

"Of course I'm serious. Are you coming?" Joey was speechless. Leanora turned to Shazad. "What do you think?"

Shazad looked back and forth between her and Joey. "You want my honest opinion? I think someone finally realized what we're up against here, and he's having second thoughts."

"That's not what this is," Joey said.

"I'm not trying to hurt your feelings. I've already said you have nothing to be ashamed of," Shazad said, extending an olive branch. "The Invisible Hand is every bit as bad as I said they were. Now you know. I think you're looking for a reason to quit without admitting you're in over your head." He turned to Leanora. "If you can help him find that reason, good. You should go. Both of you. The sooner the better."

Joey ground his teeth, cornered by his own pride. Just a few minutes ago he had seriously contemplated walking away from all of this. He had even talked to Redondo about it. But now that Joey was back and Shazad was giving him "his permission" to quit, he felt differently. Just like in the mirror world, he didn't want Shazad to be right about him. "I already told you, I'm not quitting."

"You might want to reconsider that," Leanora said. "Maybe we all should."

Shazad's face lit up at the prospect of having no more rivals left in between him and the wand. Leanora nipped that in the bud, telling him, "Don't get your hopes up. I'm not just going to walk out and forfeit my chances."

Shazad's smile faded. He looked confused. "Then what—"

"I'm going to put a stop to this," she said. Her voice was defiant and strong.

"What does that mean?" Joey asked.

Leonora's expression hardened. "If Redondo cost this boy his life, he has no business judging me. Judging any of us. I'm going to tell him that, and then I'm going to demand that he end this charade."

"No more competition?" Shazad said, putting it together. He liked the sound of that, Joey could tell.

"That's right," Leanora said. "We take a stand. Make him

decide who gets the wand before something else goes wrong. Something he can't fix. If Joey's telling the truth about what happened in the mirror world—"

"I am," Joey cut in.

"Do you realize how close we came to disaster?" Leanora asked.

"They almost got me," Joey said, appreciating her concern.

"They almost got the *wand*," Leanora said, making it clear what she was really worried about. "The longer this drags on, the higher the chance is that they're going to get it. Most likely using one of us as leverage. What is Redondo thinking, leaving himself open to that? Putting us in harm's way if he can't protect us! Especially if he's lost one assistant already?"

"We don't know if he ever lost anyone," Shazad said.

"But we can find out," Leanora countered. "If you knew that it was true, would you keep going with this? He can't force us to compete, after all."

Shazad thought about what Leanora was suggesting— refusing to take part in Redondo's competition. "If you ask me, this contest was always unnecessary," he said after some brief soul-searching. "If this is true, it's worse than that. It's reckless." Shazad nodded. "I'd prefer to be done with this. I'd tell Redondo to choose who gets the wand right now. Today. But I'd want to know what happened for a fact. And it would have to be all of us saying it. I'm not going to draw a line in the sand only to have the two of you back out on me."

Leanora nodded as if she would expect nothing less. "What about you?" she asked Joey. "You started this."

Joey put his hands up, unsure. "Look, I want to know what happened as much as you guys, maybe more, but I can't go to Siberia. My parents don't even know I'm here right now. They think I'm at school. I've got to get back. I've already been gone too long."

Leanora made a face like it was the worst excuse she had ever heard. "You worry too much. We'll be there and back before they know you're gone."

"How?"

"Follow me."

Leanora led Joey and Shazad to a fake door that was located backstage. It was a stand-alone prop from some old trick, set up on a rolling platform. As she wheeled the door into place, Joey saw that it was missing a doorknob on one side.

"What's this?" Shazad asked.

"This is how I get here." Leanora fished around inside her bag and took out a golden doorknob with a large red ruby in the handle. "This doorknob has been in my family for generations. I can use it to go anywhere—just about," she added.

Leanora fit the doorknob into place and tugged back gently, testing the connection. It locked into position without the help of any tools. She twisted it a few times and tapped the ruby until it glowed bright red. "Red means go," she said happily. "I told you it wouldn't take long." She opened the door to reveal a dense forest full of tall trees, thick with pine needles. A gentle breeze blew into the theater, announcing a pleasant spring evening.

"This is Siberia?" Joey asked, marveling at the unspoiled green world that had suddenly appeared on the other side of the door. "I thought it was all snow and ice."

"In the far north, yes. It is. This forest, however, is in the southern region, near the Podkamennaya Tunguska River. It's actually very nice this time of year." She stepped through the portal. "Are you coming?"

Shazad followed Leanora into the woods without asking any questions. Joey hesitated. He knew he should be heading back to Exemplar before he was missed, but curiosity got the better of him and he found himself going along. The opportunity was simply too amazing to pass up. No matter how scared he was of the man in the top hat and the scarf, he wasn't ready to walk away from this adventure just yet.

He stepped through the door, consciously appreciating everything he saw and felt as he crossed the threshold. The switch from day to night, the instantaneous change in temperature, the fresh smell of the forest glade . . . Despite all that he had been through in the last day and a half, he was not yet numb to the wonders of seeing magic in action.

Joey joined Leanora and Shazad on a thin forest trail. After crossing over, he turned around and saw that he had exited through a door in a small woodshed. The door was left open, and through it he could see the Majestic Theatre stage lit up like a star in the night. "Don't close that," Leanora said, leaning in to retrieve the magic doorknob from the other side of the door. "We'll need this if we want to get back home." The golden doorknob came off in her hand as easily as it had gone on. Once she had it, Leanora pulled the woodshed door shut behind her.

Unable to resist, Joey opened it back up for a quick peek. The theater was gone, replaced by stacks of firewood. Leanora returned the doorknob to her bag and took out what Joey initially thought was a pair of night-vision goggles. He made the mistake of saying so out loud, much to Shazad's and Leanora's great amusement.

"We don't use technology like that." Shazad laughed. "That's for norms who don't have magic."

I walked right into that one, Joey thought, kicking himself. Feeling an urge to defend the norms of the world, he echoed Janelle's sentiments from earlier that day. "You know, some people say magic is just science we haven't figured out yet."

"Do they?" Leanora asked, putting on the goggles. "It'll be a while before anyone figures out how to make these." Her goggles had a brown leather strap in the back and thick bronze wraparound frames with gearlike dials set on either side. Leanora turned the dials, clicking different lenses into place like some kind of steampunk optometrist. "These are time-lapse lenses," she explained. "I can use them to see who was here before us. Let's start with this morning. . . ." She turned the dials once and took a look around. Nothing. "Yesterday . . ." She slid a new lens into position and scanned the site again. Still nothing. She turned the dial one more time. "One week."

241

"Maybe I should take a look," Shazad suggested.

Leanora wasn't having it. "Quiet. I have to concentrate. There, I've got him."

"Who?" Joey asked.

"A man called Kuriev. This way," she said, choosing a direction and pointing.

Joey and Shazad followed her as she struck off, hiking through an overgrown forest path. "What are you seeing?" Joey asked.

Leanora described a ghost image of an old man carrying firewood. "It's faint, but I can see it well enough in the moonlight. We'll use it to follow him home."

"Home?" Shazad repeated. "I thought you Nomadiks didn't put down roots anywhere."

"We don't. Kuriev left our clan."

"Gave up the traveling life, did he?" Shazad asked.

"He got old," Leanora said without judgment. "He retired."

"Out here?" Joey asked, stepping carefully through the wild forest with only his socks to cover his feet. They were hundreds of miles away from civilization. "This place wouldn't have been my first choice. Unless, of course,

242

there's a secret fairy-tale village hidden around here some-where. Like a magical retirement community? Is that where we're going?"

Leanora looked at Joey. It took her a second to realize he was serious. "The things you say . . . Is that what you think it's like for us?"

Joey shrugged, wondering what was so ridiculous about the idea of a hidden magical village. "I've seen stranger things."

Leanora shook her head. "It's incredible how little you know."

"Why don't you tell me what it's like, then?"

"It's no fairy tale," Leanora said, stepping over a large, twisted tree root and pressing on through the brush. "There's no such thing as a 'magic community.' Not for retirees or anyone else. Magicians don't socialize or live together in secret storybook villages. If they did, the Invisible Hand would raid those places and steal whatever it was that made them special. People who keep magic artifacts know this. They maintain a low profile. They scatter themselves and live anonymously, jealously guarding what they have. Most of the world's magicians use their relics in secret or not at all. Like Shazad's family."

Leanora pushed a low-hanging branch out of her way, letting it whip back at Shazad. He caught it just in time.

"What's wrong with that?" Shazad asked. He snapped the branch off and left it hanging at a broken angle. "Magic *survives* in secret. There's a reason my homeland didn't suffer the same fate as yours. Don't listen to her about secret magic cities," he told Joey. "Jorako still stands."

"For how long?" Leanora asked.

"Forever," Shazad answered.

"What's Jorako?" Joey asked.

Shazad struggled with another tightly packed thicket. "My country."

Leanora snickered. "A country the size of a swimming pool," she said in a mocking tone. "Shazad's family lives there. No one else. They have relics that keep it from appearing on any map, and they watch their borders closely—most of the time, anyway."

"My family keeps its magic safe from the Invisible Hand. That's all we do. That's why Houdini's wand belongs with us, where no one can get it. No one can find Jorako unless we want them to."

"Aren't you forgetting something? My people found Jorako once."

"That was a long time ago," Shazad stressed. "And we let you find us."

"My people weren't the Nomadik back then," Leanora told Joey, ignoring the second part of Shazad's comment. "We were refugees out of Freedonya. Just beginning our traveling life."

"You should have stayed with us," Shazad told her. "We had a place for you."

"A place for us to hide." Leanora shook her head. "It never would have worked. My people couldn't stay safe behind your walls. We don't protect magic. We spread magic, traveling throughout the world, sprinkling it here and there, everywhere we go. We do the work the Order of the Majestic should have been doing all these years. That's why we can't ever stay in one place. But if we had Houdini's wand, we could stop running. We could stand and face the Invisible Hand."

"You'd lose," Shazad said matter-of-factly. "Just like your people lost Freedonya all those years ago." He tapped Joey's shoulder. "The Invisible Hand took everything they had—"

"Not everything," Leanora interjected.

"And then they erased their city from the history books,"

Shazad finished. "Have you ever heard of Freedonya before this? No. Of course you haven't. It's as if the place never existed. You try to fight them, the same thing will happen to you."

"You really think they're unbeatable?" Joey asked.

"You tell me," Shazad said. "Redondo had the wand for twenty years and didn't do a thing with it. How come?"

"That's what we're here to find out," Leanora said, forging ahead.

They walked on in silence, and Joey realized something about Redondo's deck of fortune-telling cards and what they represented. It was them. The Collector, the Traveler, and the Unknown were Shazad, Leanora, and himself. The same was true of the Shield, the Sword, and the Escape Artist cards. Shazad wanted to protect magic, Leanora wanted to fight, and Joey was looking for a safe way out. He couldn't pretend that Shazad wasn't at least a little bit right about him. It was true. Joey was in over his head. He was scared. But it was also true that he had wielded Houdini's wand, something that should have been impossible, even by a magician's standards. What did it mean? Joey wondered what he would do with the wand if it somehow ended up in his possession. He honestly didn't know. He asked himself what the right thing to do was. That path was clearer in his mind. He just wasn't sure he was strong enough. He had never seen himself as a change-the-world type of person, but he wasn't alone in that.

"You know something, Shazad?" Joey asked. "You and I have more in common than you might think."

"How's that?" Shazad asked, trudging through the forest next to Joey. Leanora was several feet in front of them.

"For one thing, no one's ever going to accuse you of being an optimist. It's the same with me. People say I'm negative too."

"I'm not negative," Shazad said instantly. "I'm just . . . realistic."

"There you go!" Joey laughed. "I told Janelle the exact same thing."

Shazad furrowed his brow. "Who's Janelle?"

Joey shook his head. "Never mind, you don't know her. But you've got to admit . . . 'realistic' is a pretty funny thing for a magician to want to be."

Shazad sighed. They walked the next few seconds in silence. "I never said it was what I wanted. You think I want a world where magic is driven into the shadows?" He shook his head. "I wish things were different. I do. It's not fair that magic has to be hidden away in places like this, but that's the reality. That's the way it's always been. Even before the Invisible Hand, in Merlin's age, there were haves and have-nots. Wizards and norms. You and I can't change that."

Joey heard himself in Shazad's rationalization of the status quo. He didn't like the sound of it. "That's the kind of thinking that got Krypton blown up."

Shazad scrunched up his face. "What are you talking about?"

"It's why nothing ever changes," Joey clarified. "That stuff you said about 'the normal world' before . . . You're not wrong. It's getting worse instead of better, but no one does anything about it. People give up before they try. If I'm being honest, that's been my attitude lately too, but not today. For whatever reason, in the mirror world, I didn't give up. Maybe that's why the wand let me use it. I needed it and it was there. I'm telling you the truth. It worked."

Shazad still looked skeptical about Joey's claim to have used Houdini's wand. "What are you saying? You want to fight the Invisible Hand too? I don't know what happened over there today, but you got lucky. Very lucky. If you come between them and the wand, they won't hesitate to kill you."

Joey made a sour face. He didn't doubt the truth of Shazad's words.

"Take my advice. If the Invisible Hand comes after you again, do the smart thing. Run."

13

Vision Quest

They came upon a clearing in the woods. There was a large cabin home in the center, handcrafted from wood and stone. It was a crooked, irregularly shaped building with a serious lack of right angles, but it seemed sturdy enough. Leanora pulled up at the edge of the forest. "We're here."

"This place looks empty," Joey said.

"No," Shazad said, pointing to the chimney, which had smoke rising out of it. "Somebody's in there."

Leanora gave the door three hard knocks, then waited. They heard movement inside the house. A slow shuffling.

"That's him," Leanora said.

A tiny hatch in the center of the door opened inward, and the upper-right-hand quadrant of an old man's face was visible on the other side, though shrouded in shadow. "Who's there?" a crotchety voice demanded. He had a thick Russian accent, much thicker than Leanora's. "What do you want?" Joey put the man's age at a hundred years old or more.

Leanora removed her goggles. "Kuriev, it's me. Leanora."

"Leanora?" the old man repeated, sounding somewhat confused.

"Valkov, Leanora Valkov. You remember."

Joey thought he saw a flicker of recognition in the eyes behind the door. "Little Lea? No . . . It can't be. . . ."

"*Dedushka*, please. Let us in. I need to talk to you. We need to talk to you."

"We?" The old man's voice turned suspicious. His eyes darted around wildly, scrutinizing Joey and Shazad before settling back on Leanora. The peephole hatch slammed shut without another word from Kuriev.

"Maybe we should have called first?" Joey asked.

"Yes, we'll text him next time," Shazad said. "Save ourselves the trip."

"Is he coming back?" Joey asked, ignoring Shazad's biting yet valid criticism.

Leanora raised her fist to knock again, but the sound of several locks unlocking and dead bolts being turned told her to relax. A moment later the door swung open, and the old man spread his arms wide.

"Lea!"

"Kuriev!"

They wrapped each other up in a mighty hug. Kuriev was a squat, grizzled old man with the remnants of white hair shaved close around his ears. He had a face creased heavily with wrinkles, a stubbly beard, gentle eyes, and a warm smile. He wore a threadbare sweater and was overjoyed to see Leanora.

"Come in. Come in! Quickly," Kuriev said, beckoning everyone to enter. Once they were all in, he pulled the door shut and turned the dials on eight different types of locks. "What are you doing here?" he asked, astonished. "Is something wrong? You are not in any trouble, I hope. . . ." He reopened the door's peephole hatch and looked out into the woods, trying to see if anyone had followed them.

"No. It's nothing like that," Leanora said, drawing Kuriev away from the door. "I'm sorry to surprise you like this, but—"

"Do not apologize to me. I will not have it," Kuriev said sternly, cutting her off. "This is a gift! The last time I saw

252

you, you were this tall." He held his hand down below his waist. "Already you were showing your talents, even then." He clapped his hands together. "Ha! Come . . . sit . . . Tell me, who are your friends?"

Kuriev guided everyone to the living room, a modest space near the front door, lit by candles and a weak fire. He tried to offer Leanora the chair closest to the fireplace, but she deferred, insisting he sit there instead. She introduced Joey and Shazad, and Kuriev shook their hands, welcoming them into his home. "Any friend of Lea's . . . ," he said, lowering himself into a chair. Beyond that, he didn't pay them much mind. He was far more concerned with Leanora.

"How are your parents?" he asked her once she had settled comfortably.

"Very well," Leanora said with a smile.

"And your grandmother?"

"The same. She sends her love."

Kuriev's eyes brightened with hope. "They know you are here? You told them?"

Leanora wavered. "Actually, no."

Kuriev bunched up his lips. He seemed to shrink an inch while processing the information. "I see. They do not think less of me, I hope. You understand, I am old enough to remember when Freedonya was more than just a place in our hearts."

"Kuriev," Leonora pleaded. "You're too hard on yourself."

"I don't have the strength I had as young man. I wish I did."

"I know that," Leonora told Kuriev. "We all know that—don't we?" She looked at Joey and Shazad, who took the hint and hastily added their own reassurances. "It's not your strong arm we need, Kuriev." Leonora tapped at her temple. "It's your strong memory."

The corners of Kuriev's mouth turned up in a knowing smile. "Listen to me . . . going on like a fool," he said, chiding himself. "You didn't come to hear an old man's excuses. You wish to know something. What can I do?"

"Do you remember a magician called Redondo the Magnificent?" Shazad asked, leaning forward.

Kuriev looked at Shazad as if he had just asked him if he spoke Russian. "Of course I remember Redondo. He led the Order of Majestic. Led it well." Kuriev shifted his jaw a bit, making a face like he had a mouth full of bad borscht. "Until he didn't."

"That's what we want to know about," Joey said. "Leanora said you might be able to show us what happened to him."

Kuriev leaned back in his chair, massaging the stubble on his cheeks and chin. "You wish to see?" he asked Leanora.

She nodded. "I want to know. It could be important."

Kuriev returned Leanora's nod and rose slowly from his seat. "Wait here." He left the room briefly, and when he came back he was carrying an antique wooden box. It was a dark walnut-brown color inlaid with light maple and rich cherry wood designs. The box was old and beautiful, and judging from Kuriev's protective hold on it, heavy with contents rare and delicate. He set the box down gently on a coffee table in the center of the room and looked up at Joey and Shazad without taking his hands off the lid. "I have a rule. I do not open this in front of strangers."

Leanora touched Kuriev's shoulder. "It's all right. We need to do this together."

The old man gave in immediately. "But you are here with Nomadik royalty, so . . ."

Leanora made a cutting motion with her hand, signaling for Kuriev to stop talking, but it was too late.

Joey gave her a look. "Royalty?"

Leanora sighed. "We didn't come here to talk about my family."

Momentarily forgetting what they did come for, Joey straightened up in his chair and looked at Shazad. "Did you know about this?" Anxious to make up for his gaffe, Kuriev opened the box before Shazad could reply, redirecting everyone's attention to the crystal ball inside. A glass orb the size of a bowling ball rose from the box and floated in place, rotating slowly at eye level.

"Is that a crystal ball?" Shazad marveled.

"Is not a disco ball." Kuriev smiled. "Then again . . ." He gave it a spin and laughed as the ball turned quickly, throwing off spots of light reflected from the fire.

"Can this really show us what happened to Grayson Manchester?" Joey asked, gawking at the mysterious floating sphere.

"If you want to see badly enough," Kuriev replied. "Like all magic, it depends on the quality of the magician. About Lea, I do not worry. As for the rest of you . . . we will see." He went around the room, dousing candles. "Look deep into crystal ball, all of you. Focus your minds on the night of Redondo's final performance. Twenty years ago in the Majestic Theatre . . ."

Joey, Leanora, and Shazad huddled close around the crystal ball. Joey stared into the center of the orb, waiting for the magic to begin. A quick glance to the left and right told him the others were doing the same, and he returned his attention to the ball, watching closely and wondering what he'd be able to see inside of it. He expected mystic vapors and blurry images to form inside the crystal ball, but it remained empty. Unblemished and unclouded. Perfectly clear.

"I see nothing," said Shazad. Beside them the fire began to die.

"Keep looking," Kuriev instructed as a tiny glow, no bigger than a snowflake, appeared deep in the crystal. "Yes, there it is."

"There what is?" asked Joey.

"What you came for. Knowledge. Also known as . . . *illumination.*" Kuriev touched the crystal ball and an intense light flared up, overtaking the room. It hit with the force of a strobe, blinding Joey momentarily. He shut his eyes instinctively, and when he blinked them clear, he did a double take at what he saw. They were no longer in Kuriev's living room. They were in the Majestic Theatre, but it was not the theater as they knew it. It was the theater of twenty years ago, in all its former glory. The Majestic, back when it was worthy of its name.

"What the . . . ?" Joey nearly fell over. "We're here?!!"

Shazad expressed similar sentiments of shock. He wasn't expecting this either. Kuriev stood behind them with the crystal ball cradled in his arms, a swirl of golden light dancing inside it. "We are not here. We are simply sharing vision of this place. The crystal ball makes the vision more real."

More real is right, Joey thought. *This is what it's supposed to look like up here.* They were onstage, but off to the side, back by the ropes for the curtain. The house was packed to capacity with thunderous applause bouncing off the walls. Joey had never seen the theater like this. The Majestic was an old and cavernous space, big enough to host an audience of three thousand or more. There were at least that many people present that night, most of them down on the main floor. There was more room in the mezzanine, upper balcony, and ritzy private boxes, all of which were occupied. Joey was struck by the vision of the Majestic as it was meant to be. Decorative molding lined the walls with an impossible level of detail, and a gilded proscenium arch sat atop the stage like a crown. Every plush red velvet seat in the theater was filled with a person who was dressed to the nines.

"This is a very good vision," Kuriev noted. "Stay here in this moment. Keep your focus. There," he said, pointing. "On him."

Joey looked across the stage. Kuriev was, of course, referring to Redondo. He was onstage with them, also in his prime. The magician onstage matched the one in the framed lobby posters and the Mystery Box instruction booklet that had first led Joey to the Majestic. He was dressed sharply in a tuxedo and top hat and stood facing the crowd with supreme confidence, a man thoroughly in his element. Watching him, Joey felt like Ebenezer Scrooge in *A Christmas Carol*, whisked back in time by the Ghost of Christmas Past.

"Can they see us?" Joey asked.

"No," Leanora said. "It's a vision, remember? We're not even really here."

"Quiet. He's talking!" Shazad said, pointing.

"Ladies and gentlemen, our time together is nearly at an end." Redondo's booming voice reached the back wall of the theater, seemingly without the aid of a microphone. "For my final trick, I'll need a volunteer to join me onstage." He

paused to stroke his pencil-thin mustache. "It has to be someone special. Preferably with a touch of magic in their soul. I
don't suppose anyone here tonight fits that description. . . ."

Hundreds of hands went up in the audience, most of
them attached to small children. They squirmed in their
seats, stretching out their arms, trying hard to reach the ceiling. Redondo smiled with effortless charm.

"I'm pleased to find so many of you feeling magical this
evening—and I'm not above taking credit for that, either! Is
that fair to say? Would it be wrong to suggest I've inspired a
theater full of future magicians here tonight?" All the kids
cheered. Joey took note of the joy in their eyes. It was just
like Redondo had said. He was hiding magic in plain sight,
doing his best to inspire wonder. There in that moment,
every child in the audience wanted to be just like him. No
doubt he had been doing the impossible all night long.

Redondo placed a hand over his heart. "Thank you. I'm
touched, but I must warn you, this last trick is dangerous. For
it to work—for you to survive it—you must possess not only a
belief in magic, but an unshakable confidence in yourself and
your own abilities. My grand finale is not intended for the weak
willed or the faint of heart. So think before you place yourself

in harm's way. Ask yourself . . . do you believe in magic? Really believe in it? Also, do you have a problem with tight spaces? Are you averse to being run through with flaming swords? Do you fear death? Most important, can you be trusted to keep inviolate the secrets of supernatural, fantastic illusion? If the answer to one of these questions is yes and the answer to several others is no, then you might be the one I need to assist me with this last trick. So! Who's feeling brave? Any takers?"

A few hands went down. A few others stayed up. The rest settled somewhere in between. The magician zeroed in on an anxious boy seated near the back of the house who dropped his hand, then half-heartedly raised it again. Before he had a chance to withdraw it a second time, the magician called on him.

"You there! In the back with the longish hair . . . is your hand up or down?"

The boy quivered as every eye in the theater turned to look at him. "It's . . . uh . . . Well, it's—"

"Can't decide, eh? Come on, then. We'll figure it out together."

The boy froze. "What?" he asked in a tiny voice.

"Good people of the Majestic Theatre, give the boy a

little encouragement, will you? Let's see if we can't get him up out of his seat."

A mixture of polite applause from adult chaperones and disappointed groans from children who had actually wanted to be chosen filled the room. The boy stood up and squeezed past the other people in his row, apologizing with every step he took. He walked up the center aisle alone, looking intimidated by the weight of the moment and the grandeur of the venue. He was small and skittish, rail thin with a pasty complexion and dark circles under his eyes. He had messy, shoulder-length black hair and wore a secondhand suit that looked even shabbier once he stood next to the magician. Side by side, the two were polar opposites—the polished and the pale.

"Don't be shy," said the magician, motioning for the boy to join him in the spotlight. "Welcome, young man. Tell the audience, what is your name?"

"Grayson, sir. Grayson Manchester."

The magician offered his hand. "A pleasure to meet you, Grayson. Everybody, put your hands together for this fine young man. Together we will perform feats of wonder to dazzle and amaze."

"This was an act, of course," Kuriev explained, standing just off the stage. "They played these parts, said these lines, countless times, but nevermore after this night."

Grayson gave a timid smile as the audience clapped for him. He looked as if he might melt under the houselights. Joey studied him and Redondo for some kind of acknowledgment between the magician and his assistant. A nod. A look. Something. Neither one of them broke character in the slightest. Joey observed in Grayson a perfect commitment to the role of "volunteer."

"How old are you, Grayson?" asked Redondo.

"Twelve, sir."

"And have you ever done magic before?"

"No, sir."

"Never? And still you volunteered to be a part of this?"

"Actually, I didn't mean to volunteer for—"

"I'm sorry. Ladies and gentlemen . . . one more round of applause for my *brave* young assistant!" Grayson gulped as the crowd saluted him once again. The magician patted him on the back. "Not to worry, lad, there's nothing to it." He pulled away a large silk drop cloth behind him, unveiling the props for his grand finale. There were swords, chains, a large wooden crate, and burning torches set on stands that had somehow managed to avoid burning through the silk. The audience cheered as Redondo shook out the silk drop cloth, transforming it into a handkerchief small enough to fit neatly inside his breast pocket. "All you have to do is stand inside this box," he said, opening the door of the crate. "I'll take care of the rest."

Grayson eyed the crate cautiously. "What's going to happen?"

"Something magnificent." The magician walked around the box, banging a fist against each side. "This may look like an ordinary wooden crate, and in many ways it is. As you can see, there are no escape hatches. No trapdoors." He stepped inside the crate and stomped on the floor, which held firm. "However, looks can be deceiving. Crafted from a special wood imported from the far-off island of Caloo-Calay, this crate is an ethereal gateway. A bona fide mystic portal. I'm about to transport you to a realm of wonderment and mystery."

"What are the swords for?" Grayson asked, unenthusiastic about the journey on which he was about to embark.

"Oh, they won't be a problem. Provided you believe in magic. You do, don't you?"

Grayson nodded, unsure.

"Good. That's very important." Redondo nudged Grayson into the box. "In you go. Hold on to this, why don't you?" he said, taking off his top hat. "For luck," he added with a wink. Having entrusted Grayson with his magic hat, Redondo closed the wooden door on him and turned to face the audience. "Now. Let's make things interesting, shall we? Watch closely as I seal—"

His voice dried up, fading into a hoarse whisper. Redondo stopped and touched two fingers to his Adam's apple. "Excuse me," he rasped, reaching for a nearby glass of ice water. Having quenched his thirst, he cleared his throat. "Let's try that again," he said, trying to keep the show moving. "Watch as I seal young Grayso—" Once again the magician's words got stuck in his throat. He tugged at his collar, unable to breathe.

"Is everything all right?" Grayson asked from inside the crate.

Everything was not all right. Redondo gagged and bent over. He punched himself in the sternum, fighting for air. Behind him, a hammer and nails floated across the stage with a mind of their own. As Redondo struggled to cough up whatever it was that was choking him, the tools went to work nailing the crate shut.

The spectacle met with a confused smattering of applause. When the last nail was pounded into place, the hammer fell to the floor with a *clunk* and Redondo spit out a playing card. It fluttered around him like a butterfly as he stood there hunched over and gasping. Eventually he regained his composure and snatched the card out of the air. Redondo turned it over, and all the color drained from his face. Joey had a pretty good idea what image he was looking at. Redondo cast the card aside, and it slid across the stage, coming to a stop at Joey's feet. Sure enough, it was the same card Joey had produced the day he'd met Redondo. The calling card of the Invisible Hand. Joey's eyes widened in alarm. Thinking about Redondo's reaction to seeing the card the day before made him deeply concerned for the boy inside the box.

Redondo rounded on the crate his assistant was trapped inside, ready for anything. The torches on either side of it erupted with geysers of flame, and the chains sprang to life, wrapping themselves around the crate. There were cheers from audience members who thought it was all part of the show, but a growing number of people began to worry that something was off. Redondo was not paying them any mind. There was no presentation . . . no showiness to what he was doing. He was focused solely on the crate.

The swords rose up into the air, and flames leaped from the torches to the blades. They circled the crate, building up a fiery barrier. Redondo waved his hands, summoning an unseen force to push the swords back. The audience *oohed* and *aah*ed. Maybe this trick was fine after all.

Redondo flashed his palms twice. The first time he did it, they were empty. The second time, a large gold skeleton key appeared inside his right hand. He rushed to the oversize padlock that held the chains in place.

"What's going on out there?" Grayson asked from inside the crate. "Is something wrong?"

"Nothing to worry about!" Redondo replied, fitting the key into the keyhole. "Just remain calm. I'll have you out of there in a mo—ahh!"

Redondo cried out as the key melted in the lock. He jumped back, shaking his hand violently. Molten gold splattered across the stage. The chains and padlock turned bright red, glowing with heat. Joey and the others gasped.

Watching Redondo get the burns that scarred his hands added to the weight of the vision for Joey, making it more real. More visceral. He wanted to run out and help Grayson, but there was nothing he could do. He wasn't even really there. Joey balled a fist, a terrible feeling of powerlessness churning in his stomach.

"Are you still there?" Grayson pounded on the door of the crate. "It's getting hot in here. I don't want to do this anymore."

Redondo clutched his badly burned hand as the swords swooped back down, surrounding the crate. They swirled in the air, spinning fast enough to create a flaming vortex. Within seconds the stage curtain was ablaze and Grayson could be heard screaming. "Help! I'm burning up! Get me out of here!"

People got out of their seats, beginning to realize this was no ordinary trick. The theater was on fire. The boy was in danger and so were they.

Parents gathered up their children and looked for the nearest exit, but Redondo stood firm. He drew Houdini's wand from his sleeve. "Don't worry," he said. "This ends now." He threw his arm forward, pointing the wand at the crate. "VALEFUEGO!" he shouted. The swords flew back. The fiery tornado dissipated.

But only for a moment.

The swords turned in midair and came down like flaming missiles. They ran through the crate, creating an explosion that blew Redondo off the stage. He landed in the orchestra pit. All around, people were screaming and running for the door. Fire spread across the theater walls, growing out of control. The theater manager, a round man with a bushy black mustache, helped Redondo up off the floor.

"What's going on? What did you do?" the manager asked.

"No! It wasn't me. . . . The Invisible Hand, they—"

"Who? What are you talking about?" The theater manager looked around the burning theater with growing alarm. He grabbed Redondo by the lapels and shook him. "What about the boy?" Redondo couldn't speak. Behind him, the charred remains of the crate broke apart and fire consumed the stage. "He wasn't actually in there, was he? Tell me you got him out!"

It was no use talking to Redondo. He was in shock as a dark shadow descended on the theater. Defying the flames, it moved from the back of the house to the front in a steady wave. A sinister laugh echoed through the room.

The theater manager spun around, still holding Redondo tight. "What is that? Who is that? What's going—"

He was interrupted by a flock of doves pouring out of Redondo's pockets and sleeves. They engulfed the theater manager, and when they passed, he found himself clutching an empty tuxedo jacket. He spun around, scanning the theater as terrified people fled the flames. Redondo was gone. The sweeping shadow kept coming. It reached the stage, and an icy chill ran through Joey's body. He shivered, and the vision of the theater shook with him. When he blinked his eyes, the vision was gone. They were back in Kuriev's cabin.

"What happened to the theater?" asked Shazad. "Where did it go?"

"Something broke the connection," Kuriev said, tapping the crystal ball as the light inside it faded down to nothing.

Joey shifted uncomfortably, feeling self-conscious about the pang of fear that had needled his gut as the shadow closed in. *Was it me?* he wondered. *Did I break it?* Fortunately, he was the only person asking that question. Everyone else was far more concerned with what they had just seen.

"He lost him," Leonora said. "Even with the wand, he

couldn't save him. And he ran. Rather than stay and fight, he ran!"

Joey was still grappling with the truth about Grayson Manchester's fiery death when he felt a cool breeze on his neck. He turned toward the door, which was wide open. "Uh, Mr. Kuriev? Didn't you lock the door? With, like . . . a bunch of locks?"

Everyone turned to look at the door, which was swinging loosely on its hinge. Before Kuriev could say anything, a man stepped forward out of the shadows and slammed the door shut from the inside. He was wearing a top hat and a scarf to hide his face. His eyes glowed with a creepy green light. "What are you watching?" he asked. "Anything good?"

14

Hat Trick

"Who the devil?" Kuriev said, a baffled expression on his face.

The man in the top hat and scarf took a bow. "Good evening, sir. I do hope I'm not intruding."

"Not again," Joey said. A skeevy chill tingled his neck as if a spider were crawling up his back. "That's him."

"Him who?" Shazad asked.

"Him! The—the guy!" Joey sputtered. "The Invisible Hand guy!"

"Is that a crystal ball?" asked the man in the top hat and scarf. "I wouldn't mind having one of those."

Kuriev snatched the crystal ball out of the air and held it close to his chest. "Go," he told Joey and the others. "Out the back door, now." His voice was steady, but the sense of urgency was unmistakable. It was an order, and Joey didn't

272

need to be told twice. He was already backing away in the other direction, but Leanora and Shazad lingered, fixated on the intruder.

"Come on!" Joey shouted, reaching out his hand and imploring them to move. The man in the top hat and scarf laughed as Kuriev fumbled with the crystal ball, putting it back into its box.

"Very kind of you to wrap that up for me," the man in the top hat and scarf told Kuriev. "I didn't come here expecting such generosity, but I'll gladly take that off your hands for you." He looked around the room. "Along with anything else you've got lying around here—and them, of course," he added, gesturing to Joey, Leanora, and Shazad. "Can't forget them, can we?"

Now Leanora and Shazad inched away from the front door, following Joey's example. Kuriev went to the fireplace and took a tiny painted wooden box off the mantel. "Let us make a deal. Leave them. You take Rasputin's Murder Box instead."

Murder box? Joey wondered. *That sounds promising.*

Kuriev opened the box, and hundreds of crows flew out, filling the room. It wasn't what Joey had expected, but he understood. A flock of crows was called a murder. Kuriev's "murder box" was a clever little piece of magic, and Joey was grateful he had it. The old man grabbed Leanora's wrist and pulled her toward the back door. Joey and Shazad dashed after them with the crows running interference. The birds provided a welcome diversion, flapping, cawing, and pecking as they swirled around the man in the top hat and scarf. Kuriev wrenched open the door and ushered the children outside. On his way out Joey saw the man with the glowing eyes remove his top hat and wave it like a net. In a single, fluid motion, he captured all the crows inside the hat and returned it to the top of his head with an artful flip. A second later he was striding toward the back door.

"Out you go," Kuriev said, shoving Leanora out the door last. She was reluctant to go once she realized he was not coming with them.

"What about you?" Leanora asked.

"Tell your grandmother I said hello." Kuriev grimaced. "And quite possibly . . . goodbye."

He slammed the door shut and locked it behind him. Leanora pounded the grainy wood with her fist. "No! What are you doing?"

"He's buying us time," Shazad said. "Will your doorknob work on this door?"

Leanora clutched at her bag, feeling for the doorknob inside. She nodded. "Yes, but—we need to get this off first," she said, rattling the back-door handle.

"Does it matter how we do that? Can we break it off?" Joey asked. He scanned the area around the house, looking for a heavy stone or a piece of firewood they could use.

"Forget this door," Shazad said, changing his mind. "We need to get out of here. The woodshed in the forest—we'll go back the way we came."

"What about him?" Leanora said, staring at the locked cabin door, behind which Kuriev surely faced mortal peril. The door jumped inside its frame. Kuriev had just been thrown up against the other side. Everyone jerked back a few feet.

"There's nothing we can do for him. We have to go!"

"We can't just leave him!" Leanora protested.

"Leanora, please," Joey said, trying to get through to her. "Shazad's right. Kuriev is giving us a chance. We have to use it. You have to show us how to get back. We need you."

Leanora wiped away tears and slid her goggles over her

eyes. Rather than lead the way to the shed, she stood there motionless.

"What's the matter?" Joey asked. "Don't you see him?"

"I see twelve of him," Leanora said. Joey instantly understood the problem. Leanora's magic lenses showed her a full week's worth of time at once. Kuriev had, of course, been outside of his cabin on numerous occasions over the last seven days, which cluttered the area around the house with visions of him and made the way forward less obvious.

"Pick one of them!" Shazad urged.

"We came out of the forest over there, didn't we?" Joey asked, trying to be helpful.

Leanora looked where Joey was pointing, hopefully tracking the image of an old man with his arms full of firewood. "Follow me," she said, her voice cracking with guilt and grief. She took off into the woods, and the two boys followed.

Whether it was due to Kuriev putting up more of a fight than anyone had expected out of him, or some kind of special magic locks he had placed on the back door, they were already deep in the forest by the time the man in the top hat and scarf got out of the house. Joey, Leanora, and Shazad were halfway down the trail when they heard the door fly off its hinges with a *bang*. Looking back through leaves and branches, Joey saw the man in the top hat and scarf standing in the doorway. He didn't see Kuriev.

"He's coming," Joey said. He urged the group on in a hoarse whisper. "Keep going!"

"This way!" Leanora said. She led them down a dark, winding path, guided by the light of the moon and a phantom vision of Kuriev only she could see. They ran as hard as they could, charging through bushes and leaping over ditches. Joey's lack of sneakers didn't slow him down, but the terrain seemed a lot rougher the second time around. It was hard to watch your step when you were running for your life. He ran until his lungs burned and every breath scorched his windpipe.

Huffing and puffing, he paused to look back again, hoping they had lost their pursuer. Listening intently, he heard rapid, light footsteps in the quiet night air. It didn't sound like the man in the top hat and scarf chasing after them. It was something else. A snarling growl came out of the shadows at the end of the trail, and a wolf came flying around the bend.

"WOLF!" Joey screamed, and started running again.

"It's his!" Shazad shouted as the wolf gave chase. "It's got to be with him. Run!"

Joey gave it all he had, but he was already tired and the wolf was way too fast. It caught him by the heel and bit down hard. Joey shrieked again, this time in pain rather than terror, as the beast's gnashing jaws brought him down. "No!" Leanora called out as he hit the dirt, but she was too far ahead to help him. Joey covered his face, trying to protect himself, but the wolf didn't go for his throat or any other part of his body. Instead, it pulled on his ankle with agonizing force, dragging him back down the trail toward Kuriev's cabin.

"Get this thing off me!" Joey screamed, struggling to twist his leg free, but it was no use. Every move he made was excruciating, and the wolf was ravenous. He wanted to pry its jaws off his ankle, but he had no leverage. Even if he had, he didn't dare put his hands anywhere near the wolf's mouth. He turned around on his belly, clawing at roots and dirt, desperate to stop the wolf from dragging him off. Looking up, Joey saw Shazad nearby and thought he was a goner, but Shazad surprised him. Joey saw him curse under his breath and come charging in. Shazad whipped off his cape and dove at the wolf without a trace of fear in his eyes. The beast relinquished its hold on Joey's ankle and turned its face up to snap at Shazad. He got the cape up to block its jaws just in time.

The wolf was much bigger than the cape, but somehow it didn't matter. Just like the time Redondo had flapped the cape open like a parachute and used it to fold Joey up like a pretzel, Shazad threw the cape over the wolf, covering its body all the way to the tail. Joey scurried out of the way as Shazad wrapped it up, capturing the wolf. It bucked hard, and he fell on top of it, using his body weight to keep the wolf trapped where it was. It fought tenaciously against Shazad's efforts to contain it. Joey heard it snarling and clawing under the cape, and then suddenly, the fighting stopped.

Shazad breathed a sigh of relief and released the animal. When he stood up and lifted the cape away, the wolf was no longer beneath it. In its place, a fluffy white bunny rabbit sat twitching its nose in silence.

"Shazad . . ." Joey breathed in shock as the bunny hopped off down the trail. "You . . . You saved me. I thought . . . I didn't think—"

"What?"

"You said you didn't want to fight."

"I don't. That doesn't mean I'm going to stand there and watch you get eaten alive. Come on, we're not out of the woods yet." He threw the cape back over his shoulder and helped Joey to his feet. "Can you run?"

"Do I have a choice?"

"No."

Joey tested his ravaged ankle. He felt like he had gotten his foot caught in a blender, but there was no time to recover. The man in the top hat and scarf was coming around the bend. He paused briefly to watch the little bunny that had once been his wolf hop past him. "Ugh," he said, loud enough for Joey and Shazad to hear. "What did they do to you?"

Leanora called out for Joey and Shazad to pick up the pace, and they started running again. Trees flew by to the left and right of Joey as he pushed himself to the limit, ignoring the pain in his ankle. The man in the top hat and scarf stalked after them. Soon they reached a clearing in the forest. The woodshed was right in front of them. "We made it," Joey said, heaving.

Shazad shook his head. "He's still with us," he said, breathing hard.

The man in the top hat and scarf was visible behind them, not too far off. He was still not running. He was toying with them. Joey wondered what tricks he had up his sleeve, but it turned out the real danger came from his hat.

"That was an ugly thing you did to my wolf. I suppose I'll have to think bigger." Joey watched as the man removed his top hat and pulled out a baby wolf by the scruff of its neck. He tossed the wolf away with a lazy motion, and the creature was full grown by the time it landed. More than full. The beast was a lion-size dire wolf, as in Joey felt a dire need to get the heck away from it as soon as possible. It padded in front of the man. He stroked its back as if it were a friendly household pet. "Too bad you don't have the wand with you this time, eh, Joey?"

Shazad looked at Joey. "You really did wield the wand," he said, stunned to hear the man in the top hat and scarf confirm Joey's story.

"Yeah," Joey said. "Not that it matters now."

"It matters," Shazad disagreed. He pinched the bridge of his nose and exhaled strongly. "How am I ever going to explain this to my parents?" He removed his cape once more, holding it at the ready like a matador. "Help Leonora get the door open. I'll hold him off."

Joey stared at Shazad. He didn't understand his new-found fighting spirit, but he wasn't complaining, either. Joey half limped, half ran to join Leanora at the woodshed door. "We have to remove the doorknob," she told him, fishing through the many pendants she wore around her neck to find the one she needed. It was the firestone pendant—the one she had threatened to use against Shazad the night they met. The giant wolf growled at the edge of the woods, paw-ing the dirt, ready to pounce. Leanora gripped the medal-lion with one hand and made a fist with the other. The last time Joey saw her do that, her fist lit up like a fireball, but this time her hand barely flickered with energy. "I just need a second to get it going," she said, looking back nervously at the wolf.

Joey wasn't sure they had a second to spare. Then he real-ized they didn't need one. "Wait a minute—my key!"

"What?" Leanora said.

Joey cursed himself for not seeing it sooner. He had been thinking only of using Leanora's doorknob to escape, because that was the way they had come. He hadn't even considered the possibility that he might have something to contribute. Joey couldn't have opened the door to Siberia, but his key could get them back home. "I have a way back into the theater," he said, holding the key up in front of the woodshed door. As before, a keyhole opened up in the wood with blue light shooting out of it. Joey inserted the key into the magical lock and opened the door. The Majestic Theatre lobby was on the other side. "Shazad, time to go!" Joey shouted.

Shazad looked back over his shoulder and saw the light of the lobby chandelier burning bright in the dark forest. "That's a sight for sore eyes."

"It certainly is," the man in the top hat and scarf agreed, standing back at the tree line. "Off you go, Fido," he said, siccing the wolf on Shazad.

Shazad backed up a few steps. He held out the cape, ready to catch the wild dog inside it, just as he had its little brother. The massive wolf bounded across the clearing in seconds and leaped through the air. Joey worried that Shazad's cape wouldn't be strong enough to hold it this time, but he never got the chance to find out. The second the wolf reached Shazad and hit the fabric of the cape, it dissolved into a thick cloud of smoke.

What the . . . ?

The man in the top hat and scarf could be heard laughing

inside the cloud. "That's just a bit of misdirection, son. I never do the same trick twice." Shazad flapped his cape to clear the smoke, and when enough of it had wafted away, the man was right on top of him. He took off his top hat and offered it to Shazad. "Here. Hold this. For luck."

Shazad didn't take the hat, but the hat took his cape, sucking it in like a vacuum cleaner. He lunged after it, trying to tug it back out, but the hat clamped down on his wrist like it was alive, quickly swallowing his arm up to the elbow.

"SHAZAD!" Joey and Leanora both screamed as the hat pulled more of him in. It was up to his shoulder now. Shazad seized the hat by the brim and struggled to pry it off, but it had him now. He made a guttural noise, straining against it, and fell to the ground, where he was momentarily hidden by the smoke. Joey and Leanora took a few steps toward Shazad, but by the time the smoke cleared, he was in the hat up to his waist. It was as if he were being swallowed by a giant python, only there was no place for him to go, no stomach for his body to fill. That didn't stop him from disappearing inch by inch into the hat.

"What do we do?" Joey asked, helpless. "We have to help him!"

There was nothing they could do. They watched in terror as Shazad's legs slid writhing past the brim of the hat and vanished into oblivion. The whole thing was over in seconds. Any shrieks that Shazad might have let out were muffled by the hat, and after he was gone, all was quiet.

Joey's knees wobbled as the hat rolled around on the ground, seemingly empty. It came to rest a few feet away from him, helped along by a gust of wind. He felt the strength drain from his legs. The situation was already critical, but this was a whole other level of bad. What were they going to do now?

"Don't worry. I'll give him back," the man from the Invisible Hand announced. "Assuming we can all be reasonable," he added, nonchalant. "We'll talk it over with Redondo. I'm sure we can work out a trade. Hold the door for me please, if you don't mind," he added, walking toward the woodshed.

Leanora tugged on Joey's sleeve. "We have to get out of here."

"Buh—but, Shazad . . . ," Joey stammered in shock.

"He's gone. We have to go now," Leanora stressed.

She was right, of course. Even in his rattled state, Joey understood the danger they were in, but he also saw the hat that Shazad was in, a few short feet from where he stood. The man from the Invisible Hand spotted Joey eyeing the hat on the ground and realized a second too late what he was thinking. His glowing eyes widened as Joey went for it.

"No! You can't do tha—" His words broke off as Joey snatched the hat and raced back toward the open woodshed door, where Leanora was waiting for him.

"Bring that back!" the man shouted. "Bring that back!"

But they were already gone.

15

Together Again

The second Joey got his key out of the lock, Leanora slammed the door on the Siberian forest. Joey opened it back up two seconds later to check that they were safely away. Several boxes tumbled down on top of him, and he jumped back. Leanora flinched too, thinking for a second that the magician from the Invisible Hand was coming in after them, but it was just the contents of an overstuffed closet in the Majestic Theatre lobby. Joey composed himself and shut the door. He leaned against it, then turned around and slid down to sit on the carpet, completely drained. "What did we do?" he asked, thumping his head lightly against the door, punishing himself. "What did we just do?"

Leanora shook her head and took a seat at the bottom of the lobby staircase. "We lost Shazad," she said in a dazed voice. "He was right. I thought I was ready, but he was right. I couldn't help him. I was useless out there."

"No, you weren't. There wasn't anything you could have done."

"That's the problem—I couldn't do anything! Look here." Leonora grabbed her firestone with her left hand. Immediately, her right began to glow. "It comes so easy now. In this place. I can turn it on and off." Grasping and releasing the pendant, she worked her magic effortlessly, demonstrating the skill that had proved so elusive in the forest. "Over there I . . . I couldn't find the fire. I panicked." She looked at Joey, crushed. "Shazad didn't. And now he's in there."

Joey's eyes fell on the top hat, which he had thrown to the floor upon entering the theater lobby. He tried not to see it as a tombstone, but it was no use.

"I don't understand," Leonora said. "He told us over and over we couldn't fight the Invisible Hand. Why did he do that?"

"It was me," Joey said, feeling awful. "He saw me in trouble, and wouldn't leave me. I never would have made it back here without him. He saved my life."

Leonora grimaced at the sight of Joey's bloody foot. "How's your ankle? It looks bad."

Joey grunted. "It feels worse." He leaned forward to peel off his sock and get a closer look at the wound, but he stopped himself midway. He felt guilty thinking of himself after what had just happened. "What are we going to do?" Joey pointed to the top hat, which was lying on the ground between them. "Is there any way to get him out of there?" Joey asked, hopeful.

Leanora shook her head, unsure. "We need Redondo."

Joey pressed a hand to his forehead. He had expected her to say that. He was dreading the conversation, but there was no avoiding it. "What do we tell him?"

"Hello?" Redondo's voice called from upstairs. Joey and Leanora looked up to the balcony overhanging the lobby. They couldn't see him yet, but he had apparently emerged from his office and heard their voices. The sound of footsteps descending the staircase came next. He was on his way.

Leanora sighed and stood back up. "We have to tell him the truth. What else can we do?"

Redondo shuffled into view and descended the steps slowly. He looked better than he had when Joey had left him—more rested—but it was clear from the way he moved that the beating he'd received in the mirror world was taking a heavy toll on him. "What's all this?" he asked in an ill-tempered voice. "What are you two up to?" Redondo looked at Joey, who was a pitiful sight, sitting on the floor to give his chewed-up ankle a rest. His consternation gave way to alarm. "Kopecky, what happened to you? What's going on?"

"We've got a problem," Joey said.

"I can see that." Redondo hobbled over to inspect Joey's injury. "Who did this?"

"Our friend from the mirror world came back."

"Here?" Redondo twisted about, scanning the lobby before dismissing the notion altogether. "Impossible."

"Not here," Joey said.

"Did he *bite* you?" Redondo was aghast.

"He had a wolf," Leanora said, clearing up the confusion. "We were in Siberia," she added.

Redondo's face contorted as he tried to make sense of what he was hearing. Leanora might as well have told him she and Joey had been visiting the moon. "What were you doing in Siberia?"

Leanora looked at Redondo, her expression grim and sad. "We wanted to find out what happened to Grayson Manchester."

"What?" Redondo said, taken aback. "Why? How did you even—" Redondo stopped himself. He was quiet for a moment. Then he looked at Joey with accusatory eyes. "What did he tell you?"

"Only what I knew," Joey said.

"That must have been a short conversation," Redondo said pointedly. "You don't know anything about Manchester."

"Because you wouldn't say anything," Joey said, unwilling to be criticized for wanting to know more about the mysterious disappearance of Redondo's old assistant. Especially after everything he had just seen. "I knew enough to be curious. I knew the Invisible Hand came after me twice in two days. Three times if you count Siberia. I also knew your old assistant died in a fire and that if we weren't careful, one of us could be next."

Redondo ground his teeth "That's not what happened."

"We watched your last performance," Leanora chimed in, backing Joey up. "We saw it in a crystal ball. We know it's true. We stood onstage and saw your last assistant burn up right here in this theater."

"No," Redondo said, adamant. "I never got anyone killed. I saved this place and everything in it."

"What about him?" Joey asked. "You couldn't save him. This place is great and all, but Redondo . . . somebody died. We saw what happened."

"You don't know what you saw," Redondo said.

"We saw you run away," Leanora said in a judgmental tone.

"No, I . . ." Redondo faltered. "Yes, I ran, but only—only because I thought—" Redondo's cough spiked his sentences with staccato-burst interruptions. "You don't understand," he said, trying to get a handle on it. "At the time everyone thought . . ." Redondo's cough intensified, momentarily sparing him the difficulty of having to go on, but every time his chest heaved it was agony for him. Joey felt sorry for the old man. It did no good to keep harping on this. No matter what had happened in the past, the fact was they needed Redondo's help now.

"Forget Manchester," Joey said. "We've got more immediate concerns. We went to find out the truth so we could decide if we wanted to keep going with this competition or not—all three of us."

"All three?" Redondo said, checking the lobby for Shazad.

"We ran into trouble." Joey grimaced, stating the obvious. "Only two of us made it back."

292

Redondo wiped his mouth with a bloody handkerchief, a dark realization setting in behind his eyes. "Shazad's not here," he said, terrified by what his absence might mean. "He's not . . . ? Please tell me he's not . . . dead," he said, stumbling over to Leanora.

"No," she said, shaking her head vigorously. "I don't think so."

"You don't think so? Where is he?"

"In there," Joey said, pointing to the top hat. His voice had gone jittery. "The guy from the mirror world, he—he sucked him into his hat! We got it though. We stole it off him."

"You what?"

Redondo turned, paying his first real attention to the hat. He picked it up and examined it briefly. Then he dropped the hat as if it had been sewn together from radioactive material. "What have you done?" Redondo's voice was barely a whisper.

Joey noticed Redondo's face had turned as white as his tuxedo shirt. "I know it's bad. We didn't mean for this to happen, but we need you to fix it. Shazad needs you. Do you think you can get him out of there? Can the wand help?"

Redondo shook his head slowly. "You shouldn't have brought this here."

"Shouldn't have—" Joey frowned. "We were lucky to get away with it. What were we supposed to do? Leave Shazad behind?"

"No. You shouldn't have been there in the first place."

"What is it?" Leanora asked, looking back and forth between Redondo and the top hat lying sideways on the floor. "What's the problem?"

Redondo took a deep, apprehensive breath. "The problem is, that's not a hat. It's a doorway. A mystic portal. And now it's in here, like a Trojan horse slipped past my defenses." He gestured to the locked theater doors as if they were useless to him now.

"What does that mean?" Joey asked, a cold feeling growing in his stomach. "What are you saying?"

"I know that hat very well, young Kopecky. It belongs to me. That is, it used to. I haven't seen it in twenty years. I gave it to Grayson Manchester the last time we shared a stage together."

"What?" Joey asked, squinting hard at Redondo. That didn't make any sense. Joey thought back to the vision in the crystal ball. He remembered Redondo handing young Grayson his hat, but how could the hat have survived the fire when the boy didn't?

"That can't be," said Leanora. "The hat would have burned up in the box with the rest of him."

"You're assuming he was in the box."

"I saw him in the box," she said.

"Looks can be deceiving."

The hat shimmied and rolled on the floor without anyone touching it. A hand sprang out from within. "Ahh!" Joey exclaimed, scrambling to his feet as the hand pawed around, searching for something to grab hold of.

"Behind me," Redondo said, steeling himself for what came next. Another hand emerged, followed by a reaching arm. Both hands soon got a firm grip on the brim of the top hat and pushed down hard. Joey's stomach did somersaults. He retreated to join Leanora at the steps as the dark magician from the Invisible Hand squeezed his way out of the hat like a genie escaping a very tight bottle. He stretched his large frame, picked his hat back up off the floor, and returned it to his head.

Joey and Leanora stared at the man in stunned silence. Redondo put an arm out in front of Joey and Leanora, silently telling them to stay back. No one said anything. The man from the Invisible Hand took a moment to get his bearings, paying more attention to the lobby than the people in it. He circled the room, examining the framed lobby posters, eventually stopping at the one with a picture of Redondo sawing his assistant in half. "Look at that," he said, appraising the image as if it belonged in an art museum. "Brings back memories, doesn't it?" he asked Redondo.

"Better days," Redondo said. "Speaking of bringing things back, where's Shazad? What have you done with him?"

"Shazad . . . Is that the boy's name? Don't worry. We'll get to him soon enough. First things first." The man began to unwind the scarf that up until that point had served him well as a mask. The face beneath the scarf shocked Joey more than any magic trick could have done.

"Mr. Gray?" he blurted, recognizing the NATL's eccentric director of alternative testing.

Leanora looked at Joey, stunned. "You know him?"

The man Joey knew as Mr. Gray grinned a wicked grin. "Not exactly. Redondo, where are your manners? Introduce me properly. You don't want to hurt my feelings, do you?"

Redondo made a queasy face like he'd just thrown up in his mouth. "Everyone, this is the person you were asking about earlier. My former assistant, Grayson Manchester."

Joey felt like his brain was broken. "Grayson Manchester?" he repeated, completely flabbergasted. "I–I don't understand."

"Of course you don't," Manchester said with a laugh. "That's why this worked so well," he added in his American accent, trying on the "Mr. Gray" persona once again. "You were able to see through all the tricks, Joey, but you didn't see through me. Maybe if you'd had a better teacher. Or any kind of teacher, really."

"You can't be Grayson Manchester," Leanora said, her voice drifting. "You died. We watched . . . We saw—"

"A trick," Manchester said in his normal voice, finishing Leanora's sentence for her. "A bloody good trick too. You saw what I wanted you to see, just like Redondo did all those years ago. Tell me, old man, how long did it take for you to figure out what really happened that night? I've always wondered."

"It took some time," Redondo admitted with all the energy of a dying man (which, of course, he was). "Too long."

Manchester smiled, clearly pleased. "And when you finally put it together . . . ?"

Redondo's expression remained dour. "I didn't feel any better about it, obviously."

As they spoke, age crept back into the lobby walls. Wall-paper peeled, lights faded, and plants shriveled up.

"Obviously," Manchester agreed, noting the changes with a critical eye. "This place has seen better days. Not that I'm complaining. It may not be the illustrious playhouse I remember, but it's still a hard ticket to come by. You need to know someone to get in here." As he spoke, he shook a grateful finger in Joey's direction. "I owe it all to you, young Kopecky."

"What's he talking about?" Leanora asked Joey. "How do you know him?"

"I don't!" Joey said as he tried to trace back in his mind just how long Manchester had been playing him. "I just . . . I met him once! He tricked me. He pretended to be someone testing me for school."

"I was testing you, Joey, but not for school—although we do that too. The Invisible Hand, I mean," Manchester explained. "It might interest you to know we've been running the National Association of Tests and Limits since the organization was founded. One of our many institutional arms. The dedicated staff working at the NATL don't know about our 'partnership' with them, but that doesn't make

298

them any less effective in their work. Controlling standardized testing is a very effective way to influence entire generations of students. Take that PMAP test you were supposed to do, for example—that helps us guide children into lives and careers where they won't make waves or upset the status quo. Of course, we weren't about to let you take the PMAP and head off to Exemplar Academy, were we? Not with your test scores. Who knows what you might have grown up to be without our guidance?"

"What I *might* have grown up to be?" The implicit threat in Manchester's choice of words made Joey uncomfortable. He didn't know how to take it, still struggling as he was to try to understand the way Manchester's mind worked and what his plan had been. "This doesn't make any sense," he said, reeling. "You were the one who gave me the Mystery Box. The Invisible Hand didn't want me to go to Exemplar, so they sent me here instead?"

Manchester grinned. "Actually, that was a bit of improvisation on my part. I sent you here. The official plan was to retest you with harder exams and send you back where you came from, but something happened when you walked in the door. Magic came in with you. Needless to say, I got curious."

"What are you talking about? What magic?" Joey thought back to the previous morning. Magic was the last thing on his mind walking into the NATL. On the train coming into the city, he had told his father he wanted to be a boy wizard, but that was just a joke. "I didn't even believe in magic before I came here."

"You've got that backward," Manchester said. "Belief in magic is what got you here. Call it what you want, a certain affinity for magic . . . your potential . . . I felt it. When you've been around magic long enough, you develop a sense for this sort of thing. I took a personal interest, and it's a good thing too!" Manchester went on, ignoring Joey's denial. "You were everything I hoped for and more. I couldn't believe my luck, but then what's luck but a touch of magic, eh, Redondo?"

"Are you finished?" Redondo asked Manchester, scowling.

"What's your hurry, old boy? This is fun catching up like this. I know you're not one for explanations, but Joey here deserves a full and frank accounting, I think. It's the least I can do for my partner in crime."

"Stop saying that," Joey said, balling a fist. "Don't listen to him. We're not partners. We're not anything."

"Joey, Joey, Joey . . . ," Manchester said in a wounded

voice. "Why deny it? We did this together. I told you, I'm your benefactor. And you were mine. I couldn't get at Redondo as long as he was hiding out in this theater. Alone I was helpless. I needed someone like you to open the door and let me in."

"Why me? Why did . . . ? What makes me so special?"

"Nothing," Manchester said happily. "Nothing at all. You're not special, Joey. You're *almost* special. I recognized it the first time we talked in the office across the street." He looked out through the glass lobby doors at Redondo's dark, cloudy realm. "Well, not *this* street, but you get the idea. You were different, Joey. The way you saw the world . . . You noticed things, details other people missed. And you had just enough imagination to inspire something in Redondo. I set things up so the two of you would meet, and by God, you didn't disappoint. You got him back onstage, thinking there was hope for people like you—for the world—but I knew you'd sabotage yourself in the end. I knew you'd sabotage him. You wanted to believe in a chance for a better future— to escape into something fantastic—but you couldn't. You were different enough to catch a glimpse of magic but too normal to fully embrace it."

Tears welled up in Joey's eyes. "That's not true."

"Oh, but it is, Joey. You didn't want to fly close to the sun for fear your wings might melt. I see you. Head in the clouds, flailing about with no direction. You want big things out of life, but you try so little, because ultimately you don't believe in yourself. You got Redondo going again, but your doubt and fear touched everything around you. Your actions literally created the opening I needed." Manchester doffed his hat and motioned to the space inside that he had just crawled out of moments earlier. "With you as my secret weapon, it was only a matter of time before we ended up right here."

Joey choked on the realization that Manchester was telling the truth. Whether Joey knew it or not, the dark magician had been manipulating his actions from the moment they had met. He had let him take the hat in Siberia. That was just the finishing touch on his con. The one that had gotten him in the door.

"How did you keep finding me?" Joey asked. "It was when you poked me in the forehead, wasn't it? What was that? Some kind of tracking spell?"

Manchester laughed. "Ha! That's very good, Joey, but

I was just messing with your mind there. It was your cell phone. You've got location services enabled. You're walking around with a GPS device in your pocket."

"What?" Joey's hand instinctively clawed at the pocket with his phone. Redondo had been right about the Invisible Hand and technology. He felt like he'd been punched in the stomach. Leanora looked at him like he deserved to be.

"Why are you doing this?" Leanora asked Manchester. "If you were Redondo's assistant, you were part of the Order of the Majestic—sworn to protect magic! How could you side with the Invisible Hand? What happened to you?"

"Redondo happened," Manchester spat. "Years of waiting for my time in the spotlight. Night after night I let Redondo cut me in half, throw knives at me while blindfolded, trap me inside mirrors, and swarm me with bees." Manchester gritted his teeth. "I'm allergic to bees, not that he ever cared. It was awful. All that work . . . all for his greater glory. The magician gets the applause. The assistant takes the risk, and if things go wrong . . . ? It's the assistant who pays the price. Time and time again, I avoided death through sheer willpower. Eight shows a week, counting the Sunday matinee. I ask you, what was the point?

All that power at his fingertips! Power he loved to put on display but refused to share or clearly teach. When I think of the lengths he went to just to keep it all to himself . . . Picture us, traveling from show to show and town to town, packed into trains and buses, when all the while he had the power to magically transport us. It was absurd. Almost as ridiculous as the performances themselves. Playing for the people . . . vying for the affection of strangers . . . trying so hard to convince himself he mattered . . ."

"That's not what the shows were for," Redondo said.

"No, of course not," Manchester said facetiously. "The man who strutted about the stage calling himself 'Redondo the Magnificent' didn't have anything to prove to anybody. Wherever did I get that idea? Stop lying to yourself, you old fraud. I know what you are. And, unlike you, I know what magic is—what it's really all about."

"And what is that?" Redondo asked.

"I'll tell you what it's not," Manchester snarled. "It's not something we use to entertain the norms in some embarrassing quest for validation. It's something we use period. A free pass for whatever we want, whenever we want. It's ours. Not theirs. Ours alone."

Redondo shook his head sadly. "You're wrong, Grayson. Everyone deserves magic. I tried to teach you—"

"You never taught me *anything*," Manchester rasped, baring his crooked teeth. "I mastered my craft in spite of you, not because of you. Can you blame me for leaving? Honestly, can you?" He looked to Joey and Leanora. "I had to free myself from life as his indentured servant, tortured for the amusement of normal people in the audience. I faked my death to give him a taste of the stress and fear I felt every night at showtime. The Invisible Hand showed me the way. They actually taught me magic, if you can imagine such a thing! It was my reward for taking Redondo out of the picture. Thanks to them, I grew strong, pulling whatever I wanted out of his old magic hat, but I could have been stronger. I should have taken Houdini's wand with me when I left. That was the real prize. Twenty years I've waited for this opportunity." Manchester sneered at Redondo. "I would have come back sooner, but you were so melodramatic, taking the theater off the map like you did. I couldn't get back in . . . until today." Manchester held out his hand. "I'll have the wand now. It's either that, or you'll never see poor Shazad again."

"What do your friends say about that?" Redondo

motioned to the lobby doors, where the shadows of the Invisible Hand were watching. "They've been out there waiting patiently to ransack this place immediately after my demise. I don't think they're going to appreciate you cutting the line like this."

Manchester barked out a laugh. "They're not my friends; they're my followers. At least, they will be. Once I have the wand, I'll be leading the Invisible Hand, and I'm going to make some changes. It's time for us to come out of the shadows, Redondo. Time to tighten our grip on the world."

"I see." Redondo grimaced. "You're still not satisfied with your role, even after all these years."

"Why should I be satisfied with anything less than greatness? The Invisible Hand may be content to wait for the walls around this place to crumble into dust before storming your castle, but I don't care to wait. I'm here now. First. The leaders of the Invisible Hand suffer from the same lack of vision you do. You used to hide magic in plain sight. They hide it away completely. . . ." Manchester clicked his tongue and shook his head in a disapproving manner. "I'm tired of being behind the scenes. Ruling the world is a center-stage, top-billing kind of job, if you ask me."

"You're going to rule the world, are you?" Redondo raised a hand, plucking Houdini's wand out of thin air. "And you think this can help you turn the Invisible Hand into an iron fist?"

"I'm going to remake the world in my image." Manchester bared his teeth in a crooked smile. "My only regret is you won't be here to see it." He held out his hand. "Now give me the wand."

"Aren't you forgetting something?" Redondo scanned the room. "Where's Shazad?"

"That's right," Manchester said, taking off his hat and scratching his head absentmindedly. "He's in here. Have a look." Manchester lobbed the hat across the room. Redondo batted it back with a swipe of his hand.

"Keep that thing away from me. Heaven only knows where it's been."

Chagrined, Manchester bent down to pick up his hat and put it back on. "It was worth a try."

"I'm not the trusting fool you think I am, Grayson. If you want to trade Shazad for the wand, he needs to be here. Let's see him."

Manchester slid his jaw around like he was chewing a

tough piece of meat. "I'm afraid that's going to be a problem," he said eventually. "You see, I stuffed him way, way down at the bottom of my hat, where even I can't reach him. Not until later tonight at the earliest. That was my insurance policy. Just in case you were able to somehow compel me to release the boy before I got what I came for."

"Very clever, Grayson," Redondo said in a mocking tone. "Congratulations. You've outsmarted everyone, including yourself."

Manchester looked daggers at Redondo, knowing he was right.

"As far as I'm concerned, this conversation is a waste of time." Redondo pressed the tip of the wand into his palm and brought his hands together. Just like that, the wand was gone. "And I don't have time to waste. Get out of my theater. Come back with Shazad, or not at all." Redondo turned around to head up the stairs.

"Stop right there," Manchester called after him. "Don't you turn your back on me. I'm no fool either. It took me twenty years to get back inside this place. I'm not leaving empty-handed."

"You don't have to worry about getting back in. Not as

long as you've got Shazad with you. Bring him back tonight—unharmed. I'll be waiting, same as always."

Redondo gave Manchester a hard, unwavering stare. Manchester glared back at him, but in the end he was the one who blinked. "You're not waiting. You're stalling," he said in a cutting tone. "It won't do you any good. What do you think? You're going to find the courage you've spent the last twenty years searching for now that it's come to this? Do make sure you check underneath the couch cushions. It's always in the last place you look." Manchester laughed at his own joke. Redondo kept quiet, refusing to let Manchester bait him. "Have it your way," he continued. "We'll finish this tonight, but don't get any ideas. If you try to run, or keep me out of here in any way, that boy is going to suffer for it."

"I won't keep you out," Redondo told Manchester. "I'll even give you a key."

He looked at Joey. It took a second for Joey to understand what was being asked of him.

"My key?" Joey said.

Redondo nodded.

"But I don't—I want—" Joey sputtered.

"There's no point in keeping it any longer. After tonight it will be just another key."

"That's right. You won't be needing it anymore," Manchester said, motioning for Joey to hand it over. Joey's heart broke as he limped over to surrender it. He placed it in Manchester's chalk-white palm. His only connection to the world of magic, gone. Manchester gripped the key, victorious. "It's been a pleasure doing business with you, Joey. To show my gratitude, I'm going to leave you be. Consider your part in the show finished. Don't bother me, and I won't bother you." Manchester rested his hand on his own chest. "You have my word."

Joey scoffed. "What's that worth?"

"More than you think. Redondo, I told you I wouldn't be leaving here empty-handed, and I meant it. This key is a lovely gesture on your part, but it's not enough. I'm going to need some assurances you won't change the locks on me while I'm gone."

"What more assurances could you possibly need? You have Shazad."

"Not just Shazad." Manchester winked and held out his hat. Black smoke came billowing out of it like pollution from a factory smokestack. The dark cloud enveloped him and spread out to fill half the room. Redondo started coughing again as the smoke aggravated his condition. Joey felt Leanora rush past him and heard her let out a sharp cry, which was quickly muffled. "Leanora?" Joey said, reaching around blindly. "LEA?" She didn't answer. Through the smoke, Joey saw a silhouetted figure wave goodbye.

"Until tonight," Manchester said. "Farewell."

When the smoke cleared, he was gone. So was Leanora.

Once he realized Manchester had taken another hostage, Redondo turned to Joey with a look of death. "I hope you're proud of yourself."

Joey was beyond devastated. He had been the one to set these events in motion. It was his fault, but Shazad and Leanora would be the ones to pay for his mistakes—either them or Redondo. "What are we going to do?" Joey asked, praying there was some way out of this.

"We?" Redondo's lip twitched. "I'm sorry, did you say 'we'? There is no 'we,' young Kopecky. We are through. Weren't you paying attention?"

"Redondo, you don't have to blame me for this, all right? I blame myself already, but you don't think . . . You can't possibly think I was working with him. Not on purpose."

Redondo looked away, unwilling to hear Joey's protestations. "Whether you meant to help him or not is irrelevant. You did his work for him."

"He tricked me!"

"Of course he tricked you," Redondo said sharply. "That's what he does. Illusions, deceptions . . . These things are his stock in trade. I don't blame Manchester for being what he is. I blame you for letting him win."

"What?"

"You can't let them win!" Redondo barked. "Isn't that what you told me?"

"He didn't win anything yet," Joey said. "You still have the wand. You're not going to give it to him, are you? Can't you use it to get Leanora and Shazad back?"

A joyless laugh escaped Redondo. "Suddenly I seem to be capable of all kinds of heroics in your eyes. You're right. I could try to save both them *and* the wand, but answer me this: What if I fail? What happens to Leanora and Shazad then? What do you think Grayson would do to them as punishment?" Redondo screwed up his face. "I don't like to think about it. I'm sure it comes as quite a shock to you, but I actually do care about their lives."

"I never thought you didn't care."

"Yes, you did. You thought I got my old assistant killed, and you were afraid that I was blindly marching the three of you toward that same fate. Don't bother denying it. I know Grayson preyed on your doubts and fears to plant those ideas in your mind, but you were the one who chose to believe his version of events. The reality he created for you with subtle hints and bits of information . . . You gave it life."

"You could have squashed it if you just told me the truth. Why didn't you? You didn't tell me anything."

Redondo gave Joey a harsh look. He was in no mood to be lectured. "I told you that you'd have to make a choice. Are you going to inspire wonder or terror? What did you inspire in Leanora and Shazad when you convinced them to go digging into my past?" Redondo shook his head, disgusted. "How little you must think of me. Do you honestly believe I would have let any of you in here if I had been responsible for the death of a child?"

"I'm sorry. I was scared. I didn't know what to believe."

"That's the problem. You didn't believe in me any more than you believed in yourself. As soon as things got difficult, you started looking for an excuse to quit. An escape. A way out. Well, now you have one."

Joey was miserable. Redondo looked the same. He started up the steps, traumatized and defeated, presumably heading back to his office.

"What about Shazad and Leonora?" Joey called after him. "What's going to happen to them?"

Redondo paused halfway up and took out his special deck of cards. "I'll get them back," he said, tapping the box against an open palm. "Whatever the cost." Redondo drew a single card: Death.

Joey swallowed hard, looking at the picture of a hooded figure, scythe in hand. "He's going to kill you."

"Redondo the Magnificent died a long time ago. Grayson's just going to finish the job." He took a sad, last look at the posters in the theater lobby. "You were right about this place. It is a ghost world." Joey didn't say anything. He didn't know what to say. A grimace formed on Redondo's lips as he fit the Death card back into his deck. "I told you at the beginning: This is the end." He raised his hand, poised to snap his fingers. "Goodbye, Joey."

Snap!

Joey felt himself losing his balance for a fraction of a second. The disorientation passed quickly, and when he recovered, he was back in Exemplar Academy. Joey recognized the hallway. He was right where Janelle had left him when she'd run off to make sure she didn't accidentally destroy the world with an artificially generated black hole. It was almost funny. Now Joey felt like he was the one more likely to bring about the end of the world as they knew it.

The lights were off inside the gymnasium. Joey didn't hear Esteban or his trainer inside. He'd been gone for hours. Joey felt as though he had aged years in those hours. Still shell-shocked, he looked around for a place to sit down. The pain in his ankle was returning. Joey had deprioritized the injury in his mind after Manchester had crawled out of his own hat, but now there was nothing to distract him. He was about to sit down in the middle of the hallway when his parents came hustling around the corner with Dr. Cho.

"There you are!" his mother said, relieved. "We've been looking all over for you. Why haven't you been answering your pho—OH MY GOD, WHAT HAPPENED TO YOU?"

16

Don't Dream It's Over

Joey's mother broke into a run, with Dr. Cho close behind, looking equal parts confused and alarmed. Joey's father brought up the rear with a *not again* look on his face. As Joey's mother fussed over his wounded ankle and rattled off questions he couldn't possibly answer truthfully, he exaggerated his pain, trying to buy himself more time to come up with a plausible explanation for both his absence and his injuries. Meanwhile, Joey's father put his hands on his hips and shook his head, unable to get over the second mysterious disappearance of his shoes—both shoes this time! He kept asking Joey what happened to them. He knew Joey had had them on when they'd left the apartment that morning. He'd checked. Joey had to know *something*. The shoes had to be here somewhere. Thankfully, the interrogation stopped when Joey's mother angrily shushed his father, pointing out that their son was a bloody mess. She forbade him from asking any more questions about the shoes until after they got him some help.

Reluctantly tabling the matter for the time being, Joey's father helped him up. They went straight to the nurse's office, where Joey's ankle was cleaned and wrapped up in a bandage. After that he had no choice but to start talking. He didn't know where to begin, but that was decided for him. The first thing everyone wanted to know was where Janelle had been when he got hurt.

"Where is she now?" Joey's father asked. "Wasn't she supposed to be showing you around?"

"Don't be mad at her," Joey said. "This isn't Janelle's fault. I kind of ditched her."

"You what?"

Not wanting to get Janelle in trouble, Joey spun a tale about feeling overcome with anxiety. He said he had a panic attack, or something close to it, and felt a sudden need to get away. Central Park was right across the street from the school, which was convenient for Joey's story. "I started feeling claustrophobic. I needed air," he said, inventing wildly. "I ducked out and went for a walk in the park. I took off my shoes," he added, throwing in important details to help sell the story. "I don't know. . . . It's a nice day out. . . . Feeling the grass under my feet . . . helped calm me down. I was on my way back when someone's dog came out of nowhere and bit me."

The last part had the benefit of being true. His parents believed him. After fending off a few more questions about the fictitious dog in the park, Joey was allowed to rest while his parents left the room to talk privately with Dr. Cho. He lay down on the cushioned bench for patients in the nurse's office, relieved his part in the conversation was over. Outside the room, he heard his mom fire off a series of questions. "What do you think? Should we be worried? Are we pushing him too hard? Is this too much too fast?" Joey's father tried to allay her fears, but she shushed him again, wanting to hear what Dr. Cho thought. Joey sat up, trying to eavesdrop, but Janelle appeared in the doorway with a few questions of her own.

"There you are! I've been looking all over for you."

"Sorry." Joey dropped back down. "I didn't mean to worry you."

"Forget about me—look at you! Are you okay?"

"Eh." Joey jangled his foot, testing his ankle. The bandage and athletic tape constricted his movement, which helped with the pain. "I'll live."

"What the heck happened?"

"I don't really want to talk about it," Joey said, sullen. "What about you? Everything okay in the basement? Don't worry. I didn't say anything about your project." He had actually forgotten about Janelle's glitching supercollider until he'd gotten back to Exemplar. At the moment Joey was strangely numb to the prospect of a black hole swallowing up the universe. He might have even viewed it as a welcome escape.

Janelle hedged a bit. "Things didn't exactly go as planned, but it's all good. Completely unstable."

"Unstable is good?"

"Unstable black holes are. They shrink away to nothing and collapse. What we don't want is a stable black hole that's going to stick around for any real amount of time."

"Right."

"Don't tell anyone. I'll get in so much trouble." Janelle looked over her shoulder. The grown-ups were returning.

"I've got to go check on it. I'll show you tomorrow if it's still here. Are you coming back?"

Joey didn't say anything. He didn't know the answer. There was no telling what tomorrow held now.

Dr. Cho offered to send the family home in a car service so Joey wouldn't have to limp through the streets of New York without any shoes on. Joey was grateful for that, because it enabled him to pretend to sleep the whole ride back to Hoboken and avoid discussing what had happened any further with his parents. It was hard enough enduring his mother's worried looks and his father's judgmental glare without actually talking about it. All the excitement and positivity his mom and dad had exhibited on the way in that morning was gone. The last thing Joey saw before he closed his eyes was his father looking at him like Joey had blown his shot at the big time. Joey couldn't blame him for being disappointed. He had to admit, Exemplar was cooler than he had expected. Janelle had been right about that. Any place the Invisible Hand wanted to keep Joey out of had to have something going for it, but that was the real problem for Joey—Manchester and the Invisible Hand. Exemplar

Academy didn't matter anymore. Joey thought back to what Manchester had said, wondering what was going to happen when the man finally got hold of Houdini's wand. Could he really take over the world? It seemed impossible, but then, there wasn't a single thing that had happened to Joey in the last forty-eight hours that wasn't impossible.

Joey remembered how he had felt wielding Houdini's wand, and he was a novice! Manchester had twenty years of magical experience or more. Surely he'd be able to take charge of the Invisible Hand with that kind of power at his fingertips, and with their support, he was capable of anything. The Invisible Hand was made up of the most ruthless, powerful, and manipulative magicians in the world. If Redondo, Leanora, and Shazad were to be believed (and Joey had no reason to doubt them), the group was practically running the planet already. Manchester had told Redondo he wanted to come out of the shadows and take his rightful place center stage. The more Joey thought about it, the more he became convinced that a comic-book supervillain-style global takeover was in the works and there was nothing he could do about it. There wasn't anyone he could tell. The only people he knew who would believe him were Redondo,

Leanora, and Shazad. Redondo had kicked him out, and Leanora and Shazad were in no position to help.

Joey felt a fresh pang of guilt thinking about Leanora and Shazad trapped in Manchester's magic top hat. *It should be me in that hat*, he thought. It *would* have been him if Shazad had not stepped up to rescue him from the wolf. Joey blamed himself for everything that had gone wrong that day. They wouldn't have even been in Siberia if not for him. Manchester had been right—his doubt and fear had infected everyone.

Joey cursed himself for letting Manchester get inside his head. Why did he have to go digging into Redondo's past? If he was afraid about what Redondo had done, or what might happen to him if he stayed on, he should have just left. Taken himself out of the competition for the wand. Either Shazad or Leanora would have won it, and everything would have been fine. Shazad would have kept the wand safe in Jorako. Leonora would have taken the wand on the road and used it against people like Manchester.

What would you have done with it? Joey asked himself. He still didn't have an answer for that, any more than he had an answer for what he could do to fix things. He wanted to make up for what he had done and help Redondo in some way, but how? He couldn't even get back into the theater. He was out, and it was over. Manchester was going to kill Redondo and take the wand. There was nothing to stop him now.

The car pulled up in front of Joey's apartment building and he "woke up" without needing to be roused. His ankle still hurt when he put pressure on it, but he declined his parents' offers of assistance and went inside under his own steam. He was determined to keep his mom and dad at arm's length until he was ready to talk, and he couldn't do that if he was using one of them as a crutch.

As soon as they were back in the apartment, Joey said he was still tired and wanted to go lie down. His mother said she thought that was a good idea. His father didn't say anything, but he stepped aside and gave Joey his space as he went to his room and closed the door. Joey collapsed onto his bed. He wasn't lying about being tired. He really was exhausted, both mentally and physically. Joey reached for his phone, but stopped himself before he got it out of his pocket. Ordinarily he would have cycled through various social media and video apps until he nodded off, but now he felt like the phone was one of the Invisible Hand's digital fingers. He powered it down (after turning off the location services feature).

Depressed and dejected, Joey pulled a pillow over his face. Hiding away from the world, he tried to go to sleep for real. At least then he wouldn't have to think about his problems. Or so he thought. Sleep came to Joey quickly, but it brought him no relief, as Manchester haunted his dreams. Joey had nightmares about Manchester taking over New York, standing in Times Square and using the wand to call down tornadoes and hurricane-force winds as shadows overran the streets. In his dream Manchester thanked Joey once again for his invaluable assistance, saying that he couldn't have done this without him. "You made this possible, Joey. You were the one!"

"No," Joey moaned in his sleep, denying the truth his subconscious mind knew all too well. "I didn't know! You did it—you tricked me!"

Manchester laughed. "You didn't make it very difficult, did you? After all, I met you only yesterday. Some genius you turned out to be!"

The words cut Joey deep. He already felt responsible, but in his dream he felt ridiculous, too. How had things gone so wrong so fast? Why had he fallen for Manchester's tricks so easily? He had always been the one who saw through the tricks.

"If you're wondering how this happened, it's simple really. I'm a magician. You're a norm. This is the way the world works. It's always been like this—you just never knew it before now. A magical life was never in the cards for you, Joey. You finding magic is like being the one dog at the pound who's not color-blind. Naturally you're very proud and excited, but what does it amount to in the end? You're still a dog when all's said and done, and dogs are meant to obey." The magical winds that Manchester was controlling swept Joey up into the air. The silhouetted magicians of the Invisible Hand took to the sky as well, soaring over the city and out into the world beyond. Manchester waved at them like the flying monkeys from *The Wizard of Oz*. "Fly, my pretties! Fly! Fly!" He cackled. "Oh, and, Joey? Remember when I said I would leave you alone after this?" he asked. "I lied."

Manchester waved the wand, and Joey flew out over the Hudson River, where the wind released its hold on him. He dropped like a stone into the water, which had suddenly transformed into a giant version of the whirlpool-mouthed monster from the incident with the Water of Life.

Joey screamed, waking up in bed.

His father was at the door seconds later. "You okay?"

"Wha—" Joey rubbed his eyes and blinked his way back into the waking world. "Yeah," he mumbled. "I'm fine. I just . . . bad dream."

"You hungry?" his father asked. "We got takeout."

"Is it dinnertime already?" Joey asked in a disoriented voice. Checking his window, he saw that it was dark outside.

"It's past dinner. We let you sleep. Figured you needed the rest. You've had a lot on your mind the last couple of days." Joey nodded, thinking his father didn't know the half of it. "We ordered from that burger place you like," his father volunteered.

Joey's ears perked up. "Taco-Pizza-Burger? You guys hate that place."

"It's growing on me. I had a pepperoni burrito burger, myself. Wasn't terrible." His father held up a take-out bag with the TPB logo on it. "This one's yours. You want it?"

Joey's stomach growled. He hadn't eaten anything since breakfast. "I could eat."

"Dig in," his father said, handing over the bag.

"Thanks." Joey tore into his food right there on the bed. Normally his father would tell him, "No eating in your room," or "Take it to the kitchen," but instead he pulled out Joey's desk chair and pointed. "Mind if I join you?"

Joey shook his head with his mouth full of taco fries. He wasn't looking forward to the conversation his father no doubt wanted to have, but he figured he couldn't put it off forever, and the burger had softened him up a bit. Catching him half asleep and surprising him with his favorite food had been a savvy move on his father's part.

"Listen, Joey, your mom and I were talking. This school . . . You don't have to go if you don't want to."

Joey stopped chewing. If he had been drinking his soda, he might have done a spit take. "Really?"

"Really," his father said, looking him straight in the eye. "If you don't think you can do it," he added with an air of surrender, "we're not going to force you."

Joey sat up in bed. His father had managed to surprise him again. Yesterday morning Joey would have killed to hear him say those words, and for a second his spirits lifted, but then his groggy mind remembered that he had actually liked what little he had seen of Exemplar Academy. On top of that, where he went to school was the least of his problems right now. Joey slumped back against his pillows. "It doesn't matter."

Now it was Joey's father's turn to be surprised. "What do you mean?"

Joey shook his head. "It's not the school that's bothering me."

"It's not?" His father furrowed his brow. "What's the problem, then?"

Joey put his food down for a second, thinking about how he had screwed up his chance to have magic in his life. Maybe everybody's chance. "I blew it, Dad," he said, his voice cracking a little. He didn't want to cry. He willed the tears back into his eye sockets.

"Joey . . ." His father tried to put a hand on his shoulder. "You didn't blow anything."

"Yes, I did," Joey said, pulling away. "I had a chance to do something—to be a part of something amazing, but I was afraid. I thought I could do it for a second, but I was wrong. I messed it up. I ruined everything."

"Come on, now . . . Don't be so hard on yourself. You didn't ruin anything. Tomorrow's another day. You can try again."

"I can't. It's too late."

"It's not. Joey, what happened today . . . It's not the end of the world."

"You don't know," Joey said. His father still thought

they were talking about Exemplar Academy. "You don't understand."

"That's true, I don't," his father agreed, but there was compassion in his voice. "I want to though. More than anything, I want to understand. Talk to me, Joey."

"I can't. That's the problem," Joey said, adamant. "I can't explain, and you just—you don't know what's going on, Dad. You still want me to go to Exemplar. I know you do, but you don't get it. I don't belong there, okay? I don't belong anywhere."

"That's not true," Joey's father said. "Hey. Look at me. That's not true at all. Yes, I do want you to go to that school. I think it's a great opportunity. I said that from day one. But I don't want you to go there if it's going to make you miserable. You don't need that school to do something special with your life. You can do that on your own. I know you can. And I'm not gonna force you to go to Exemplar, but you *do* belong there. Get that through your head. You belong anywhere you decide you belong. You have unlimited potential. You have to know that."

Joey sniffed. "You just think that because I did well on a bunch of tests."

"I don't need those tests to tell me what I already know. What I see out of you every day. You may think you played some kind of trick to figure out the answers on those tests, but you're not giving yourself enough credit. That takes real intelligence, Joey. You're a special kind of special. I look at you and I say, 'This kid can do anything.' You see things other people don't. In fact, you saw something I missed in all this. You're right. Exemplar Academy doesn't matter. Believing in yourself is what matters. I know I've been pushing you really hard, and I'm sorry for that. I just don't want you to end up like me."

Joey wiped his eyes and looked up at his father. "What are you talking about?"

His father sighed. "Can I steal some of your fries?"

Joey offered them up. "Sure."

"They have good fries at this place. As long as I'm opening up here, I might as well admit that, too." His father grabbed a handful of fries and a napkin to use as a plate. "I told you yesterday that I didn't want to be an accountant when I was your age, right? I'm guessing that didn't come as an earth-shattering revelation. I mean, what kid wants that? Nobody wants that. Don't get me wrong. I don't hate my job or anything. It's fine. It helps me do my part to take care of this family, but it doesn't give me . . . I don't know. . . ." Joey's father gestured at the air, searching for the right word. He settled at last on: "It doesn't give me energy. It's just a job. It's not where my heart is at."

"What did you want to be when you were my age?" Joey asked.

Joey's father snickered to himself. It was almost like he couldn't say it out loud. "You're gonna laugh."

Joey was intrigued. He had never talked to his father like this. "What did you want to do, join the circus?"

"Close." His father smiled. "I wanted to be a magician."

Joey nearly fell off the bed. "*What?*"

"You heard me. I loved magic when I was a kid. I loved magicians. It was a different time back then. Magicians used to be a bigger deal. There was the Great Mysterio . . . Ella the Enchantress . . . Redondo the Magnificent—he was the best." Joey's father turned around halfway and tapped the lid of the Mystery Box, which was still there on Joey's desk. "I really can't believe they gave this to you at the testing center. Did I mention I had one of these when I was a kid?"

"You told me," Joey said, leaning forward, suddenly engaged.

"I watched Redondo make the Lincoln Memorial disappear on TV when I was ten years old. Blew my mind. I used to practice his tricks and put on shows for my family. . . . You used to do the same thing. We got you a children's magic set when you were in the first grade, remember?"

"I remember," Joey said.

"We loved it. My parents loved it when I did it too. They were actually fine with me wanting to be a magician, if you can believe that. Maybe they were just humoring me. I don't know. If they were, they had me fooled. They said anything I was that into, I couldn't help but succeed at."

"No kidding."

"Didn't know your grandma and grandpa were so cool, did you?"

"What happened? Why'd you stop?"

Joey's father lifted a hand up and let it drop. "I got scared. We never had a lot of money growing up. I decided to go for something safer. Think about it: It's not easy to make a living onstage. How many successful world-famous magicians do you know? There are no Houdinis out there anymore.

There aren't even any Redondos. That guy fell off the face of the earth."

He kind of did, Joey thought.

"I didn't want to try and fail. Sound familiar?"

Joey nodded reluctantly. His father understood his situation better than he thought. Something clicked in his brain. Maybe Joey and his father had more in common than they realized.

"Hey, Dad, did you ever do all the tricks in one sitting, like I did with that test?"

"It's funny you ask that." Joey's dad took out his lucky coin. "I never told you where I got this. I was your age, maybe a little older. I was up late one night. I couldn't sleep, and I didn't have anything to read, so I took out Redondo's Mystery Box here. I had a desk in my room just like this one, and I sat there late into the night, doing every trick in the box, one after the other until I got through them all. It was just like that test you took, except I didn't get a grade at the end. By the way, did you ever get the results of that test back? Dr. Cho was asking."

"Dad! Forget the test. Finish the story," Joey said excitedly.

"Right, right . . . It doesn't matter," Joey's father said,

remembering that Exemplar Academy was off the table now. "Okay, when I was done, I found this coin tied to a string at the bottom of the box. Somehow I'd missed it up until then. There was a note about the coin being the 'price of admission' for an audience with Redondo. So I pulled the string, and I must have finally fallen asleep, because I had this dream where I was transported to some carnival in some faraway land. Somewhere in Europe, I think. There was this big tent for Redondo. I was going to go in and watch his act in person."

"The coin was the cost of a ticket," Joey said, mesmerized.

"Exactly. I was going to pay and go in, but—"

"What happened?" Joey blurted out. He couldn't believe what he was hearing. It was the coin! Manchester had said that when he walked into the NATL office, magic had walked in with him. He didn't understand then, but it made perfect sense now. It was his father's lucky coin! The item at the bottom of the Mystery Box was supposed to bring people with magic potential to Redondo, wherever he was. Joey's father had passed the test the same as him! From the sound of it, he'd done it before Redondo had gone into hiding, too! "You were actually there?"

"No, Joey. It was a dream," his father said, finding it funny that Joey needed to be reminded of that little detail. "But in my dream there was this guy outside the tent . . . just a kid, really—a creepy British kid," he added, with an unpleasant grimace. "That's why I thought the carnival was somewhere in Europe. He was manning the ticket window. I don't remember exactly what he said to me, but I didn't like his vibe, you know? He kind of scared me off. I didn't go in the tent."

"You didn't?" Joey asked, eager for more. "What'd you do?"

"I woke up. That's it. That's the dream."

"That's it?" Joey was blown away. His father was talking about Grayson Manchester. He had to be. It made perfect sense. Manchester wouldn't have wanted to share magic or Redondo with anyone else, even back then. He would have tried to scare off the competition—people like his father—before they ever got to meet his boss. Joey wondered how many other kids Manchester had turned away during his years as Redondo's assistant. How many other potentially extraordinary magicians had grown up to live ordinary lives instead?

"Don't look so upset, kiddo. It's not like any of this actually happened."

"I know that," Joey said, covering. "But you kept the coin. How come?"

Joey's father gave a shrug. "I just liked it, same as you. I told myself it was lucky. Who knows? Maybe it is, but you get older, and you learn a few things. We make our own luck, Joey. I look at this coin now and I see a reminder to not be afraid. Or better yet, to try to do the things that I'm afraid of. You have to go after the things you want in life. I didn't do that when I was your age because I was scared. People used to say I was a magician with numbers. . . . Somehow I ended up in accounting. I'm still not exactly sure how that happened. I played it safe. I guess I got it in my head it was the next best thing, but I don't want that to be you, Joey. Don't settle for your next best life. Not when you have got a shot like this in front of you."

Joey looked at the coin in his father's hand, an idea forming in his head. "I do have a shot, don't I?"

Joey's father finished his fries and stood up. "That's up to you." He tapped Joey on the shoulder. "Finish your food. You need to eat."

"Dad?" Joey called out just before his father left the room. "Do you still believe in magic?"

"Still?"

"You had to believe at some point."

Joey's father flipped the coin in the air and caught it. "How could I stop believing in magic when I see it every day in this apartment? When I see it right here in this room?"

Joey watched as his father moved the coin across his knuckles back and forth. "I think I see it too, Dad. Could I borrow that coin again?"

"I'll tell you what. Keep it." He flipped the coin to Joey. "No strings attached this time."

Joey caught the coin and smiled wide. *Not yet, but give me a few minutes.*

17

The Final Curtain

Joey wolfed down the rest of his food and threw out the wrappers and crumbs in the kitchen. His parents were surprised to see that he was already dressed in his pajamas when he came out of his room, considering he had slept much of the afternoon. He told them he just wanted to pack it in for the day and maybe things would look better in the morning. They had no objection to that. Joey just hoped they wouldn't check on him after he went to bed, because he didn't plan to be there very long.

Back in his room, Joey changed his clothes and put on an old pair of sneakers. They were a little tight, but he got them on. He had kept them for rainy days and other things that might get messy. What Joey had in mind for the rest of the evening definitely qualified. He emptied the Mystery

Box, found the golden string at the bottom, and tied it to his father's coin, through the hole in the middle. It was old, but he didn't think that would be a problem. Houdini's wand was a hundred years old at least. All that mattered was what he believed.

It's go time, Joey told himself. *No doubt. No fear.*

And no more waiting. He pulled the string, and there was a loud *crack* as the walls of his room fell away. Once again he was back on the foggy street of Redondo's depressed, Off-Broadway realm. The shadows of the Invisible Hand were there too, blocking the entrance to the theater. One of them spotted Joey and screeched to its brethren. Joey steeled his nerves as they drifted over to swarm him. "You're not really here," he said, standing his ground and waving them off. He didn't pick up the Mystery Box and swing it at them this time. He didn't need one. His hand was enough. Swatting at the shadows, Joey split them apart and strode through their midst unafraid. The only real threat here was Manchester. When he got to the theater door, it was locked, as usual. Joey didn't have a key to get in anymore, but he didn't think he needed that either. He looked at the coin in his hand—the token that should have facilitated his father's meeting with

Redondo. It was meant for another time and place, but Joey believed it would work here. "It's not a coin," he told himself, gripping it tight in front of the locked door. "It's a key. It just looks like a coin."

Joey heard an audible *click* as the door unlocked for him. He opened it just enough to quickly squeeze through the gap before the shadow creatures regrouped. He didn't think they could do any real damage if they followed him in, but he figured it couldn't hurt to be a little bit careful. He had already let one member of the Invisible Hand into the theater. That was enough.

The lobby was quiet, dark, and empty. Joey hoped he wasn't too late. He opened the door to the main auditorium of the theater, but the houselights were off in there as well. He didn't see Redondo. He didn't see anyone. Joey was about to call out for him, but thought better of it. If Redondo didn't want him there, he could send him home with a snap of his fingers. And if Manchester was stalking around backstage, Joey was better off keeping his mouth shut.

Joey backed away from the lobby doors and went up the staircase to the second level. It creaked beneath his feet, so he walked close to the banister, minimizing the weight distribution on each step and staying as quiet as possible. On the second-floor landing, he found another staircase that led up to Redondo's private office. Pausing outside the door, Joey thought about what he was going to say to Redondo when he saw him. He didn't have anything prepared. He didn't have anything beyond a strong desire to make things right. He wanted to help and he wasn't going to take no for an answer. Unfortunately, Redondo wasn't there to say yes or no.

The office was not only empty; it was immaculate. Cleaner than Joey had ever seen it before. Joey switched on a lamp and saw that various magical relics, texts, and instruments were all neatly arranged on Redondo's shelves. His cluttered desk had been cleared save for a leather-bound book and a deck of cards. Joey took a look. It was Redondo's magic deck. The one he always had on him. *Why would he leave this up here?* As the question drifted through Joey's brain, a likely answer followed close behind. The last card Joey had seen Redondo pull was Death. After drawing that from the deck, the art of fortune-telling probably lost its luster. Joey leafed through the pages of the book and found it was an inventory of every magical artifact in the theater. Knowing death was near, Redondo had apparently put his house in order. This he had a harder time understanding. Redondo had originally intended to destroy Houdini's wand before he succumbed to his illness rather than let it fall into the Invisible Hand's clutches. Why had he organized all of this? He was practically gift wrapping everything in the theater for Manchester and his cronies. Joey speculated that Redondo perhaps couldn't bring himself to get rid of it all. Or maybe he was being cautious, in case Manchester demanded something more than the wand in return for Leanora and Shazad. Or maybe Joey was too late and he was looking at Manchester's handiwork, not Redondo's.

He scanned the room again, suddenly feeling vulnerable, worrying that Redondo was already dead. Joey held his breath and listened, but he heard nothing. "He's not dead yet," Joey whispered, trying to reassure himself. "This place wouldn't even be here if he were." He went to the office windows and opened them up, looking out on the dark, decrepit theater. For better or worse, this place was a part of Redondo. He had to be here somewhere. Joey was about to give in and call out for him, but Manchester beat him to the punch.

"Honey, I'm ho-oome!" Manchester's voice echoed up

from the theater lobby with a mocking, melodic tone. The sound grated on Joey, boiling his blood. He ducked low and withdrew from the window overlooking the theater as he heard Manchester moving around downstairs.

"Redondo! Where are you?" Manchester shouted, pushing the lobby doors open and entering the main house of the theater. "It's showtime, old man. You mustn't keep your public waiting. Come out, come out, wherever you are. . . ."

"I'm right here, Grayson," Redondo's voice called out, filling the room.

Joey's head whipped around as a spotlight switched on, illuminating Redondo. He was standing onstage with his hands clasped behind his back and his eyes fixed firmly on Manchester. Heartened, Joey crept back to the window and peeked over the sill. Redondo was dressed in his usual outfit, a black tuxedo with a white vest, a dress shirt, and a bow tie. However, for the first time that Joey could recall, Redondo's bow tie was tied up in place, not hanging loose around his neck. His rumpled tuxedo had been neatly pressed, his dress shirt and vest were as crisp and clean as a fresh layer of snow. His hair, slick with pomade, looked practically bulletproof. He looked confident and ready. Seeing Redondo like this gave Joey a tiny spark of hope. Was it possible the old man had a plan to save Leanora and Shazad without giving up the wand? Or was he just looking to die with dignity?

"Back onstage at last. How does it feel? Not too large a turnout for your big comeback, though. You don't have much of a following anymore, do you?"

"I'm not here for applause."

"No, you're here to die. You look different, by the way. Did you change your hair?" Manchester asked. "I'm kidding. It's nice to see you dressed up for the occasion. I take it as a compliment. I'd say they can bury you in that suit, but there isn't going to be anything left to bury after I'm finished with you."

Redondo's lips flattened out in a tight smile. "I understand you're trying to be menacing, but you might want to give it a rest. If nothing else, it will save us time. Or don't you realize death threats have very little effect on the terminally ill?"

"Fair enough," Manchester said, walking down the aisle toward the stage. "But it's not just you dying tonight, Redondo. It's your entire brand of magic. The last vestiges of the Order of the Majestic, a group you failed both personally and profoundly."

"You forgot publicly," Redondo said, unaffected.

344

"Heh." Manchester chuckled. "At least you have a sense of humor about it."

"Did you bring the children?"

Manchester joined Redondo onstage and circled him like a lion sizing up its prey. "Did you bring the wand?" he asked, evading Redondo's question.

Redondo pressed his hands together and slowly drew them apart. Houdini's wand materialized between his palms, glowing with magical energy. "I'm the master of the wand. I'm never without it." Manchester's eyes lit up, but Redondo clapped his hands, and the wand disappeared from sight. "I want to see Leanora and Shazad. Now."

Manchester put on a patronizing smile. "Never let it be said that I denied a dying man his last wish." He took off his hat, reached his arm deep inside, and pulled out . . . a sword. "No, that's not it." He reached back in and pulled out another sword. And another. "That's not it, either. I know they're in here somewhere." Digging his arm all the way up to the shoulder, he felt around inside until he found something, but it wasn't Leanora or Shazad. It was a fiery, blazing torch. "Make yourself useful, would you? Hold that," he told Redondo, trying to pass him the torch.

Redondo crossed his arms and turned away, unamused.

"Must you be so petty?" Manchester asked, shaking a stand for the torch out of the hat. "I'm only thinking about fire safety. The theater is flammable, in case you've forgotten," he added in a self-righteous voice. Once the torch was safely holstered, Manchester continued rummaging around in the hat for Leanora and Shazad. Smoke started pouring out of the hat once more. Redondo's cough kicked in, raspy as ever. "I'm sorry about the smoke. I know it aggravates your condition. Consider it a necessary evil."

"Not unlike yourself," Redondo said, hacking up a lung.

Manchester snickered. "Same old Redondo. You see everything in black-and-white. No room for gray. I'm not evil. I just refuse to live my life ruled by fear, forever asking permission. But I'm not interested in a philosophical discussion about the nature of magic. Our transaction here tonight closes off all future debate. Until our business is concluded, we'll just have to agree to disagree."

When the smoke dissipated, there was a large crate in the center of the stage. It looked very much like the one Manchester had supposedly died in twenty years ago. Manchester sauntered over to it and opened the door. Leanora and Shazad fell out and collapsed to the floor. Redondo rushed over to check on them as they lay there, clutching their arms and shivering.

"There we are. Happy now?" asked Manchester.

"I'll tell you what would make me happy . . . ," Redondo said in a gravelly voice.

"Manners, please. I can always put them back where I found them."

Redondo scowled and turned his attention back to the children. "Leanora? Shazad? Are you all right? Has he harmed you in any way?"

"C-c-cold . . . ," Leanora said through chattering teeth. "So cold." Shazad, who had been stuck in the hat longer, was lying on his side, clutching his knees to his chest. Watching the scene play out, Joey gripped the office windowsill hard enough to leave fingerprints in the wood finish.

Manchester used his hat as a fan to wave away the rest of the smoke. "They'll be fine," he reassured Redondo. "You might have to give them a minute, but they'll be back on their feet in no time. You, on the other hand, are out of time. I held up my end of the bargain, Redondo. It's time for you to hold up yours."

"Yes." Redondo stood up, appearing satisfied that Leanora and Shazad were all right, or at least that they would be in time. "The wand, then," he said. Producing it once more from between his palms, he held it up but didn't hand it over. "You remember that it only obeys one master."

"As long as that person lives," Manchester replied with a smarmy darkness. "I realize your days are already numbered, but patience has never been my strong suit." He rested his hand on the lid of the crate and drummed his fingers. "Remember our closing number? Back when we worked together, you used to put me in a box just like this one, drive swords through it, and set it on fire. I couldn't wait to get out of it. Tonight it's your turn in the box. If not . . ." Manchester picked up the swords by their hilts and positioned them in the air above Leanora and Shazad. The swords dangled there as if hung by invisible strings. They were heavy, gruesome blades cast from black iron, with sharp, jagged edges. The kind of weapons an orc might swing at a knight in shining armor.

"These aren't the blades we used to use in our act," Redondo observed, inspecting their choppy, serrated edges.

"They're the fabled Swords of Damocles," Manchester said proudly. "Just a little something I picked up in my travels. They'll hang over these children's heads until I decide they shouldn't." Manchester gave a nod, and the swords dropped an inch closer to Leanora and Shazad. They yelped and scuttled away, but the swords followed them wherever they went. "Then again, you could say the choice is yours." He nodded to the crate, implying that Redondo should get in before he got tired of waiting.

"I see." Redondo stroked his mustache. "It's time, then."

Desperate to help, Joey searched Redondo's office for something he could use against Manchester. He grabbed the index of magical items off the desk and started reading pages at random, hoping something useful would jump out at him. Surely Redondo had something worthwhile in his office, but even if he did, what were the odds that Joey would be able to find it and master it in the next few minutes? And then surprise Manchester with it? He wanted to spring out of the trapdoor and take Manchester by surprise, but even if he managed to strike a blow, what was to stop the swords from falling on Leanora and Shazad and chopping them to bits? He couldn't risk that, could he? He was the reason they were in this mess. If they were to die because he tried to be a hero and did something reckless, he couldn't live with that. But what if Redondo died because he did nothing? And Leanora and Shazad died too? They weren't exactly safe where they were at the moment. He didn't come here just to be another norm in the audience. Looking around the room once more, Joey's eyes fell on a short length of rope and a tiny blue bottle sitting on a shelf behind Redondo's desk. An idea started to form.

A few short seconds later, Joey took Redondo's cane with the silver raven handle from its place in the umbrella stand. His hand shook as he reached up toward the attic door in the ceiling and hooked the shiny bird through the steel ring in its center. *This is it*, Joey told himself. *I'm going in.*

Only he wasn't.

The door wouldn't open. Stealth was a priority, so Joey had pulled down gently at first, but then he tried harder—and harder—going as far as to pick up his legs and hang down on the cane like a piece of playground equipment. But the door wouldn't budge. Foiled, Joey returned to the window, unable to do anything but watch.

Redondo was staring up at the window to his office. Joey wondered if he had felt him trying to open the attic door. The theater was a part of him after all. Then again, it could just be that he saw the open office window with a light on inside and noticed things were not as he had left them. Redondo looked like he was about to give the wand to Manchester but had stopped halfway through the motion. Manchester had his hand out, impatient to receive it. "I'm waiting . . . ," he droned.

Redondo seemed to snap back into the moment. "Of course," he said, but he didn't hand the wand over just yet. "It occurs to me that if I do what you say, I'll be dead and will have no way of knowing if you let these two go or not. Am I supposed to just trust you on this?"

"You can trust me to kill them if you don't do as you're told," Manchester snapped, dropping the swords another half inch.

"That part I believe," Redondo said. "But the rest . . . You're asking me for a lot of faith."

"What can I say?" Manchester flashed a guilty smile. "It's a chance either way, but one you have to take. The only thing that will save these two from the sword is you sacrificing yourself and passing that wand to a worthy heir."

"Too late," Shazad said, sitting up onstage. "H-he's . . . already d-done that."

"Quiet, you," Manchester sneered. "I didn't give you permission to speak."

"I know how you feel. I d-didn't want to believe it either," Shazad said, still shivering. "You're not the only one who w-wanted the wand. When I think about how much time I spent studying . . . How hard I t-trained?" Shazad shook his head. "My parents are going to be so disappointed when I tell them I didn't win it. You'll probably have even more explaining to do."

"What are you babbling about?" Manchester asked, annoyed. "The wand's right there. He has it."

"Doesn't matter," Shazad said, rubbing his arms to warm up. "It's got a new m-master now. You were there. You should know."

"You're talking about the mirror world," Redondo realized. "Young Kopecky." He stole another glance up at the office window.

"Him?" Manchester said, suppressing the urge to laugh. "You're not serious."

"He actually d-did it," Leanora said, coming around. "Joey used the wand—against you," she told Manchester. "That's why you fought for him," she added, turning to Shazad.

Shazad nodded. "There was no place left to hide. It was t-time to fight."

Joey couldn't believe what he was hearing. The room was spinning. He cast about inside Redondo's office, safe for the moment, wondering what to think. Could it be true? Was the wand already his, or was Shazad just trying to buy time and the others were playing along? He didn't know what to believe. Joey tried to remember if he had seen Redondo use the wand again after the fight in the mirror world. He hadn't.

"It doesn't matter," Manchester spat. "Even if you're right, the boy's nothing. He's a norm, a loose end easily tied up. I know just where to find him. You kicked him out, remember? He's probably at home, hiding under his bed-sheets crying."

"I expect he's hiding somewhere," Redondo agreed. "But not the way you think. You didn't see him for what he was, Grayson. Neither did I, not at first. He was hiding in plain sight, like all the best magic. A hidden gem."

Redondo glanced quickly at the window one last time.

Did he just wink at me? Joey wondered.

"You know, I used to have this special deck of cards,"

Redondo continued. "When I was a young man—not much older than these two, in fact—a woman I had never met before used them to tell my fortune. She told me I would inspire a new age of magical wonder. Even let me keep the deck. It was my first magical relic."

"Is there a point to this story, or is it just dementia setting in?" Manchester asked.

Joey turned around and looked at the cards on the desk. Redondo was trying to tell him something.

"No more stalling!" Manchester barked, and he moved the blades dangerously close to Leanora's and Shazad's throats. "Do the right thing and get in the crate. Now."

"I will, but first . . ." Redondo paused, and something subtle in his expression shifted. He had a gleam in his eye. "Grayson, I want to thank you."

"You want to thank me?" Manchester asked, confused.

"I do. For helping me figure out what my last great trick will be. Who knows? You might get something out of it after all."

"I'll get something out of it all right. The wand."

"Yes, the wand." Redondo took the wand back out and held it up. "You know I always intended to destroy this rather than let you and yours get your hands on it. You changed all that."

354

"Obviously."

"I don't mean this." Redondo motioned to Leanora and Shazad, held hostage by magical weaponry. "I mean sending Joey to find me. You made me realize something important. Something I missed."

"What's that?"

Redondo smiled. "It's not about me. All your scheming . . . All you've done is lead me to a grand epiphany. I don't need to come up with some magnificent illusion that inspires the world to believe in magic again. That isn't my responsibility. My responsibility is to a much smaller group of people."

"The people you're responsible for are sitting here with swords at their throats." Manchester waved a hand, and the blades pressed into Leanora's and Shazad's necks, drawing blood. It was just a drop from each of them, but the message was clear. Manchester was through talking. "Your move, old man."

"Right you are, Grayson," Redondo said. "On with the show!"

He strode past Manchester into the crate and spun around to face Leanora and Shazad. "Good luck, children. Don't worry. You're in good hands." He touched two fingers to his hairline, bowing his head slightly in a gesture that was one-part salute and one-part farewell. From there things happened quickly. The crate sealed itself up without any help from anyone. The swords flew away from Leonora and Shazad and sprang to life as flames leaped from the torches to the blades. They swirled through the air, surrounding the crate with a flaming vortex, just as they had done twenty years ago. History went on to repeat itself as the fiery cyclone converged on the crate and its unfortunate occupant. Flaming swords ran through the wooden box, reducing it to a pile of blazing sticks. Joey should have been horrified, but the spark of confidence he'd seen in Redondo as he entered the crate had lifted his spirits. He was onto something. Joey didn't know what it was, but from the sound of it, Redondo knew what he had to do to beat Manchester! If one's eyes could be trusted, the blaze was a funeral pyre for Redondo, but Joey refused to believe what he saw. Redondo wasn't dead. It was a trick. It had to be.

Joey rushed across the room to Redondo's desk and the magic deck of cards. Recognizing what Redondo had intended for him to do, Joey turned over the topmost card. The image on the other side made his spirit soar. It was a large red bird with its wings spread wide, flying out of a fiery conflagration: the Phoenix. New hope rising from the ashes . . . Joey pocketed the cards and returned to the window.

Down onstage, the fire burned itself out, and the swords clattered to the floorboards, their blades crumbling into dust. Leanora and Shazad helped each other up, and together they staggered to the edge of the stage, moving away from Manchester.

"There," Manchester said, very much relieved. "That wasn't so hard, was it?" He removed his top hat, pressed it to his chest, and bowed his head in false reverence. "A moment of silence for the dearly departed. Redondo the Magnificent is magnificent no more."

You wish, Joey thought.

"The king is dead!" Manchester laughed, kicking through the ashes of the crate, looking for Houdini's wand. "Long live the . . ." His voice trailed off as the object of his search eluded him. "Long live . . ." He looked harder. Ashes and blackened wood flew away to expose the floorboards beneath. Nothing. The wand wasn't there.

That's right, Joey thought, enjoying the confused look on Manchester's face. *You think you're the only one who can fake your death in that box?* He stood up in the window, eager to see Manchester get his comeuppance. *Here it comes. . . .*

Manchester went through every inch of the crate's charred remains, growing increasingly frustrated in his fruitless search for the wand.

Any second now, Joey thought, eager for Redondo's triumphant return.

But Redondo didn't show. And then Manchester found the wand among the ashes.

What?

"Finally!" Manchester rejoiced, holding up the wand as if he were King Arthur hoisting up Excalibur, having just drawn the fabled sword from its stone. Joey was mortified by the sight of Manchester with the wand.

"Where is *he?*" Joey whispered to himself, clinging to the hope that things couldn't end this way. He held his breath, staring at the stage, waiting for the other shoe to drop. Where was the magical twist ending? Redondo's master stroke? It didn't make sense. *Unless . . .*

The realization hit Joey like a bucket of ice water: Redondo wasn't coming back. Joey felt hollow and cold inside. Redondo was dead, and he had done nothing to stop it. As a famous Sith Lord had once said on-screen, his failure was now complete. But Shazad didn't share Joey's dejected outlook. Joey heard him onstage, reassuring Leanora. "It's all right," he told her. "It doesn't matter. He can't do a thing with it."

"Is that so?" Manchester said, turning toward Shazad, galled by his nerve. "What say we test your theory with a killing curse? It just so happens I know quite a few. I've always wanted to try them out but never had the means to do so . . . until now."

"You told Redondo you'd let us go!" Leanora shouted.

"And he was right not to trust me." He waved the wand in their direction, taking aim. . . .

"NO!" Joey shouted, and all eyes turned up to Redondo's office window, where Joey now stood in plain view.

"Look who's here," Manchester said, a Cheshire cat grin on his face. "Don't move, Joey. I'll be with you in just a moment." He returned his focus to Leanora and Shazad. "First things first." With a graceful angling of the wrist, he spoke a chilling word: "Morté."

Nothing happened. Manchester waited a moment, then tried again.

"Silentes!" he said, waving the wand, raising his voice just a touch.

Once again there was no magic to be found.

"Leto!" Manchester shouted, getting agitated.

He might as well have been waving a drumstick. Manchester looked at the useless wand as if it had betrayed him, and in his mind it probably had. A satisfied, know-it-all expression emerged on Shazad's face. Leanora gave a short laugh of relief, and Joey did the same.

"I don't believe this," Manchester said, still staring at the wand. "It chose him?" As he looked up at Joey, his disbelief morphed into murderous resentment. "I can deal with that."

"Deal with *this*," Leanora said, striding across the stage in big, sweeping steps. She had the firestone pendant clutched in her left hand, and her right hand was lit up like a torch. Leanora took a swing at Manchester, leaving a trail of fire like a comet. The impact was explosive. As she drove her fist into Manchester's stomach, there was a flash of light. The next thing Joey knew, Manchester was flying across the stage. He hit the backstage wall and the wand tumbled from his hand.

As soon as Joey saw that, he grabbed the cane that was

still hooked through the ring of the attic door in the ceil-ing. He pulled down hard, and the door swung open freely. There wasn't any room in Joey's mind for doubt, because there wasn't any time for it. Had he stopped to think about what he could and could not do, maybe nothing would have happened. Instead, what happened was he scurried up the ladder as fast as he could, and a half second later, the trap-door opened in the center of the stage. Charred debris from the crate and ashes from the fire fell away as Joey pushed it open and rushed toward the wand.

18

The Magician's Duel

Manchester went for the wand at the same time as Joey, but Joey was ready for him. He tossed out the Gordian rope. Manchester caught it instinctively.

Gotcha.

Manchester tried to toss the rope away, but it was too late. He gasped as it wrapped around his wrists and slithered up his arms. Rapidly growing longer from both ends, it looped around his body, squeezing him like the tentacles of a giant squid. Within seconds, he was completely enveloped, and Joey had the wand in his hand.

He felt no burst of energy when he picked it up this time. No hulking superpower growing inside him. Instead, Joey felt a terrible weight on his shoulders. An incredible burden and responsibility. The spotlight was on him now.

Manchester looked up at Joey with a sneer. "I hope you're not expecting this to hold me. Do you have any idea how many times I escaped these ropes when I was your age? Right here on this very stage?"

"That's all right. They just need to restrain you long enough for me to get this," Joey said, holding up the wand.

"What do you think you're going to do with that?" Manchester asked, working to free himself. The ropes were already loosening up. "Nice punch, by the way," he told Leonora. "But you should have come at me harder. It'll take more than you've got to keep me down. More than any of you have got. I'll be out of this in no time. Do the sensible thing and give me the wand, Joey. I promise I'll kill you quickly."

Joey held the wand down by his side, keeping his distance from Manchester and the enchanted rope. "For some reason that doesn't sound like a great deal to me."

"That's true enough, but you won't get a better offer from me."

"I'm the one with the wand," Joey said, pointing it at Manchester.

"Redondo had the wand a few minutes ago," Manchester

said, unfazed. "You might want to take a few steps back. Brush whatever's left of him off your shoes."

Joey looked down. He was standing in the remnants of the crate. The fires had burned hot enough to turn everything into dust and cinders. He backed away from the trapdoor, struck by a profound sense of loss. Joey had always known they were going to lose Redondo, but not like this. He turned to Leanora and Shazad, keeping one eye on Manchester and the wand at the ready. "Are you guys okay?"

"They're fine," Manchester said, answering for them. "For now," he added. "I asked you a question, Joey. What are you going to do?" As he spoke, he disentangled one of his arms from the massive knot he was bound in. He'd be free soon.

Joey's eyes swept the backstage area, looking for something specific. Redondo had cleaned up here, too, save for the crowbar and the shattered aquarium.

"Your part in this is over, boy. Redondo's gone. There's no one coming to rescue you this time."

"*I* rescued *him* last time, remember?"

"I hope you're not planning to make me float away again. That's not going to get the job done. I'll keep coming back.

I'll never stop. You're going to have to kill me. Tell me, have you ever killed someone before? Don't bother answering; it's a rhetorical question. Of course you haven't. That's why I've got nothing to fear from you and that wand. You don't want this responsibility. You know you don't. As long as I'm alive, you'll never know peace, and that's no way to live. Do yourself a favor. End this now. Tonight. While I'm still in the mood to be merciful."

Joey was trembling, but he did his best to project confidence. He needed to be brave, and if he couldn't do that, he decided that pretending to be brave was the next best thing. At the moment it was the only thing.

"Is that what you told my father?"

Manchester squinted at Joey. "Your father?"

"When he was my age. He passed Redondo's test too." Joey took out the coin he used to access the theater. "Turns out I'm not such a norm after all. Magic runs in the family."

Manchester recognized the coin. A light bulb went on in his mind. "That's the bit of magic you carried with you into the testing center. I thought it felt familiar. I take it that's how you got back in here without a key."

"My father's lucky coin," Joey said. He gripped it tightly,

as if channeling its strength. "He thought it was luck, but it was magic. He should have had more of it. He would have if not for you. I wonder how different the world would be right now if Redondo had my dad for an assistant instead of you."

Manchester gave a tiny shrug, unapologetic. "We'll never know," he said as he got his other arm free.

"Because you got rid of him. Even then you were scared of the competition."

"Sounds to me like your father was the one who was scared. I wish I could tell you I remember him, but I don't. He wasn't the only child to find Redondo's sad little sideshow back in those days. Far from it. But if I was able to convince your father he wasn't a magician and send him on his way, then he wasn't a magician, now, was he? It all comes down to what you believe. Be grateful he folded so easily. Other children required permanent convincing." He was pushing down on the ropes now, sliding them down his chest.

Shazad's face contorted in revulsion. "What are you saying? You killed them?"

"I never did like to share." Manchester smiled, flashing his crooked teeth.

Joey felt queasy. He didn't know why that surprised him so

much. He'd known Manchester was a killer—he was responsible for the death of Redondo, after all. But to think he had started at such a young age and with other children . . . for what? Just to keep magic to himself? That was a whole other level of evil.

"Joey, what are you waiting for?" Leanora asked as Manchester stepped out of the ropes and kicked them away. "Use the wand. Finish him!"

Joey said nothing. He stood motionless, like a mannequin in a store window. Manchester spread his arms wide in a taunting gesture, boldly inviting the death blow. Joey's fingers tightened on the wand. Sweat beaded on his forehead as he contemplated cold-blooded murder. There was no getting around it. It would be murder, however much Manchester deserved it. He had killed Redondo, and Joey had heard him attempt three different killing spells on Leanora and Shazad. It would be easy enough to repeat those words, but Joey doubted they would work for him. His heart wasn't in that kind of magic. It was no use pretending. Manchester was right. He wasn't a killer.

Manchester laughed as Joey lowered the wand. "I told you he can't do it. He's too scared."

Joey swallowed hard. There wasn't any doubt about it. Manchester did scare him. The idea of facing him alone—without Redondo there to protect him—terrified Joey, but he had to do it. He was the only one who could. He had to learn his father's lesson and do the thing that scared him. The question was, what scared *Manchester?* Joey put the wand in his pocket and felt Redondo's deck of cards. He had an idea.

"Give me the wand," Manchester said, holding out a stiff hand. "I won't ask again."

Joey shook his head. "Redondo had a competition for the wand. If you want in, that's one thing, but I'm not just going to hand it over. You've got to earn it."

Manchester's eyebrows went up. He paused a moment, then leaned forward, tapping a finger to his ear. "I'm sorry. My hearing must be off. It sounds like you're saying you want to duel. Against me?"

Joey nodded. "May the best magician win."

Manchester burst out laughing as if that were the funniest thing he had ever heard.

Joey let Manchester have his fun, grateful for the extra time to psych himself up. *He wants me scared,* Joey thought. *He's trying to get inside my head so I can't do this. But I can do it.* Joey told himself he had to get out of his own head. This was just another test. He had to cut away the distractions and solve the problem. Nothing killed magic dead like doubt and fear, but he wasn't the only one who could feel those feelings.

"We'll keep it simple. I'll do one trick. Something to make you disappear for good. If it doesn't work, I lose. You get the wand. But if I pull this off, you leave us alone—all of us. And you agree to never set foot inside the Majestic Theatre again."

Manchester's eyes narrowed. He appeared both baffled and insulted by Joey's suggestion. "You're delusional."

"Do we have a deal or not?"

"Oh yes," Manchester said facetiously. "Why not?" He raised his right hand and swore an oath in front of everyone: "On my honor, if you can best me, may the magic drain from my body and strike me dead if I ever return to this place."

"All right," Joey said, taking Manchester's pledge with a grain of salt. He didn't think Manchester had any honor, but it didn't really matter. If Joey played his cards right, Manchester wouldn't be in a position to come back to the Majestic anyway. He reached into his pocket, but not for the wand. "This is Redondo's magic deck. The one he told you about. Let's see what's in the cards for you." Joey fanned the deck and offered it to Manchester.

"This is the best you can do?"

"Pick a card. Any card."

"Just one?"

"I only need one."

Manchester selected a card from the middle of the pack. When he turned it over, it was not one of Redondo's strange fortune-telling cards, but rather the card Joey had pulled from the deck the previous morning—the one with the symbol of the Invisible Hand.

Manchester smiled. "My own card. What does that signify?"

"It's not your card. Not exactly. Look again."

Holding the card close to his face, Manchester inspected the card, noting a red dot on the palm of the hand. "I see. What's this red dot supposed to be? Blood on my hands? If you think that's going to make me feel bad, you don't know who you're dealing with."

"I know who I'm dealing with. Do you?" Backing away, Joey took the wand out of his pocket and pointed it at Manchester. "*Apis Melifera.*"

Manchester crooked an eyebrow. "What was that?"

"You'll see. They sound like magic words, don't they? It's actually binary nomenclature. That's a scientific naming system for animals. First you list the genus, then the species. Don't ask me why I remember that. I learned it in biology class."

"What are you talking about?"

"I'm talking about the western honeybee. You're allergic to bees, right? Me too. I don't like them, but we do need them. They're important to the environment, now more than ever."

Manchester shut his mouth. His eyes darted left and right. A faint buzzing noise was clearly audible. Where was it coming from? Joey nodded toward the card in his hand. Manchester looked down at it. A live bee was sitting on the upper-left corner of the card. Startled, Manchester shook his hand immediately, casting the bee off. It was an involuntary, spastic reaction. There was no doubt about it—Manchester was afraid.

"That's not blood on the hand in that card." Joey smiled. "It's a sting."

Soon more bees were there, orbiting Manchester's hand in slow, looping circles. He dropped the card and waved the bees off. It didn't help. For every bee he chased away, two more appeared, and the more he tried to get rid of them, the more aggressive they became. "What is this?" he asked, swinging his arms wildly. "Where are they coming from?"

"Sorry. A magician never reveals his secrets." Joey tapped his forearm. "I think they like your coat."

Confused, Manchester twisted his arm around for a look. What he saw made the little color he had in his already pale face drain completely away. The underside of his arm, from the elbow to the wrist, was positively crawling with bees. There had to be a hundred or more, packed in tight, as if his sleeve were the interior wall of a hive.

"GAH!" he blurted out in utter terror. Desperate to get away from his own arm, he lost all sense of where he was and backpedaled until he tripped on the twisted lines of rope that were strewn about the stage. Manchester landed in the ash heap and flailed around in an agitated frenzy. He tore his coat off and threw it away, but that did nothing to get rid of the bees. Angry now, they swarmed him like a sentient cloud. With Manchester otherwise occupied, Joey returned to Leanora and Shazad.

"Come on. We've got to get out of here," he said.

"We can't leave," Leanora said. "Those bees aren't going to stop him."

"They might," Joey said. "Bee stings are no joke when you've got allergies. Believe me, I know."

"But if you're allergic too, aren't you in danger as well?" Shazad asked.

"Not if I stay focused," Joey said, holding up the wand and silently willing the bees to stay away from him. "Can you guys swim?"

"Can we swim?" Leanora repeated, baffled.

"What are you talking about?" Shazad asked, echoing her sentiments.

"Never mind," Joey said. "I'll take care of it."

"We've got to take care of him!" Leanora said, pointing at Manchester. "Even if your bees run him out of here, you can't honestly believe he's going to honor the deal you made."

"That's what this is for." Joey took the tiny blue bottle he had found in Redondo's office and set it on the ground. Leaving Shazad and Leanora for a moment, he ran backstage to grab the crowbar he spotted earlier.

"What are you doing?" Leanora asked Joey, thinking he

meant to hit Manchester with the crowbar. "Don't use that. Use the wand!"

"I will, but we have to be smart about how we do it."

"This is smart?" Shazad asked.

"This is genius." Joey raised the crowbar high in the air. "I think," he added. "Stay close."

He brought the heavy metal bar down with all his might, shattering the tiny bottle that contained the Water of Life. A rush of liquid exploded from the point of impact as if a dam had burst, blasting Joey, Shazad, and Leonora all the way to the back of the theater. Fortunately, Joey remembered Redondo's protective spell and had shielded the three of them inside an airtight bubble, shouting, "Encapsulato!" the second before they were washed away. When the wave settled, the bubble dissolved and the three of them stood up, knee-deep in water. Joey looked down at the wand in his hand. "I think I'm getting the hang of this."

The water sloshed around inside the theater. Joey spotted Manchester in the third row. The force of the wave had thrown him into the seats. "This was all in that tiny bottle?" Shazad asked.

"Unbelievable, right?" Joey replied.

An ominous swell of water rose in the center of the flooded theater, defying the laws of physics. Glowing sapphire eyes materialized within the liquid mass, making it look like the head of a giant rising from the deep. A mouth opened up on the water giant's face, and the water they were standing in rushed back to fill the void. Leanora faltered against the freshly created current but used the last row of theater seats to steady herself. "What is that?"

"Aqua de Vida," Joey explained. "Also known as the Water of Life. We'd better get out of here." He guided Leanora and Shazad out the theater doors and into the lobby. They moved quickly as the water shallowed out this far from the stage, but a second wave blasted the lobby doors off the hinges and washed them out into the street.

The water settled again. Joey and the others stood up, soaking wet. The shadow creatures of the Invisible Hand rushed them, reaching out with long arms and sharp fingers. Leanora and Shazad put up their hands to protect themselves, but Joey wasn't fazed. "These guys never learn," he said, shaking his head. "Don't worry. They can't hurt you. They're not even he—"

Joey was interrupted by one of the shadow creatures

knocking him off his feet. He splashed down on wet pavement, shocked to the core.

"You were saying?" Shazad asked as more shadows rushed in. They swarmed Joey on the ground, trying to jerk the wand out of his hands. He rolled over, getting the wand underneath him and guarding it with his body. As Leanora and Shazad tried to pull the shadow creatures off Joey, he realized what was happening. Redondo was gone. The protections around his Off-Broadway realm were breaking down. The shadows were gaining strength. He had to take them out before they got stronger. Thinking about what got rid of shadows, Joey spun around with the wand, shouting, "Nova!"

A blinding light flashed out to fill the street. It was as if Joey were balancing a tiny star on the tip of the wand. The world went white for several seconds, and when it faded, everyone's vision was hopelessly blurred. Leanora and Shazad were staggering about, rubbing their eyes. Joey was also seeing spots, but from what he was able to make out, they were alone. The shadows had all been vaporized.

"What was that you said?" Leanora asked Joey, blinking hard.

"Nova," Joey repeated. "It's the term for a sudden increase in the brightness of a star."

"How do you know that?"

Joey blinked his eyes clear, grateful he had not called for a supernova. "Just a little something I learned in science class."

"Does science class have an answer for that?" Shazad asked. A gurgling moan poured out of the theater. Water flowed like raging rapids beneath the marquee and rose to assume a ghostlike form. The Water of Life had followed them out into the street.

"Okay, maybe this wasn't such a genius idea," Joey admitted.

"I would have thought something called the Water of Life would be friendlier," Leanora said.

"We got off on the wrong foot, me and this thing," Joey replied. "This isn't the first time I hit it with a crowbar."

"Now you tell us."

The ankle-deep water they were standing in grew deeper, and the current started up again. Soon they were submerged up to their necks. Joey tried in vain to swim away as the water carried him back toward the theater entrance where the water creature waited. His plan was backfiring. He had hoped to rile up the Water of Life and leave it to swallow Manchester—and maybe it had—but it clearly wasn't content to stop there. It still had an ax to grind with him.

"This is a great plan!" Shazad shouted, swimming alongside him. "I'm so glad you came to our rescue!"

Joey couldn't blame him for being upset. So far Joey had succeeded only in trading one form of danger for another. The water creature expanded its form into that of a wide, hungry mouth, but before it could swallow Joey, Leanora, and Shazad, everything changed. The clouds lifted and the temperature climbed. The world shook off its gloom and Joey's feet found the pavement once again as the water shallowed out. He could have kissed the city street as it solidified beneath him. Redondo's phantom realm had collapsed just in time. They were back in New York—the real New York. The Majestic Theatre splashed down its rightful place with a booming *thud*, and torrents of water spilled out everywhere. Cars screeched to a halt and spun out in the street. Pedestrians made sounds of confusion and alarm, cursing the sudden deluge and the damage done to their outfits.

"Guurgh?" croaked a bubbling puddle near Joey's

feet. He looked down and saw a pair of glowing blue eyes swirling in confusion. "Are you all right?" Joey asked the puddle. The eyeballs rounded on him, heavy with suspicion. Joey put his hands up. "Look, I'm sorry. Really. No hard feelings? I didn't mean to hurt you. I just . . . I just didn't know what else to do." The luminous eyes narrowed, still unsure. Shazad took hold of a signpost, just in case the water creature tried to suck them in again. Leanora did the same. Joey looked around for something he could latch on to as a precaution when he heard the sound of running water. The spillage in the street was draining into the sewers. "Hey, you hear that?" Joey asked. He put a hand to his ear. "Listen! You're free. You don't have to go back in the bottle. You can go anywhere. What do you say? Bygones?"

The sentient puddle pondered Joey's words briefly before gliding toward the street. After that the water was gone. Every last drop. Even the liquid that had saturated Joey's clothes and hair had vanished, leaving him completely dry. Leanora and Shazad were dry as well.

Joey stood up and ran a free hand through his hair. "I'm glad that worked."

"You let it go to the sewer?" asked Shazad. "Was that wise?"

Joey shook his head. "I don't think I could have stopped it if I tried."

"You guys . . . ," Leanora said, pointing. Manchester had stumbled into the lobby, hat in hand. He looked like he had been through the wringer, and he was angrier than Joey had ever seen him.

Joey brought the wand up like a gunslinger drawing his weapon. "Quixote!" Manchester spun around like a psychotic ballerina, slamming hard into the lobby wall. Disoriented, he bounced back and fell, but he wasn't giving up. A moment later he was up again. The fight wasn't over.

"You're going to have to do better than that," Shazad told Joey.

He shook his head. "I don't . . . I don't know what to do."

"He's going to keep coming," Leanora told Joey. "If you want to stop him, I think you're going to have to stop him for good."

"You mean kill him? I can't do that."

"Before he kills you," Leanora warned. "Before he kills all of us!"

Joey looked down at the wand in his hand. He knew he could make the wand into a lethal weapon if he wanted to. He had practically done so already with the bees. But using the wand specifically to kill . . . like a gun . . . that was different somehow. He just couldn't cross that line.

"You better do something," Shazad said, backing away from the theater. "I don't want to end up in that hat again. It was like being stuck in a black hole."

Joey looked at Leanora as an idea clicked in his brain. "Leanora! Do you still have that doorknob?"

She clutched at her bag from the outside, feeling around for it. "Right here!"

Thank goodness, Joey thought. "Come on, then! Follow me!" He took off down the street, and Leanora and Shazad ran after him.

"Where are we going?" Leanora called out.

"We need a door," Joey said, checking the buildings as they passed them. Halfway down the street he found what he was looking for, a shop with a standard doorknob on its entrance. "Here!" he shouted.

Leanora used her firestone necklace to charge up her fist with magical energy. This time she had no trouble powering up and knocking the doorknob off the door. A clean karate-chop motion severed the handle, and the next thing Joey knew, she had the gold-and-ruby doorknob out of her bag. She pressed it into place on the door and turned the knob, checking the connection. The ruby lit up, signifying the magical bond was secure and the door was ready for action. "Where are we going?" Leanora asked Joey, stepping aside to let him do the honors.

"How does this work?" Joey asked.

"You have to visualize where you want to go. Picture it in your mind, clear as you can."

Joey grimaced. "What if I've never seen the place before?"

"It doesn't matter. You just have to focus."

"He's coming," Shazad said, pointing down the street. Manchester had staggered out of the theater. "He sees us."

"Okay," Joey said, reaching tentatively for the doorknob. *You can do this.* He closed his eyes and turned the knob. The door opened inward on what looked to be a dark basement storage area.

"Is this it?" Leanora asked. "Is this what you wanted?"

"I don't know," Joey said, venturing inside. "I think so." Everything was dark and quiet. Leanora and Shazad followed Joey in.

"What is this place?" Shazad asked, not yet closing the door behind them.

Joey was about to say he hoped it was the basement of Exemplar Academy, when Janelle came around the corner with a flashlight. She and Joey bumped into each other, and they both sprang back, shouting out in surprise.

"This is the place," Joey said afterward, relieved.

"Joey?" Janelle asked. She was patting her chest, still getting over the shock of running into him. "You scared me to death! What are you doing here?"

"What am I doing here?" Joey had no idea how to explain his sudden appearance and no time to waste trying. "What are *you* doing here this late?"

"I'm keeping an eye on my project," Janelle said defensively. "I couldn't just leave it. Not after what happened today. What if someone stumbled across it at random? Where did you come from?"

"Are you here by yourself?" Joey asked.

Janelle nodded. "I told my parents I was pulling an all-nighter in my lab."

"You can do that?"

"I do it all the time. What's going on here?" Janelle looked past Joey, Leanora, and Shazad, mystified by their sudden appearance. Her mouth fell open when she glimpsed the portal behind them. "Is that the street out there? In the basement?!!"

"I should get the door," Leanora said, going back to retrieve the magic doorknob.

"No!" Joey put a hand up. "We want him to follow us."

"We do?" Shazad asked.

"What are you talking about?" asked Janelle. "What is this? Who are they?" she added, gesturing to Leanora and Shazad.

"Shazad, Leanora . . . meet Janelle," Joey said quickly. "She's a genius. Janelle, this is Leanora and Shazad. They're . . ." He was going to say "magicians" but went another way at the last second. "They're my friends. I don't expect you to understand this, and I'm sorry I can't explain—at all—but I need to see your project. Now. And you need to get out of here five minutes ago."

Janelle looked at Joey like he was out of his mind. "Are you kidding? I'm not going anywhere."

"Please," Joey begged. "You have to trust me. It's not safe here."

"You want to talk about safe? I've got this whole basement sealed off. You know what's going to happen to you if you open that door?" She pointed across the basement, past assorted heat and air-conditioning equipment to a door on the opposite wall marked STORAGE. Joey went straight to it. "Don't bother. It's locked," said Janelle.

Joey turned toward her, eyes full of hope. "It's still in there?" he asked, pointing at the door.

"For a few more minutes," Janelle said, checking her phone. "Assuming my calculations are correct. You can't go in there. Look, I had to hook myself up to a safety line just to take a peek."

Everyone looked and saw a line of cable lashed around the base of a hot water heater. "What are you going to do?" Leanora asked Joey. "What's behind that door?"

"Why do you have a magic wand?" Janelle asked Joey. He pocketed the wand as soon as she mentioned it, but it hardly mattered. It wasn't as if he would be able to keep it a secret much longer. Janelle glanced back at the door that Joey and the others had used to enter the basement and flinched. "Who's that?"

"Just get ready to grab that lifeline—all of you," Joey said,

385

eyeing the door. Manchester was coming through it. He collected Leanora's golden doorknob on the way in and nudged the door shut with his foot.

"Well, well, well . . . isn't this cozy?" Manchester said, strutting around like he owned the place. "Who's this, now?" he asked, noticing Janelle. "More new friends? Joey, I had no idea you were so popular. You're going to be missed. Who knew?"

Joey took the wand back out and held it in front of his body, ready to snap it in two. "Don't take another step."

The threat did nothing to dent Manchester's confidence. "Why not?" he asked, lazily tossing and catching Leanora's doorknob in one hand like a baseball. "You're not going to break that wand."

"Stay back!" Joey ordered, bending the wand almost to the breaking point. He could practically hear the strain in the wood as it reached the upper limits of its endurance. Manchester stopped advancing. "You don't know what I'm going to do," Joey said. "I'm not like you. I'm not even like them," he added, nodding toward Leanora and Shazad. "I didn't get into this because I had to have this wand. I didn't want to change the world, remember? I didn't want to fight bad guys and go through life with a target on my back. I just wanted Redondo to teach me magic."

Manchester smiled as if Joey should have known better. "That was your mistake, not mine. I told you, magic isn't for everybody. I warned you it was dangerous, but you wouldn't listen, would you? It didn't have to be like this. If you had only done as you were told, you wouldn't be in this position, but that's not the case. You *are* in this position, Joey. You put yourself here. There's only one way out, and I promise you, breaking that wand in half isn't it."

"It's one way out," Joey said. "Giving the wand to you is another. But I've got to tell you, I'm not loving that idea, either."

"I'm not having this conversation with you." Manchester sneered. "Give me the wand now, or so help me, I'll—"

"What? Kill me? You're going to do that anyway."

"I was going to say I'll kill *them*." Manchester took off his hat and held a hand over the opening, ready to pull out something truly terrible and throw it at Leanora, Shazad, and Janelle. Joey looked over at them. They were huddled together, the line of cable at their feet. Janelle looked especially confused and frightened. "It's your choice," Manchester said. "What's it going to be?"

Joey cursed under his breath and relaxed his grip on the wand. "All right. I'm not going to break it." He held the wand up with one hand. "I choose door number three."

Manchester squinted. "What?"

Joey whirled around and aimed the wand at the door behind him, shouting:

"OPEN SESAME!"

With that, the closet that had once housed Janelle's supercollider project opened. Inside, hovering in midair, was a black hole the size of a dinner plate and absolutely nothing else. The black hole's gravitational pull had sucked everything that had once lined the closet into the void, and now that the door was open, it went to work on the rest of the basement. As the door flew open, Joey dove for the lifeline and let the wand go.

"What the—NO!" shouted Manchester as the wand flew back into the closet and disappeared into the abyss. He lurched after it, immediately realizing that he had made a fatal mistake. As the black hole pulled Manchester toward the closet, Joey caught the end of the cable and held on tight. Leanora, Shazad, and Janelle were all closer to the wall, holding fast to the same line. It was like being caught in the Water of Life's current, only stronger. Joey prayed that Janelle's calculations had been correct and the black hole would soon be gone. He didn't know how much more of this he could take. He tried climbing up the cable hand over hand, but he didn't get very far. The gravitational forces at work behind him were too strong.

"YOU!" Manchester bellowed at Joey, bracing himself in the closet door. "You . . . You threw it away!" he sputtered. "How . . . ? I don't believe . . . You ruined everything!"

"Believe it!" Joey shouted back. "You want the wand so bad? Go get it!"

"You worthless piece of—" Manchester cut himself off mid-insult as his hand slipped on the doorframe. He nearly fell back into the closet (and beyond). Still clutching his top hat tight in his fist, he growled and leaped forward, latching on to Joey with his free hand.

"AHH!" Joey cried out as Manchester grabbed hold of his wounded ankle. He slipped all the way back to the end of the line, pain shooting up through his leg.

"Joey!" screamed Leanora. The others wanted to help him, but they were too far away. Together they started moving down the line to Joey, but they had to go slowly and carefully so as not to lose their own grip. Looking up at them, Joey knew they wouldn't reach him in time. Manchester's weight was too much, especially on top of the cosmic force of the black hole. It was like being caught in a tractor beam. He couldn't get away. Manchester's fingernails dug into Joey's skin, stabbing through the soft bandage on his ankle. The pain was too much. He was going to let go. He could feel himself getting ready to give up.

Then the black hole flickered. It was only for a fraction of a second. It was barely even noticeable, but Joey felt the pull of death rest behind him and knew that the end was near. That knowledge gave him strength. He didn't have to hold on forever. Just a few more seconds, that was all. This was it. His one chance to get rid of Manchester.

"Joey, hang on!" Shazad shouted as they worked their way down to him.

"Don't let go!" Janelle shouted.

"You're coming with me," Manchester said through gritted teeth. "I told you before, Joey, we're in this together."

"Sorry, Grayson!" Joey threw his foot back at Manchester's face. "I'm breaking up the act!" He kicked at Manchester once . . . twice . . . three times. The first two blows missed as

Manchester twisted to avoid Joey's wild kicks, but the third kick landed squarely on his nose. With each kick that followed, and each subsequent turn from Manchester, the bandage on Joey's ankle loosened. Finally it came undone. Joey's shoe popped off, and Manchester screamed, clutching the bandage as he went sliding backward into the center of the black hole. His cry cut off mid-shriek as he disappeared into nothingness. It was as if someone had hit the mute button on his voice.

As glad as Joey was to see him go, he couldn't celebrate just yet. The black hole was still active and still pulling on him with all the force of a rocket trying to leave the atmosphere. Joey was just barely holding on. The black hole flickered again, just for a second, and Shazad inched closer, with Leonora holding tight to his cape and Janelle holding on to Leonora. Shazad reached out to Joey. Their fingers touched. Shazad almost had him, but Joey slipped away before he got there. Joey went flying backward . . .

. . . and slammed into the closet wall with a *whack*.

Huh?

Joey sat up, looking around in a daze. He was shocked but grateful to still be alive. The black hole had blinked out of existence just in time. He sighed and melted into the wall, grinning broadly.

After a few seconds, Janelle crept away from the wall. "Is . . . whatever just happened . . . over?"

Joey blinked his eyes open and took stock of his surroundings. The black hole was gone, and Manchester had gone away with it. The threat was in their rear view. There was no one there but the four of them. "It's over," he confirmed, feeling like he could sleep for a year. "It's all over," he added, thinking about what they had lost.

"The wand . . . ," Shazad said, edging toward the empty closet. "You . . . You just let it go."

Joey's face was grim. "I had to."

"Why didn't you use it?" Leanora exclaimed.

"I did use it—as bait. I knew he'd go after it. When you've got a problem you can't solve and no time to work out the answer, all you can do is simplify the equation. You look for values that cancel each other out, like Manchester and the wand."

"That's no solution," Shazad said, mourning the loss of the world's most powerful magical object.

"It worked, didn't it?" Joey asked. "It's better this way,

Shazad. You said yourself, the wand had more power than any one person should have."

"You seemed to manage it pretty well," Shazad replied, simultaneously giving Joey credit and condemning his decision to abandon the wand.

"Who taught you how to do all that?" Leanora asked.

Joey shrugged. "Some of it I learned by watching Redondo. The rest of it . . . 'open sesame,' 'nova,' the thing with the bees . . . I used my imagination. By the way, Janelle, you can tell your friend Sandy she doesn't have a bee problem anymore. I took care of it for her."

"This is too much," Janelle said. "What the heck did I just see? Were you all just fighting over a wand? Like, a real magic wand? Who was that guy who just . . . ? He just . . ." Janelle gulped and trailed off, pointing a shaky finger at the empty closet that Joey was still sitting in.

All things considered, Joey thought she was handling the situation very well. Naturally, she had questions. She had just seen a grown man get sucked into a black hole, and she was smart enough to realize it had been Joey's plan to get rid of him that way, but she wasn't hysterical. The fact that Manchester had threatened to kill everyone in the room had probably muted any sympathy she had for him, but still, Joey was impressed by how well she was keeping it together.

Leanora was impressed with her as well. "I'd like to know what *that* was," she said, pointing to the spot where the black hole had been. "Joey never told us he knew any other magicians."

Janelle looked at Joey, impossible realizations forming in her head. "I'm starting to understand why you weren't sufficiently freaked out by the idea of a localized unstable black hole in a basement closet."

Joey smiled. "You're doing pretty good in the not-freaking-out department yourself."

"I'm getting there. We need to talk, Joey."

"Tomorrow," he said, completely drained. "I'll tell you all about it tomorrow."

"You're coming back, then?" she asked.

"I'll be here," Joey promised. "But first . . . there's something I have to show these two." He turned to Leanora and Shazad. "We need to go back to the theater."

19

The Majestic Legacy

Leanora was visibly relieved to find that Manchester had dropped her magic doorknob when he had reached for the wand. It had rolled underneath Exemplar Academy's furnace and narrowly avoided the black hole's gravitational pull. Joey was even more relieved to learn that his shoe had followed a similar safe trajectory, sliding back to the wall beside the closet rather than into the closet itself.

"Thank God," he had said, lacing his sneakers back up. "I can't afford to lose any more shoes. My father would be out of his mind."

They used Leanora's golden doorknob to return to the street where the Majestic Theatre stood once more. Back on the street, Joey, Leanora, and Shazad found the Majestic Theatre right where they had left it. The empty lot and plywood fencing were gone, but the three of them were the only people who seemed to notice anything had changed. People walked by it, oblivious. For all they knew, the theater had been there forever. It was still run-down, the letters on its marquee only half lit up. Joey, Leanora, and Shazad stared up in silence at their fractured glow:

_ _ _ MAJ_ _ _IC

The front door was open. They let themselves in. Joey locked the door behind them, just in case. The lobby was dark and empty, as he had expected. He led the way up the stairs to the office, clinging to a hope he didn't dare say out loud. Thinking of the Phoenix card he had pulled from Redondo's deck before he had entered the crate, Joey imagined Redondo might be there sitting behind his desk when they opened the door, ready to applaud them on a job well done. But the office was empty, just as before. The mess of Redondo's ideas and procrastinations . . . the playing cards, Post-its, and papers . . . They had all been cleared away. The partly sketched-out tricks on the chalkboard had been erased, and the desk, once buried beneath a mountain of notebooks, letters, and half-assembled magical props, was now completely bare save for the book he had left behind.

Joey looked around, struck by how un-Redondo-like the office now felt.

"He's really gone," Leanora said. "He sacrificed himself to save us."

"To save the wand," Shazad corrected her. "It was all for nothing." He hung his head. "What a waste."

Joey wiped a tear from his eyes with the heel of his palm and sniffed. The idea of Redondo sacrificing himself in vain weighed on Joey like a cannonball strapped to his heart. He wondered if he had failed him, as Shazad surely thought he had. When Manchester was breathing down his neck, Joey didn't have time to think about what to do with the wand. He had just acted. Now that he did have time, he didn't know how to act—or how to feel. Without question, the wand was the most wondrous magical object in the world, but it was also heavy with a power he had never once craved and the kind of responsibility he had shied away from all his life. "I don't know if I did the right thing, Shazad, but I know one thing for sure. It wasn't all for nothing." Joey handed him the book on Redondo's desk. "This is what I wanted to show you. Redondo told me this theater was a treasure trove of magical objects. Take a look; he wrote them all down."

Shazad turned the pages with wide-eyed interest. "There must be hundreds of relics here in this book."

Joey nodded. "I think he wanted us to take care of them after he died. Magic still needs protecting, right? This here . . ." Joey blinked back tears. "This is Redondo's legacy."

"That's not my legacy," a familiar voice called out. "You are."

Joey turned toward the voice, afraid he might be imagining it. "Redondo? You're alive?"

The matter was open for debate. Redondo was not there in the flesh. "I wouldn't exactly say *alive*," he replied. It was his reflection in the office mirror speaking. "I will say this much. I'm feeling better than I have in years." The faded, partially transparent image beckoned them to come closer. Puzzled, Joey and the others approached the mirror.

"I don't understand. What is this?" asked Leanora.

"Didn't expect to see me again, did you?" Redondo asked.

Joey shook his head. "I wouldn't say I expected it, no. But I did hope a little. Very little," he added, a smile forming on his lips. He held his thumb and forefinger close together. "This much." He didn't know how this was possible, but he didn't care. So what if Redondo wasn't 100 percent alive? Right now he'd take what he could get.

Redondo smiled back at Joey. "I had my own hopes as well. Seeing the three of you here together, it's clear that they were well-founded. Now I want to hear all about what happened after I blew up. Please. Tell me everything."

They told Redondo the story of how Joey defeated Manchester first in the theater and then again in the basement of Exemplar Academy. The fact that it was Grayson Manchester they had been fighting came as an incredible shock to Shazad, who was still under the impression that Redondo's old assistant had burned to death onstage twenty years ago. Redondo, Joey, and Leanora had to pause to catch him up on everything he had missed by being the first one sucked into Manchester's top hat. Once the truth about Manchester came out, Shazad apologized profusely to Redondo for thinking he had gotten his old assistant killed. Redondo assured him his apologies were completely unnecessary, especially now.

"Where are you?" Shazad wanted to know. "How are you still here?"

"It's the wand," Redondo explained. "When it changes hands, the memory of its former master stays behind long enough to pass on any wisdom they wish to share."

"But I lost the wand," Joey said, feeling awkward. "I gave it up."

"I know. That's why I won't be allowed to linger much longer. Just enough for a proper goodbye, and then I'll be gone."

"But not forgotten," Leanora said. "You saved our lives. We can't ever repay you."

"Never," Shazad agreed.

"You don't owe me anything," Redondo said. "Just make them good lives, all of you. Full of magic for yourself and others. That's payment enough."

"Redondo," Joey began, not knowing what to say to someone who was not dying but was already dead. "I . . . I hate to see you like this."

"Don't be sad," Redondo said. "For a long time I didn't like what I saw when I looked in this mirror either. It's all right, really. Thanks to you . . ." He paused. "Thanks to all of you, I finally stopped hiding. I spent years in this theater, right here in this room, thinking about how to make a comeback. How to restore the Order of the Majestic. I told myself that's what I was doing, at least. Really, I had no intention of doing any such thing. Don't get me wrong. I *thought* I was trying my best. But I recently realized there was something . . . someone holding me back. That person was me."

"I don't understand," Leanora said. "Why did you hide away all those years if you knew you didn't get Manchester killed?"

"For a long time I thought I had killed him," Redondo explained. "Later, when I realized the truth . . . that knowledge only added insult to injury. Manchester had fooled me. Me! The greatest magician alive!" Redondo let out a grim laugh. "If you want an honest answer, I was embarrassed, and not just about that. I had inspired such hatred in that boy, unwittingly. He was so angry . . . I had no idea. Perhaps if I had been less concerned with myself and paid more attention to the world around me . . ."

"No. He made his own choices," Joey said. "What he turned into wasn't your fault."

Redondo disagreed. "I should have seen it. I thought Grayson would be my successor, but he never understood why we put on shows and played for people in the audience. I failed to teach him that working magic for yourself isn't enough. You have to share it with others if you want to give it meaning. There's a reason he could never pull anything out of my old hat to fill that hole he had inside him. It's the same reason why he thought the wand was the thing he'd been lacking all these years. I knew better, but I figured it out too late. After Grayson left, I didn't want to start over. I didn't trust anyone, myself included. Magic had always come easy to me. Grayson's betrayal was the first real failure I had ever met with. Then I met a boy who found magic in a world that had none. Who dealt with failure at every turn in this theater and kept coming back for more. Even though he was scared. Even after I threw him out! You never stopped trying, young Kopecky. I needed to see that kind of fire again. Thank you."

"Did I do the right thing?" Joey asked. "With the wand? I still don't know."

"You did what was right for you. That's all that matters."

"Why did the wand pick me?" Joey asked. "Leanora and Shazad know way more about magic than I do. What if they were the ones in the mirror world fighting Manchester with you? Maybe it would have picked one of them. Maybe it *should* have been one of them."

"I know this is hard to understand, but I don't think the

wand chose you because of anything you did. I think it chose you because of what you were going to do."

"But, what did I do with the wand?" Joey asked. "I lost it."

"Who knows?" Redondo countered. "Maybe there's something more you're still meant to do. You're young. . . . I don't think you're done making magic just yet. I don't think any of you are. The show must go on. You all have your parts to play. As for what they will be, who can say? Don't go thinking you have to know everything right now. That was my mistake. I lost years wondering how to dazzle audiences . . . how to make them fall in love with magic again . . . how to help the world see the magic that exists in every breath we take. I didn't know how to do it. I didn't know where to begin. I wasted so much time trying to put it all perfectly together in my head before starting." Redondo shook his head ruefully. "Trying to be perfect? That is a recipe for doing nothing. I tried, but I never really went for it, because I was scared. Once we try to create something, it becomes real. And we worry, what if it's not good enough? If we never start, an idea can forever retain the promising, boundless potential it has here in this environment." He tapped at his temple. "Up here, it remains a pure, perfect intention, before it gets muddied up with action and failed attempts. But until we do that—stain and tarnish an idea in an effort to bring it to life—it is nothing. It's just an idea, and ideas are easy. It's the execution that makes them matter. That is what makes them special. The magic gets mixed in during the process. There is magic to be found in figuring things out! I understand that now. You can spend all your life waiting for inspiration and the right moment, but in the end there is no right moment. You just have to find your way. And you will. You'll make your magic. They'll help," Redondo added, gesturing to Leanora and Shazad. "I'm leaving the theater to all of you."

"What?" Shazad said, shocked.

"You're leaving us the theater?" Leanora added, struggling to comprehend the breadth of Redondo's postmortem generosity.

Redondo pointed at the desk. "Center drawer."

Leanora was closest. She opened the drawer and took out an envelope. Opening it, she read aloud: "The final will and testament of Melvin Kamitsky."

The three of them looked at Redondo: "Melvin Kamitsky?!!"

Redondo shrugged. "What, you thought my parents named me Redondo the Magnificent?"

"If you're Melvin, where did Redondo come from?" Joey asked.

"Melvin came from Massapequa, Long Island. Redondo Beach is out in California somewhere. I think it's technically part of Los Angeles, but I don't know. I've never visited. I just liked the way it sounded."

Joey had to laugh. He had always assumed that Redondo had some fantastical magical origin. "You think you know a guy . . . ," he said, pleasantly surprised to learn that Redondo's past was every bit as normal as his own.

"I don't get it," Shazad said, frowning.

"What's to get? I thought it was catchier than Melvin the Magnificent."

"Not that," Shazad said. "Why are you leaving the theater to all of us? Joey won your competition, even if he did lose the wand. Leonora and I . . . We didn't even get that far. We failed."

"Failed?" Redondo made a face like he'd just been hit in the forehead with a Ping-Pong ball. "Shazad . . . you didn't fail anything. The competition was never just about the

405

wand. It was about bringing the three of you together. I had to learn who you were . . . what you were made of . . . and you three had to learn about each other."

"Why?" Shazad asked.

"Because the purest, most powerful form of magic cannot be created alone. It's going to take all three of you to change the world and to take it back from the Invisible Hand. They're still out there. Grayson Manchester was just a cog in the machine. There are other, faster-moving parts—with sharper edges! When the time comes for you to meet them, you're going to need one another. And you'll be there for one another. I know you will. I look at you, and I don't see failure. I see three phoenixes. Hope for the future." Redondo pointed to Shazad. "Your instinct is to safeguard magic. Protect it. That's good. You saw that book. This theater has a few items that need protecting." He turned to Leonora. "You want to use magic to fight injustice. I like the sound of that. This theater has a few things that can help on that front as well." Finally, he turned to Joey. "As for you, Joey . . . you just love magic. That's what it's all about. The Invisible Hand, they think it's all about power. Magic is so much more than that. Magic is that thing that lies just out of our reach, but we reach for it anyway, despite all reason and common sense. And when we reach, we do so in the spirit of giving, not taking. The idea is to create wonders that will amaze, astound, and delight. To bring that feeling into the world takes a magician, and the world needs you—all three of you—to make it a magical place."

"I've only been doing this for two days," Joey argued. "What am I going to do without you there to teach me?"

"I never taught you anything, and yet you learned so much."

Joey would not be deterred. He wasn't ready to let Redondo go. "There's so much I still don't know."

"You know enough to begin," Redondo said. "That's the hardest part. Magnificence is a decision, young man. Speaking of which . . ." Redondo clapped his hands inside the mirror. The sound triggered a miraculous, instantaneous restoration of the Majestic. The effect was breathtaking. Joey and the others looked out the open office window, as every bulb lit up with brilliant light, every crack in the wall healed, and every chipped piece of molding re-formed good as new—better than Joey had ever seen it before. The spectacle of the transformation filled Joey with wonder and inspiration. Everything magic was supposed to do.

"What do you think?" Redondo asked, rubbing his hands together. "Did I get everything?"

"I don't understand," Joey said, still marveling at the change. "You told me this theater was a part of you. Shouldn't it get worse instead of better, now that you're . . . you know, now that you're . . . ?"

"Dead?" Redondo said, supplying the word Joey was awkwardly avoiding. The word he couldn't bring himself to say out loud. "What can I tell you? I'm in good spirits," he said with a laugh. "Lighten up, Joey. I was on my way out anyway, remember? It's all right. Even if a piece of this old place is dying with me, there's three phoenixes rising from the ashes of my life." A great smile spread out across his face. "I couldn't have asked for a better final act. First thing you learn onstage is that all people ever remember is the last thing you do. Before this I would have been remembered as the man who let the Order of the Majestic fall apart. Now I am the man who restored it."

Joey, Leanora, and Shazad looked at one another, then back at Redondo, whose reflection was beginning to fade. "Redondo . . . ," Joey began. "You're not talking about us. Are you?"

"Aren't you the one who asked me if there could be another Order of the Majestic someday? You're the one who has to answer that question. It's up to you, young Kopecky. It's up to all of you."

Redondo's reflection faded away. The children kept staring straight ahead into the mirror. The first three members of the newly restored Order of the Majestic stared back.

20
The Great Game

After everything incredible that had happened to Joey, the hardest thing for him to believe was that the next day was only Wednesday. He had traveled to other dimensions, battled evil magicians, released water monsters into the New York City sewer system, and destroyed priceless magical artifacts. His whole world had changed in forty-eight hours, and the week wasn't even half over.

When Joey got up the next morning, he told his parents he was ready to give Exemplar Academy another try. After they picked their jaws up off the floor, they asked him what it was that had changed his mind. He said he didn't think it would be impossible to succeed there anymore. It turned out, he was good at impossible. Joey went to school that day with a smile on his face, looking forward to seeing Janelle again.

Dr. Cho met him at the gate, and the first thing he did was apologize for the previous day's incident. "Oh please, don't waste another second thinking about that," she said before he could finish saying he was sorry. "You're hardly the first student to get overwhelmed on a visit to our school. Believe it or not, I've seen worse." Joey didn't see how that could be true, but he thanked Dr. Cho for understanding just the same.

On the walk to her office, Dr. Cho mentioned that the school had yet to receive Joey's PMAP test results. He wasn't the least bit surprised. After all, "Mr. Gray" had turned out to be Grayson Manchester, and the test he'd taken was a sham. It was a safe bet no test scores would be forthcoming from the NATL.

"Here's the thing, Dr. Cho. I didn't actually take the PMAP test."

"Jules," she said instantly. "I told you, Joey, please. Call me Jules. And your father told me all about your . . . alternative test. It sounded very interesting." She said the word "interesting" the way people usually did when they were too polite to say what they really meant. "I called the NATL yesterday to find out more."

"What did they tell you?" Joey asked. He assumed she had hit a dead end and that he'd be taking the real PMAP test later that morning.

"I ended up speaking with the head of the NATL. He said he was incredibly sorry for the delay and that he'd take care of everything. He actually came by to personally deliver your test results this morning."

Joey stopped short. "What? Who came by? When—"

Dr. Cho laughed. "You're famous, Joey. He said he wanted to meet the boy who did so well on all their tests. He's right in here." She opened the door to her office. A man in a suit and tie was sitting in one of the chairs across from her desk. He stood up as they entered. "This is Mr. Black, chief administrator of the National Association of Tests and Limits. Say hello."

"Mr. Black?" Joey asked, instantly wary of the man. For one thing, he knew the Invisible Hand secretly ran the NATL, and for another, he had already met Mr. Gray and Mrs. White. Joey backed away a step, sensing danger, but the man was fast. He reached out to shake Joey's hand, got ahold of Joey's arm, and pulled him in close.

"Joey Kopecky! At last, I'm in the presence of greatness."

Mr. Black gave Joey's hand a vigorous shake, grinning broadly. He was a handsome man with movie-star good looks and wavy blond hair. He couldn't have been more than thirty years old. When he let go of Joey's hand, Joey noticed he had placed a small hourglass on the edge of Dr. Cho's desk.

Out of the corner of Joey's eye, he saw Dr. Cho's body turn rigid. Joey looked over his shoulder and flinched. She had stopped dead at the door to her office. It was as if she had been hit with a freeze ray. "What the . . . ?" Joey checked the clock on the wall. It had stopped ticking. All around Joey, time stood still. There was magic at work, and it wasn't his.

"Pretty cool, don't you think?" Mr. Black asked. He gestured to the hourglass as if he were presenting a work of art. "I give you the Sands of Time. Most people think they stop time, but in fact it's the opposite. The hourglass actually speeds up time within a two-foot radius. It's not much, but it's enough for you and me to squeeze a few extra minutes out of the space between this second and the next. Sit down, Joey. Let's chat. We've got until the sands run out to get to know each other better."

Looking right at home, Mr. Black sat back down and waited for Joey to follow suit. Feeling decidedly less comfortable, Joey took the seat across from him. "Who are you?" he asked, trying to sound in control. "Manchester's boss?" he guessed. "The guy behind the guy?"

The man smiled. "Something like that."

"Is 'Mr. Black' the best fake name you could come up with?"

"It's not that I can't come up with anything better. I just can't be bothered to try. There's no point in getting creative when the norms will fall for just about anything. My real name, which I'm happy to tell *you*, is Ledger DeMayne. My card." He offered Joey a card with the Invisible Hand symbol on the back.

"You can go ahead and keep that," Joey said. "What do you want?" He held his breath and hoped DeMayne wasn't there to pick a fight.

"I just came to talk," DeMayne said behind a reassuring smile. "I wanted to meet the boy who caused so much trouble. Wait. That's not true," he said, correcting himself. "Technically, we've met before. We've just never been formally introduced. Don't hate me, but I was one of the shadows who tackled you outside the Majestic Theatre last night. My colleagues and I have been attempting to enter Redondo's sanctuary through the shadow realm for months. We would have gotten away with it, too, if not for you meddling kids!" he added, quoting *Scooby-Doo*. DeMayne chuckled. "I'm joking, of course. You didn't ruin my plans. Manchester did. It's my own fault. I should have seen it coming. Once a traitor, always a traitor. Shame."

"If it makes you feel any better, he won't be stabbing anyone else in the back. He's gone. We dropped him down a black hole last night."

DeMayne's eyebrows went up. "A black hole? Really?"

Joey nodded. "Really."

DeMayne thought about that for a second, then motioned with his hands as if such things happened all the time. "What can I say? I'm sorry I missed that."

Joey was perplexed by DeMayne's affable manner, acting like they were old friends or something. "We dropped the wand down there too, in case you were wondering."

At this DeMayne's smile faded. He straightened up in his seat and studied Joey for a moment. "You're serious."

Joey nodded, staring straight into DeMayne's bright blue eyes. Joey was afraid he might get angry, but he took the wand's loss in stride. "That's too bad. Sounds like I wasted my time coming here."

"You thought I still had the wand?"

"I did."

Joey shook his head. "Sorry. You can threaten me all you want, but it's gone. You're too late."

"So you said." DeMayne grimaced. "It's quite a loss, but you're mistaken. I didn't come here to threaten you. I came to do what Manchester should have done the moment he realized your potential. Recruit you."

Joey twitched slightly. He wasn't prepared for that. He shifted in his seat, trying to hide his surprise. DeMayne took an envelope with the NATL seal out of his pocket and offered it to Joey.

"What's that?"

"Open it up. Find out."

Joey opened the envelope. Inside were his PMAP test results.

POTENTIAL MAPPING TEST RESULTS FOR:

Kopecky, Joseph J.*

*Alternative testing candidate

JOB RECOMMENDATION:

Subject is ideally suited to pursue

anything he wants.

Joey stared at the test score printout. "Anything I want?" he whispered. After a few seconds of stunned silence, he looked up at DeMayne. "I don't understand."

DeMayne smiled like a salesman. "That's how it is for people like us. Rules don't apply. We can do anything we want. What part of that don't you understand?"

"You're telling me to drop out of school and join the Invisible Hand?"

"You have other plans?" DeMayne probed. It was a simple question, but Joey detected a warning layered underneath it. A subtle threat:

If you're not with us, you're against us.

"What's it going to be, Joey?"

Joey folded up the paper with the test results and put it back in the envelope. He didn't know how DeMayne would react if he refused, but he put on his most convincing tough-guy face and hoped for the best. Just like with Manchester, if he couldn't be fearless, he would pretend to be brave, and that would have to do. "Manchester already asked me to join your little club. I remember because it was right before he tried to kill me. Thanks, but no thanks. I'll pass."

DeMayne had an injured expression on his face. "You can't let Manchester color your opinion of us. The man was completely unhinged. Surely you picked up on that. He wasn't looking at the big picture. He was only thinking about himself."

"Like the rest of you are any different?" Joey asked. "You keep all the world's magic to yourselves."

"You say that like it's a bad thing."

"Of course it is! You could make the world a better place, but you don't do it."

"My world's a better place, Joey. Yours could be too. If you want it bad enough."

"I'm not going to join you," Joey said definitively. "What do you think? I root for the Empire when I watch Star Wars? You think I want Sauron to get the ring back from Frodo? Forget it. I'm the guy who gave up the wand. I'm not going to join the dark side."

"The dark side?" DeMayne laughed out loud. "That's adorable. Now I understand why you were able to find Redondo and wield that wand. You might come from New Jersey, but you live in a fantasy world. We're not evil. We're just the people in charge. I understand how that can be confusing to you. The powerful always look sinister to the powerless. Especially the young and idealistic. I was like you once. I didn't understand. You've got a lot to learn."

"What do I have to learn?"

"That you're not one of *them* anymore." DeMayne pointed at the frozen figure of Dr. Cho. "You're in the show now, Joey. The great game. The prize is nothing less than mastery over magic and everything that comes with it, but you're not playing to win. You don't have the killer instinct. If you did, you would have kept the wand for yourself."

"I kept it from Manchester," Joey said. "And from you. That's a pretty big win."

"Is it? Because based on what you've told me, Houdini's wand isn't gone. It's lost. And lost things can be found—by anyone."

Joey's stomach tightened. He wanted to laugh off the notion of someone tracking down the wand inside a black hole that wasn't even there anymore, but he couldn't bring himself to do it. Sitting there in DeMayne's magic time bubble, it dawned on Joey that there was no idea "out there" enough that he could dismiss it out of hand. For all he knew, every black hole in the universe was a doorway to some magic kingdom. What if that was true and DeMayne knew the way in? Joey prayed it wasn't.

"Do you understand what happened now?" DeMayne asked Joey. "You didn't win. Manchester *lost*. Try to appreciate the difference, because you won't get so lucky next time. Speaking of which, that's all the time we have for today."

The last few grains of sand fell through the hourglass and DeMayne snatched the relic off the desk. Time immediately returned to normal. Dr. Cho unfroze and did a slight double take, no doubt wondering when Joey and "Mr. Black" had sat down. A half a second earlier, they had all been standing together.

"I wish I could stay longer, but I have to be going," DeMayne said, rising to his feet. "Dr. Cho, thank you for introducing me to this young man. It was good to finally put a face to the name. And now I'll know where to find him if I ever have a need."

Joey grated at what was clearly another veiled threat from DeMayne. Dr. Cho missed it. "You're not leaving already?" she said, confused. "What about Joey's test scores?"

"He's got them." DeMayne flicked the envelope in Joey's hand. "I've made my recommendations. It'll be interesting to see where Joey goes from here."

"I'll be sure to keep it interesting, then," Joey said, standing up. He nodded toward an inspirational poster on Dr. Cho's wall with the Exemplar Academy motto written on it: OUR STUDENTS CHANGE THE WORLD. Joey locked eyes with DeMayne. "That's the plan, anyway."

DeMayne met Joey's gaze. He smiled, but there was no warmth in it. "Good luck with that," he said without feeling. As he left the room, Joey knew there would be more tests in his future, but he wasn't afraid. He was good with tests, and he wouldn't face them alone.

Onward, young magicians, Joey thought to himself. *We've got work to do.*

Acknowledgments

"Where do you get your ideas?"

That's the question I get more than any other. Like most authors, I don't usually have an answer for it. However, this book was different. I remember the exact moment the light bulb lit up for me.

The fact is, I didn't plan on writing this book. I was actually going to write something completely different. I had this other idea, something that had been sitting in the back of my brain for years, waiting patiently and growing over time. I was finally going to get around to it when all of a sudden, *this* story came out of nowhere and pushed its way to the front of the line. Here's what happened.

My wife and I had bought our children a magic set. My older son was playing with it. He was five years old at the time.

I was going to show him how to do one of the tricks, which involved the illusion of twisting your hand all the way around on your wrist in a full 180-degree turn. My son jumped back and looked at me like I was crazy. He didn't want me going anywhere near his wrist. That's when it hit me. . . . He thought it was real. Of course he did. All children believe in magic. Until they don't. I wondered what would happen if we could hold on to that belief. Wouldn't that be nice?

Just like that, an idea was born. A boy comes across an old magic set and finds out that magic is real—but only if you believe in it. He gets pulled into a secret magical world, and . . . that's it. That's all I had. But that was enough to begin. And that beginning kept me going. That spark of magic in a kindergartner's eyes. This story wouldn't exist without that.

From there, I had a lot of stuff to figure out. It's a real magic trick, bringing a story into the world. Making it appear out of thin air. Out of nothing. But in the words of Redondo the Magnificent, "There is magic to be found in figuring things out." The trick is making people think I do it all by myself. I'm a lot like a magician standing onstage, taking a bow after the show's over. That's me when this book comes out. The truth is, there's an army of people working behind the scenes to support that illusion, and it's my privilege to thank everyone who helps bring my imagination to life here in this pages.

First, I want to thank you, the reader, for picking this book up. Making sure these stories are worthy of your time and attention is something I think about every single day, so I hope you had fun with this one. With any luck, I managed to surprise you with a few twists and keep you coming back for more. From the bottom of my heart, thank you for reading.

I want to thank my agent, Danielle Chiotti, who was on board with the idea for *Order of the Majestic* from the very beginning. Through all my false starts, writing, rewriting, and delays, she had faith in this story and in me. Her guidance and support was invaluable. I'm so grateful for her and everyone at Upstart Crow Literary.

My editor, Liesa Abrams, is another person I am extremely lucky to be working with. Some people see possibilities others can't see, and Liesa is one of them. Always asking thought-provoking questions and sharing challenging ideas, Liesa has a gift for knowing exactly what a story needs. She is a joy to collaborate with, and her input makes everything I write better.

On that same note, Samira Iravani was instrumental in helping me craft this story. Her contributions and insights are greatly appreciated. I want to thank art director Karin Paprocki and artist Owen Richardson for their work on this book's stunning cover. I owe a great debt to them, publisher Mara Anastas, production editor Rebecca Vitkus, copy editor Penina Lopez, proofreader Stacey Sakal, and everyone at Simon & Schuster/Aladdin.

Finally, none of my books would be complete without a special thank-you to my family. My mom and dad, who always encouraged my imagination growing up, but also taught me to work hard and find a way to make things happen in the real world. My children, who, in addition to giving me ideas for books, are the best things I ever had a hand in creating. Saving the best for last, thank you to my amazing wife, Rebecca, whose love and support brings magic into my world every day. I can't imagine life without it, or her.

Thank you all for being there for me and for making this book possible.